Tony Saint was born in Northumberland in 1968 and educated at the taxpayers' expense. After attending university in Bristol and Hamilton, Ontario, he joined the United Kingdom Immigration Service in 1993. He lives in South London. His first novel, *Refusal Shoes*, was published to great acclaim in 1993.

Also by Tony Saint and published by Serpent's Tail

Refusal Shoes

'*Refusal Shoes* comes on like a cross between *Airport* and *League of Gentlemen* . . . Saint writes some very funny dialogue and offers sharp observation' *Independent on Sunday*

'A gruesomely comic account of an immigration service . . . *Refusal Shoes* brings a new perspective to a big current topic while also being highly entertaining' *Daily Telegraph*

'Henry shares many characteristics with Yossarian and Hawkeye, the protagonists and anti-heroes of Heller's *Catch 22* and Altman's *MASH*. They are non-heroes or anti-heroes who use cynicism and humour to cope with intense danger and pressure, rampant mediocrity, and petty authority figures' *Bookmunch.co.uk*

'So successful in its depiction of the flickering-fluorescent petty-politicking of immigration officers – where productivity is measured in "refused leave to enter" stamps – that you almost start worrying whether your own papers are in order' Tony White

'A brutally funny first novel which refuses to pull any punches' Ben Richards

'A high-farce, fast and funny debut thriller...When you take this book on holiday, get someone to bring it back for you through customs' Arnold Brown

blag

....

Tony Saint

For Catherine

Library of Congress Catalog Card Number: 2004100910

A complete catalogue record for this book can be
obtained from the British Library on request

The right of Tony Saint to be identified as
the author of this work has been asserted by him
in accordance with the Copyright, Designs and
Patents Act 1988

First published in 2004 by Serpent's Tail,
4 Blackstock Mews, London N4 2BT

website: www.serpentstail.com

Printed by Mackays of Chatham, plc

10 9 8 7 6 5 4 3 2 1

part one

....

1

....

The leader, three lengths ahead, got a little close to the second last fence, went through the top of it. It dipped hard on landing, nose scraping the soft ground. For a second, Harry Verma thought it was staying up. His fists and shoulders tightened in sympathy. He bent his knees, willing the nag to pull itself back on its legs, but the strain of the jockey (unforgivably putting up three pounds overweight) pushing down his long neck was too much and he hit the deck.

'Shit!' said Harry. He crumpled his pink betting slip, £50 win, into a ball, letting it drop and swinging a buckled boot at it in anger. 'Wanker!'

The kick turned him around, so that he faced Tommy, a permanent exhibit at the bookies. Tommy sat bent and thin on his regular high chair, legs crossed, rolled cigarette bobbing between pale cracked lips.

'Sometimes,' said Tommy, 'the power of prayer is simply not enough.'

Four hundred pounds down now on the afternoon, Harry ignored the outcome of the race but darted across to the corner, where the greyhound form was pinned up. Next race: 4.12, Perry Barr. 480 metres. Dipping a hand into his jacket pocket, his fingers wrestled the plastic bag within to locate a jellybean, which he popped into his mouth. Meanwhile, he scanned the runners with a stubby plastic pen.

Trap 3. Indian Boy.

'It's got to be Indian Boy,' he said over his jellybean, glancing across at Tommy.

'That'll be very scientific,' offered Tommy.

'Piss off,' said Harry, preparing to scribble his wager. 'You saw a dog called Irish Idler or Navvy's Breath or something, you wouldn't back it?'

Tommy rolled his eyes, recrossed his legs.

'Such a dog would clearly have the Lord on his side. The one true Lord, not one of these seven-armed fellers you boys go for.'

Harry was about to reply, but he heard a footfall coming down the stairs into the basement betting shop. It was slow, calculated. Harry smelled a rat. This wasn't the step of a punter, who would always hurry down just in case there was a good thing he was about to miss. No, this was way too measured a step. It signalled a different intent. Something told Harry he didn't want to be at the end of it.

He went to the counter and motioned silently towards the locked door of the adjacent toilet. Through the hatch was pushed a long key with a piece of string attached to a luminous green tennis ball.

'I'm not here,' he whispered to Donna, the girl behind the counter, and turned to Tommy, giving the same information with hand signals. Tommy looked back at him as if he were a dodgy piece of DIY.

Harry slid into the lavatory and waited as the footsteps hit the bottom of the stairs, paused and headed over to the counter.

'Looking for someone,' Harry heard a voice say. It was deep, not too bright, definitely Asian, but with a hint of Birmingham, he thought. 'Looking for Harry. Verma.'

Donna didn't answer straight away. *Good girl*, thought Harry, ear pressed to the bog door, a fresh red jellybean gripped between his front teeth. *Not too keen.*

'No,' he heard her say faintly. 'He's not here.'

'Have you seen him?'

Harry visualised Donna shaking her head.

'I heard say,' said the voice, 'that he come here a lot.'

'Dunno, love,' said Donna. 'I'm new here, you see,' she lied expertly.

A pause. Harry dropped to his haunches to look through the keyhole. He saw a body, big belly, blue shirt, leather jacket, turn towards Tommy.

'Who is it you'll be looking for?' he asked.

Harry heard his name repeated. Tommy thought about it.

'The name rings a bell, but I can't quite place it.'

'Asian bloke. Fancies himself. Calls himself a lawyer.'

Tommy mimed recognition. Harry held his breath.

'I know the feller you're on about. You describe him well, if I may say so.'

Always the smartarse, Tommy.

'Have you seen him?'

Tommy shook his head.

'Not for a little while. But listen. If it's a tip on the horses you're after, take my advice. Don't ask him.'

Ha ha.

The body was at rest for a moment.

'Tell him, if you see him,' said the voice. 'Tell him Mr Bohra would like to speak to him.'

'Regarding . . .?'

Harry felt his mouth tighten.

'Regarding business,' replied the body after a pause.

Tommy nodded and tapped his head.

'I've stored it in there,' he said, and Harry saw a portion of the body move behind him and on up the stairs. He waited for the telltale increase in traffic noise from outside to come and go before emerging.

'Tosser,' he said to Tommy, slipping the key back under the window.

Unmoved, Tommy nodded towards the bank of screens on the opposite wall. 'They're puttin' 'em in the traps. You'd better get a move on.'

Harry scribbled the bet. *£100 win. Trap 3*. One step to the left and he slipped the bet through the window, two fifties under it. Time to win some of Bohra's money back . . .

'*Hare running at Perry Barr* . . .'

Harry stepped back, arms folded around his chest. From his waist a mobile phone trill disturbed him. 'Yes . . . ?'

The traps sprang up. Trap 3 got away well . . .

'Harry?'

It was Carla, his secretary.

'What?'

First corner. 3 Dog gets in behind the leader, keeping up with the pace . . .

'Where are you?'

'I'm busy.'

3 Dog pushed wide around the second bend, backed into third.

'Well, listen. I've got a client here . . .'

3 Dog fading down the back straight . . .

'Shit,' Harry muttered between clenched teeth. 'What do they want?' he asked the phone, moving over to get a better view of the prices for the next race: six-furlong handicap on the all-weather at Wolverhampton.

'It's Miss Sharma. She's got an immigration interview tomorrow. She thinks they're going to refuse her.'

'Yeah, well, that's normally what they do.'

Twelve runners. Harry scanned the form. More zeros than his overdraft. Nothing jumped out at him.

'She wants your advice, Harry . . .'

Harry looked down to the bottom of the weights, looking for a horse ahead of the handicapper.

'Remind me. What's she look like?'

A pause.

'Yes, that's correct. She's here with me now . . .'

'OK, I've got you . . .'

He stopped at the second bottom weight, Borninthebayou by name, carrying eight stone two, a four-year-old, in the frame a couple of times in the last three out, might be on the upgrade . . .

'Is she the one with the limp?'

'Don't think so, Harry . . .'

Harry stepped back, threw his head up to check the prices.

'All right, Sharma, Sharma . . . She's not that fat one, is she?'

BORNINTHEBAY . . . 10 to 1, in from 14. That meant there was money for it . . .

'That would be correct . . .'

Harry grabbed a slip.

'I thought she was getting married.'

'Yeah, well,' Carla answered, her voice a tense hiss now. 'You were supposed to be finding her a husband . . .'

They were going into the stalls at Wolverhampton. Harry rammed the phone between chin and shoulder, pulled the rolled bundle of notes from his pocket.

'Husbands are proving a little difficult to come by right now. They want more money than they used to. Tell her I'm working on it.'

He loosened four fifties, make it five, let them fall on the counter.

'You're her lawyer, Harry. She's got a sodding interview tomorrow.' Carla's voice was barely audible now. 'They're going to deport her and she's threatening to go barmy here. She's a big girl, Harry. You don't pay me enough to start wrestling her . . .'

Harry scribbled runes on the slip:

WLV 4.15
#11 £250 win

Last horse going in.

'Harry? . . .'

Harry slid on his heels across the lino to the betting counter, forced the slip and the money through.

'Harry?'

'Listen. Get on the phone to that doctor, what's his name?'

'Which one?'

'You know,' Harry answered, dropping his voice. 'The pillow-biter.'

'Dr Barry?'

'That's him. Get him to do her a sick note, then we'll fling it at immigration tomorrow.'

On the big screen the stalls snapped open. Horse 11, white jacket with green chevrons on the jockey, tucks in on the inside, moving nicely . . .

'Sick note for what exactly?'

'It doesn't matter. Something serious enough to buy us a couple of weeks, better a month. Pneumonia, depression, whatever . . .'

Two furlongs, still on the bridle, got a run on the inside . . .

'And he'll do that if I just ring him up?'

'Tell him it's for me. He owes me a favour. I got his Brazilian boyfriend residency and a hospital bed for what remains of his sweet short life. He'll do it. Got to go.'

He folded his arms again, gnawing at the tip of the phone's aerial, eyes fixed up.

. . . two furlongs out now, moving up to the leader, starting to race now, kicking up wet sand, moving ahead a furlong from home . . .

'Too early,' muttered Tommy. 'Taking it up too early . . .'

Harry stared up, brow furrowed, eyelids heavy, contemptuous at the pounding pulse in his chest and his own wheezing breath. His horse hit the front but never made a break. With two hundred yards to go it was hauled in by two others on its outside. It was behind more than a neck down when the jockey chose to give it a slap with the whip. Harry wished it was his fist that the crop was in, wanted to smash it off the beast's flanks himself, wanted to draw blood, wanted his eight hundred pounds' worth of frustration to at least buy him that.

He shoved the last handful of jellybeans into his mouth and bit on them hard.

Tommy, face screwed up, slowly pulled a slip out of his shirt pocket; his daily fifty-pence Yankee. He looked at it for a few seconds and sighed philosophically.

'Would you credit it?' he said, gently dismounting his stool and heading for the PAY window. 'The Lord smiles on those who are pure of heart. That must be it.'

But Harry wasn't listening. He was already back over at the greyhound numbers, picking one out for the 4.22 at Hall Green.

2

....

Sean Carlyle checked the time.

4.22 p.m.

He had the shakes. Again. He couldn't tell whether it was fear or being forced to make it this late into the day without a drink. Probably both. After all, he was shaking pretty badly. And there was no question of popping a downer now. He needed to be on his mettle for this blag.

He leaned forward and peered up, saw the sky was darkening, felt the humidity in the clamminess at the back of his neck and around his crotch.

Thirsty.

Stretching across the passenger seat, he opened the glove compartment to get at the half-bottle of Smirnoff Blue Label inside. Keeping his head below the windscreen, he took one, two slugs. The alcohol cut into the mouth ulcer that had been on his lower gum for about a week, stung tears into his eyes.

A book had fallen from the glove compartment and on to the passenger seat. *501 Spanish Verbs*. Somebody else must have left it there when they'd had this car from the pool. He remembered having the same edition, the time when . . .

It was starting again, the cascade of memory distilling itself to the one recollection he least wanted. Like being in quicksand, the harder he struggled to avoid it, the sharper it came back at him, that image of himself, sitting on the beach . . .

Maria . . .

Don't get out of the car . . .

He rubbed his face hard with both hands, managing to fracture the image in his mind. He picked up the book and leafed through it. *Spanish*, he thought, stopping at one page and reading through a conjugated verb. *Nice language . . .*

>me quebranto
>te quebrantas
>se quebranta

He glanced up to see what it meant.

>quebrantarse – to fall apart

He threw the fucker back on to the passenger seat.

He'd been parked there twenty minutes, as arranged, waiting for the Old Bill to turn up. They were cutting it a bit fine. At times like these he wished he could just go in there by himself or, better still, not bother going in at all. With his regular tag team partner Dixon spending more time on the sick than ever, there was always that possibility, but not when the rozzers had been called in by some hard-on in the office.

His mind drifted. In the vacuum of thought he remembered his little secret, his *big* problem . . .

He shook his head, blinked a couple of times and looked down at the case file which lay on his lap, opened. It referred to William 'Sweet Bill' Cameron, Liberian national, known to be in the UK illegally. It was Sean's job to pick him up, *spin his drum*, make the *blag* and serve deportation papers on him. On file there were only two documents, an unsigned letter written in a childish scrawl. Whoever had written it had probably done so with their wrong hand, to further assure anonymity. Understandable when you saw the second piece of paper on file, a police intelligence report, citing Sweet Bill as being 'of interest' for drugs offences, robbery, indecent assault, you name it . . .

In his rear view he saw a blue van pull up across the street, about fifty yards away. Somehow, only an unmarked police vehicle could be quite so conspicuous.

Quickly, he checked the contents of his Home Office-issued briefcase, more like a box, opened and closed by two sturdy metal clasps. It was all there: mobile; pager; Polaroid camera; a sleeveless luminous jacket marked IMMIGRATION, his blagging jacket; Swiss army knife; handcuffs and, of course, forms. Form APP104, Form IS151A, Form IS101, Form IS96, Form IS91. All present and correct.

He got out of the car, feeling a little dizzy, and walked across the front of the van. There were two men up front in short-sleeved white shirts. Sean reached inside his windcheater and pulled out his immigration warrant to show them before carrying on around the side. As he reached the van's rear, the door windows blacked out, slid back. Eight more coppers were inside, two rows of four on either side. All big bastards. Sean could tell they'd all been pumping each other up for the last half-hour. They were looking forward to it. The fact that they were all wearing bulletproof vests recalibrated his pulse a couple of notches up.

'Immigration,' said Sean.

'You immigration?' asked one of the grunts, short, spiky blond hair.

'Immigration,' repeated Sean.

'Just the one of you?' another asked.

'Yeah. My partner's gone sick.'

A couple of them nodded solemnly at this. They obviously took what Sean said at face value. The thought of someone crying off as a result of sheer cowardice wasn't something they would admit to being aware of.

'His loss,' said Blondie. 'This is going to be fucking tasty,' he added, baring his teeth. 'I'm right up for a ruck . . .'

Sean squeezed up on the left-hand bench, sliding the door shut behind him. The exhaust expectorated and the van moved off.

'So how we going to play this one?'

Sean's question caused a few laughs, Blondie pushing his bottom lip out with his tongue, making a *durr* noise.

'What do you think? We're going to smash the fucking door down, charge in and pull the slag out by the bollocks. Same as usual.'

More laughter. Sean felt forced to join in with a weak smile.

'Why so many of you, though?'

The one furthest away on the opposite bench, a little older than average, answered. 'We want to make it nice and quick,' he said, leaning down to pick something up. Another flak jacket, which he flung at Sean. 'The word is he may have firearms.'

Sean caught it late, tight to his chest, blinked slowly.

'So you lot are carrying, then?'

Heads shook regretfully.

'No need,' said Blondie, putting a brave face on the lack of heaters. 'These hands,' he explained, 'lethal weapons,' and set about attacking his neighbour with a few karate chops to the neck and shoulder.

'Gerroff,' shouted his victim. 'Gerroff, you poof.'

'Cut that out,' said the senior man before addressing Sean again. 'There's enough of us. We should be able to overpower him if we maintain an element of surprise.'

Sean nodded, detected the quality in his voice that signified the mix of weariness and fear that he knew himself all too well. With nowhere else for them both to look, their eyes stayed fixed for a second across the vanload of uniformed psychos. Sean figured that this one must have a wife, kids maybe. He knew a look that said *What the fuck am I doing here?* when he saw one.

The van lurched to a stop.

'Right, everyone knows their position,' said the sane one. 'What's your name?' he asked Sean. Sean told him.

'All right, Sean. We thought you might fancy the Dragonlight?'

'Sure,' said Sean. *Shit*, he thought.

The Dragonlight was passed down, a giant lamp, like off a movie set, with two handles on the back, designed to be shone in an assailant's face, temporarily blinding him and making apprehension an easy matter. What it meant was that Sean would have to go in early. He had rather fancied being able to hang back, have more time to gauge the situation. He preferred that course of action when entering the abode of a gun-toting crackhead. As a rule.

His throat felt dry. He wanted a drink. *Beer and chaser*, he kept thinking, *Beer and Chaser. Chaser, chaser, chaser.*

Sean heard one of the doors at the front slam and footsteps from around the outside of the vehicle. The door was snapped back from that side and daylight blew in, momentarily confusing him. Pressure from behind forced Sean to jump out of the van, clutching the Dragonlight in both hands, his calves hurting slightly as he landed flat-footed on the road. He barely had time to look around, acclimatise himself to the narrow street, the row of identical two-storey houses, before he was pushed along by the coppers' barely controlled panic.

They moved left out of the van, boots clicking against the tarmac, all nine of them pelting directly across the road to the door, all standing in the small porch that led into the building. Stuck there crammed in with almost a dozen lunatic coppers, Sean felt the urge to shit, started to feel the blood pumping again, all his frayed senses honing in on the need for self-preservation.

Blondie had charged to the front, carrying the hydraulic press used for forced entrance, which he had quickly attached at eye level with small vice attachments to the front door.

'Ready with that Dragonlight!' someone whispered.

Holding it down at knee level, Sean switched it on.

'Everyone down,' said Blondie.

They all ducked down, except Sean, whose reactions were slowed by something he had noticed.

'Fucking hell, you're blinding me!' shouted one of the grunts, the Dragonlight right in his face.

'Switch it off!'

'Get down!'

'Can't see!'

'Switch it off!'

'Get down!'

Sean felt himself being hauled to the ground by the knee of his trousers just as the hydraulic press went off with a sudden hiss and pop, blowing the door in and flying back, giving him a centre parting as he fell, just avoiding it.

'You all right?'

Sean nodded.

'I'm blind!' screamed Blondie.

Another of the grunts stood up, hands shielding eyes, and fell over backwards, sending empty milk bottles clattering.

'Point that fucking thing to the ground!'

Sean let go of the Dragonlight with one hand, the weight of the thing almost hauling him down.

'Let's get in there!'

'Hang on,' said Sean.

'Hang on what? Let's fucking do it!'

Sean pointed to something on the inside of the porch, next to the gaping door space. Three bells.

'Which flat is it?'

'Nobody said anything about it being a fucking flat!'

'We just got this address.'

'What's it say on the bells?'

One of the grunts perused the three slips of paper inserted behind plastic strips next to each buzzer.

'None of them say him.'

'Of course none of them say him. What's he going to have on his buzzer? "Sweet Bill. All-Round Scrote"?'

Looking around, Sean could see half the street come out of

their front doors, most looking on disapprovingly, arms folded across chests.

'So much for the element of surprise,' he muttered.

'Two upstairs are women. Bottom one's blank.'

'All right. Move it!'

All impetus gone, they shuffled in. Being a pretty low-standard house conversion in Sean's eyes, he could see that the door to the flat itself wouldn't cause much of a problem. But by now who-ever – *whatever* – was on the other side would have a pretty good idea they were coming and would be ready. The plan obsolete, Sean was aware that the blag was in a state of terminal, possibly fatal, drift. He thought about the time a twenty-stone Guyanese woman had fired a starting pistol at him and he had pissed him-self. Never did work out what a twenty-stone woman was doing with a starting pistol . . . The memory gave him a sharp tickle in his palms. He realised he was struggling for breath, sweating badly. *Need a downer*, he was thinking, *downer* . . . The lithium tablets were rattling in his pocket, but keeping the Dragonlight steady was taking up both hands.

'What now?' said a grunt.

'Fuck knows.'

'If he's a shooter, he's going to be waiting for us.'

'We'll be sitting ducks.'

'Maybe we should call for back-up?'

'What you mean? There are ten of us here already.'

'Shut up,' said the sane one.

Taking a cautionary step back, Sean felt a tap on his shoulder.

Blondie. Eyes wide, pupils the size of pinheads, nostrils flared. 'Stand aside.'

'It's all right, Barry,' the sane one said, palms out, trying to calm. 'We're just taking stock . . .'

'Stand aside,' said Blondie, taking a step back for a run-up.

'Take stock, Barry . . .'

'Fuck stock,' said Barry.

'Barry!'

'STAND-A-FUCKING-SIDE!'

'BARRY!'

But Blondie was already on the charge, screaming like a fucking banshee, dropping a shoulder at the last minute and ripping the chipboard door off its hinges on his way in.

'Dragonliiiiiight!'

They charged into a narrow corridor, Sean maybe third or fourth, heart tripping like a ringing tone. Even after only a few months of this, his experience told him that they were in the right place, that there was an illegal here; something to do with the smell, sweat and boiled cabbage, and the half-hearted decoration.

He swung the Dragonlight into each room as they went.

Bedroom, curtains drawn, sheets unkempt.

Sitting room, TV on, sound down.

Bathroom. Window open, air clammy.

Galley kitchen. Nothing.

'Nobody home,' said Sean, relieved. He let the Dragonlight down.

Around him, the posse of wound-up coppers was still making him nervous.

'Fuck,' snarled Blondie, kicking over a carefully built pyramid of empty chocolate malt cans, punching the conspiring toaster.

'I'll go back out front,' said the sane one. 'Radio in. The rest of you, have a look around, see what you can find.'

The cops drifted back through to root around, nick any money or cigarettes they could find. Sean needed fresh air. He walked through the kitchen and tried the back door. Unlocked.

There was a small yard at the back. Three metal dustbins, each one with a flat number painted on it, stood against the back wall, next to a padlocked door that led to a back lane. Sean stepped out, breathing deeply, trying to slow down his ticker. Hurriedly, he dug into the pocket of his windcheater and grabbed the bottle of pills, swallowed two dry, kept trying to breathe. But he remained bad, couldn't relax, felt a fist of delayed anxiety shoot up from his gut, making him gulp for air, doubling him over . . .

He puked up over his shoes and the hem of his trousers, liquid mainly from mouth and nose, a slight acid burn of vodka wafting through his nostrils as he sniffed back.

This, he told himself, *can't go on.*

Planting both hands on the wall in front of him, he hauled himself up with a groan, scraping his shoes clean against the back of his trousers, letting his head rest against the brickwork . . .

Brickwork.

He took a step back. From the kitchen, this had looked like the external wall to the yard, but it wasn't.

It was an outhouse.

Sean crept round to the edge, saw there was a door, put a hand out towards it . . .

He stopped himself, looking at his own hand shaking an inch above the wrought-iron handle.

Why do it, Sean? Why risk it? Forget about it, Just walk . . .

The door was kicked outwards, catching Sean a screaming blow to his wrist, sending him spinning back. He slipped in the pool of his own vomit and hit the deck, knee cracking into concrete.

Looking up, he caught sight of William 'Sweet Bill' Cameron emerge from the outhouse, unarmed, stark bollock naked except for a collection of gold chains around his neck, and leap on to the dustbins and over the wall.

'RUNNER!' screamed Sean, instinct overcoming him. As soon as he shouted he regretted it.

He clambered up, leaning on his wrist, which gave him a long, stinging reminder of his injury. By the time the first police grunt was in the yard, Sean was already atop the dustbins, ready to clamber over the wall.

'Round the front,' he shouted. 'Try and cut him off!'

He launched himself down, landing on feet and hands, keeping the weight off the dodgy wrist. He started running, pleased that his sore knee didn't hold him up much. Ahead, he could see that

Sweet Bill had a decent head start, but running barefoot down the rough surface of the lane was slowing him up, making him dance. When Sweet Bill turned his body to look back, Sean caught a view of his dick flapping up and down like an oil-soaked bird trying to take off.

Chasing him down the alley, Sean didn't have time to think about what exactly he was doing. Suddenly, all he wanted was to catch up, to collar the toerag, haul him in.

After all, it was his blag.

He was gaining, picking up maybe ten yards in every fifty they were running. That still meant Sweet Bill was going to make it to the end of the lane about thirty yards ahead. But beyond him a whelp of brakes signalled the arrival of the blue police van. Still running, Sean could see that it was a simple enough operation to block off the lane with the whole side of the vehicle, but the grunt driving wanted points for artistic impression. Arriving on the scene, he shunted the front of the van outwards, trying to leave the back door facing down the lane, allowing his colleagues in the back to jump out and take Sweet Bill out.

But he left the swing of the steering wheel too late, and the van careered in reverse into the furthest wall, buckling the back door shut and leaving Bill with an inviting corridor to continue his escape down.

'Fuck!' muttered Sean over the sound of his own troubled res-piration. Out of the back lane, the road surface was smoother and that, combined with the sniff of freedom, was starting to give Sweet Bill the advantage. Sean made it to the end of the lane, ran past the human groans from the van and the sound of the engine trying to grind itself free. Darting a look right, he was just in time to see his quarry knock an old woman to the ground and dart off the street into a road on the left. Skidding on the heels of his boots, he continued to give chase, followed by a couple of dazed coppers from the front of the van.

'Hurry,' shouted Sean. 'He's heading for the High Street.'

3

....

Harry climbed the steps out of the bookie's, feeling sick. Sick
only the way losing nearly a thousand pounds in twenty minutes
can make you feel. Each bend of the leg to negotiate the next
stair felt like a kneecapping, every footfall brought a death-rat-
tle sigh. The jangle of the few coppers left in his pocket mocked
him like a nutter's laugh.

Looking up, he could see through the door that the grim
afternoon sky afforded him no solace. Reaching the top of the
flight, the gloom allowed him to see his own reflection in the
glass of the door.

He stared hard.

'My name is Harmendra Verma,' he said. 'And I am . . .'

He stopped, biting his lip, holding his own reflection in a stare.

'My name is Harmendra Verma and I am . . .'

Fists clenched, jaw out.

'. . . an utter twat.'

Stepping out, he felt the warm air smother him. Storm coming, he thought.

Away to his left, he noticed that the clientele of one of the
local pubs, serving Caribbeans mainly, had spilled out on to the
High Street, half-blocking the pavement in a flurry of dreds,
cans of Red Stripe and manic conversation.

Seeing them, alongside the dry throat normally associated
with haemorrhaging money, made Harry thirsty. He searched
his pockets for enough silver to buy a pint of shandy but felt he

needed the insurance of a trip to the cashpoint. He leaned for-
wards, scanning the street for an appropriate bank, where he
could tap the one account he had that might have twenty quid
left in it.

That was when he saw the naked man running, *hopping*,
down the middle of the street, halting traffic, his dick threatening to fly off as he came pelting down the street, arms and legs
pumping.

This apparition was greeted with cheers and elaborate
high fives by the pub crowd next door, followed by boos of
derision for the two coppers who were gaining, themselves
ahead of a geezer in civvies, jeans and a plastic windcheater,
who didn't look like he had much running left in him. Harry
pegged him for immigration straight off. Too unhealthy to be
anything else.

'Go, Billy,' shouted one muscular drinker, his dreadlocks inefficiently shoved under a leather flat cap. 'Run, man.
Run!'

Harry felt the blood pumping again, his downstairs debacle
momentarily forgotten. Time to go to work.

He approached the Rasta. 'Here, mate,' he said. 'You know
him?'

Rasta eschewed eye contact, crunching his beer can and
dropping it, a petulant piece of delinquency.

'Name be Bill,' he said.

'Know his surname?'

A slow blink. 'Bill is all. Who is axing the question?'

Harry smirked. 'I'm his lawyer.'

Now the Rasta turned his head, looked him up and down.
'What you talking, blaaaahdcloth? Sweet Billy Cameron got no
brief, man!'

Harry grabbed a biro from his inside pocket, clicked out the
ballpoint, wrote BILL CAMERON on the palm of his hand.

'He does now,' said Harry, heading off towards his car.

Game on.

*

Sean was tying up fast. His run had deteriorated into a trot favouring his good knee, so he limped, one shoulder ahead of the other, Quasimodo on speed, red-faced, sweating Smirnoff like a bastard. The chest pains were back, joined by voodoo pins shoved behind his left shoulder blade.

He lost sight of Sweet Bill as he had allowed the swing of his dick to steer him left and towards the Metcalf Housing Estate, an unnaturally occurring labyrinth of shit-brown brick, disused lifts and stairs that led nowhere. The perfect hiding place.

The glass broke on a fire alarm in his lungs and he slowed to a trot, leaving the now-futile chase to the two grunts. By the time he got to the junction where Bill had made his turn, he expected to see them leaning on one another, panting for breath, the chase over and declared a failure.

Not so.

The grunts were standing apart with their back to him, circling Sweet Bill, who was lying face first on the ground with another man on top of him, his forearm grinding Bill's half-turned face deep into the road surface. If Bill was Sweet before, now he was positively frothing, twitching like a lighted banger. But his captor's knee, dug deep in the small of his back, kept his thrashings in their place. Sean noticed the first drops of rain from the threatened storm fall and slither down Sweet Bill's muscular flanks.

The man on top was wiry, bone near his surface. He wore a pair of painstakingly pleated serge trousers, tight around the crotch, a cream polo neck sweater beneath a checked sports jacket. His hair was thinning, brushed across a lumpen forehead, an intent gaze made more insistent by the black-plastic-framed mullioned windows he wore on his nose. He looked like a woodwork teacher.

'Yur a bit fuckin' testy, aren't ya?' he addressed Sweet Bill in a Caledonian hiss. 'Yu fancy a bit of a rumble, ya slag . . . ?'

One of the grunts put the flat of his hands out in a suppli-catory gesture at Bill's attacker.

'Now, look, we don't want this to get out of hand . . .'

'Just take it easy, mate. We don't want you to get hurt,' said the other.

Sean stepped forward. The man on top of Sweet Bill peered through his glasses at him and sniffed.

'You,' he said, matter-of-factly. 'Where you been?'

'It's all right,' Sean told the coppers. 'He's one of mine. Eric,' he added by way of greeting.

Keeping one hand on Sweet Bill, Eric McCleish took the opportunity to flash his warrant, jab a Marlboro into his mouth and push his NHS specs back on to his nose.

'Are you just going to stand there or are you going to cuff this fucking ratbag?'

Sean nodded to the two coppers, who set about restraining Sweet Bill, telling him he was arrested, reading him his rights. Eric moved across to Sean, who was still catching his breath, bent forward, hands on knees.

'What were you doing here?' Sean asked, pulling himself back upright, declining a fag, rubbing his bad wrist.

'I was in the neighbourhood. At the Crown Court.'

'Oh, yeah? Sending somebody down?'

Eric shook his head, hissed out a mouthful of smoke between clenched teeth.

'No. I just got banned for three years for drink-driving.'

'Right,' Sean said, watching as a marked police car pulled up. 'So how did you get here?'

'I drove,' said Eric, no hint of the ironic. Over his shoulder, Sean saw one of their office pool cars. 'I heard that you needed a bit of help on the police frequency, so I thought, Fuck it, if it's a blag, I'll get myself over in a hurry. Should have known it was one of yours. It's been a while,' he added with a little shiver of pleasure, 'since I decked a runner. Still got the old magic.'

Truth was, Sean was in the presence of an immigration service legend here. Eric McCleish was a name Sean had heard years before ever joining enforcement. But his actual presence, that was something again. The little sanity Eric had once had was now utterly extinguished by working for three years on the Yardie desk. During this period he had earned his nickname of Crazy Horse, living up to it with scrotes and colleagues alike. Half-truths of his excesses were legion, but anything was possible when you got to the plateau Eric was at, somewhere between religious zeal and sociopathic dysfunction. Drinking, drugging, embezzling, whoring and above all blagging . . . Eric wasn't just living the job any more. He *was* the job, a fucking force of nature.

Sean looked hard at Crazy Horse, trying to spot a gleam of empathy from behind the aquarium glass of his specs, but he saw nothing.

'You all right?' McCleish asked him, with a hint of derision. Sean hadn't been in the job long enough to get anything but contempt.

'Fine, fine,' he answered, drawing in a long breath.

'Right,' accepted Eric, turning in towards Sean to keep the two coppers out of vision. He produced a small tin with CURIOUSLY STRONG MINTS written olde worlde on the lid. Inside were a half dozen two-tone pills, rolling innocently.

'Want one?'

'What are they?'

'Not sure. Phenobarbital derivative, summat like that. Bloke I took 'em off, a squeal called Dog, you know him?'

Sean shook his head. Nobody else touched Eric's elaborate network of informers, not if they knew what was good for them.

'I'll pass,' said Sean. 'Got some of my own.'

'. . . anyway, he was calling them Busters.'

Eric popped one, two and put the tin away.

'Busters,' he repeated with a laugh. 'I like that. It's a good name.' He stared at Sean again. 'It's a fucking *appropriate* name.'

Looking back, they both saw Sweet Bill being dragged to the police car. He was still struggling, so one grunt moved in behind and gave him a nice chop to the back of the legs with his truncheon. As Bill's knee buckled, they shoved him on to the back seat. Eric looked on for a moment before heading back to his car.

'Listen, mate, what did you say your name was again?'

'Sean.'

'Aye, right, Sean. Sean, mate, could you do us a favour?' he said, throwing Sean the keys. 'Drop me off, will ya? I need to get down that fuckin' pub, drown me sorrows,' he said, throwing Sean the keys. 'Banned for three years. Christ knows what Mrs McCleish'll say,' he added, getting into the passenger seat as the rain suddenly got heavier. 'Three years? Can you fuckin' believe it?'

4

....

Through the gradual blur on his windscreen as the rain began to fall hard, Harry watched the two immigration hard-knocks get into the car, playing at Starsky and Hutch as they loved to do. He had parked on a red zone still on the High Street, looking from a safe distance. From here, William looked like he might be more trouble than he was worth once the legal aid had dried up. He was worth the legal aid trouble. *Anybody* was worth the legal aid trouble. Money for old rope.

He wound down the window as the police car turned back on to the High Street. He was pleased to see the immigration boys going in the opposite direction. That meant he had some time to play with, time to get William onside. A gentle breaker of storm air swabbed the back of his neck, kept him cool as he put his BMW, personalised number plates to disguise its age, into drive.

Leaning across, one hand on the wheel, he picked up the mobile phone and tapped in a number. He waited until the first junction, when he would know which nick they were taking Bill to, before pressing DIAL, slipping the phone on to its cradle and putting the call through to the in-car speaker.

It rang three times, and then an agonising fourth. Four times meant Carla had left the office, unless she was taking a piss or having a fag or making a cup of tea or just being a lazy bitch . . .

She picked it up on the fifth ring.

'What?'

Harry laughed derisively.

'What the hell is that? *What?* Is that how you answer the phone to everybody?'

'I knew it was you.'

'How the hell did you know it was me?'

'I just knew.'

'Women's intuition? That's our new business plan? Barclays are going to love that.'

'Sod off, Harry. Of course it's you. Who else is going to call me now, when I'm on my way out and you haven't paid me for a month?'

'You keep answering it like that and I'll never have any fucking income to pay you from.'

A pause. Carla didn't like swearing. Except when . . .

'What?' she repeated, *worrrrrrr*, in the Cockney drone she copied from the telly.

'I need you to do something for me.'

'I'm on my way home, Harry. It's after half-five.'

'I know, I know. It's not going to take long.'

'I have to get home to my husband and baby, Harry. Darren's working tonight and I would like to spend a few minutes with him, if that's all right with you.'

Harry noted the information, stored it in short-term advantage. He carried on as if she hadn't spoken.

'Here's what I want you to do,' he said, ignoring her groan. 'Knock up a quick fax, letter of representation. Name of William Cameron.'

'Date of birth?'

'Don't worry about that,' replied Harry, smiling at the thought that she was staying on to help him out.

'Nationality?'

Harry thought. He didn't want to risk a guess. 'Put down Stateless. Then fax it as soon as you can to the custody sergeant at Battersea nick. Have you got that number?'

'I don't suppose it's an official secret.'

'Maybe not,' shouted Harry into the microphone attached to the sunshield above his head. 'But you, darling, are a national treasure.'

'Just pay me,' said the voice, sounding sexy he thought, followed by the click of excommunication.

'I'll pay you, all right,' he smiled, taking a left.

Harry parked just out of view of the nick, left it a few minutes before getting out of the car. Didn't want to turn up too soon, make it too obvious. He took the opportunity to sort out his briefcase, make sure he had paper, pens, jellybeans, the packet of fags he carried to offer to clients and, all-importantly, enough of the magic legal aid forms, the licence to print money and help get Bohra off his back. He felt the increasingly frequent shiver of self-hatred that all gamblers know when he thought about the five thousand he'd borrowed, ostensibly to help with relocating his office, the five thousand that now nestled comfortably in the coffers of his local turf accountants. And – oh, yeah – he couldn't have chosen a nicer bloke to be behind on his repayments with . . .

Still, he could make it back, even if it meant dodging Bohra and having to keep his nose in the trough of immigration work for a little longer.

Just a little longer . . .

He got out of the car and started walking to the station, holding his leather briefcase over his head as protection against the sheeting rain.

Through the main door, which swung stiffly, was a small enquiries area, with a few plastic chairs and a guichet, unmanned.

PLEASE PRESS FOR SERVICE announced an old laminated sign attached to the reinforced glass. An arrow pointed down to a horizontal tit fixed to the desk. Harry gave the nipple a poke. A nasty buzz went off somewhere in the building.

A tired-looking uniform stepped out into the space behind the guichet.

'Yes?'

Harry cleared his throat. 'My name is Harmendra Verma, from Verma Carter Associates at Law.'

He slid one of the business cards he'd got from the machine in the shopping arcade through the small gap below the window. The copper didn't even give it a cursory look.

'And?' he asked, squinting.

'I'm here to see my client.'

The policeman stood back, picked something from between his teeth. 'You're a brief?'

'Solicitor, yes.'

'You?'

'Look at the card. LLB. You know what that means?'

The constable puffed out his cheeks, a gesture of stagy surprise suggesting Harry would be better off behind a shop counter or driving a cab. 'Who is your client, then?'

'His name is William Cameron.'

'What, the naked feller?'

Harry flicked a look over his own shoulder. 'I don't know anything about his state of dress. I would like to see my client.'

'He hasn't even made his phone call yet. How come you're here?'

Harry had a ready-made answer. 'I received a call from a friend, informing me that he needed legal representation.'

The copper shook his head. 'Wouldn't be turning up on spec, would you? Little spot of ambulance chasing, is it? We've got duty briefs for the likes of him. We don't need any more vultures, mate.'

Harry's eyes narrowed. 'Just let me see him, or you'll have an official complaint to contend with.'

The copper leaned forward again, resting his forearm on the desk and sucked through his teeth. 'You don't come into my station and threaten me, understood? Now, I haven't been told that this suspect has a lawyer, wants a lawyer or can even spell the word lawyer. Until I have that information, my friend, I think the best place for you is out in the rain.'

He turned and headed back into the office. Harry was left, choosing to stand his ground but equally with nowhere to go. He felt the frustration of his self-inflicted mauling at the bookie's seize him by the throat again, making him want to curse, to bounce his fist off the lead-laced glass keeping him out.

The sergeant had slammed the door shut behind him, but a dodgy catch had let it swing back open, giving Harry a partial view of the office behind. Harry could see the fax machine in the far corner begin to spill out a received message. The one who had just told him to fuck off came into view to pick it up off the tray where it had landed. Harry stayed where he was, held his breath as the rozzer read it then – *yes!* – looked across sourly.

'I'd like to see my client,' shouted Harry. 'Now!'

He was led through and down to the interview rooms, shown into one and left alone there. After a couple of minutes Sweet Bill was ushered in, looking cowed. They had found him one of the pairs of white overalls normally reserved for serial killers, with a zip that pulled from the crotch right up the front.

Sweet Bill tilted his head back as he looked at Harry. Harry rolled his eyes, knowing that Bill was just warming himself up for the full Malcolm X bit. As if he'd been waiting his whole life for this chance . . .

Harry turned to the constable who'd brought Bill in, still lurking by the door. 'I'm going to take instruction from my client,' he said. 'If you could leave.'

Another unimpressed look, but the door clunked shut and left him in there with his latest meal ticket. Harry pointed to a chair and Bill suspiciously sat down.

'You understand English?' Harry asked.

'Maybe,' grunted Bill.

Harry sighed, bored of him already.

'I didn't ask you whether you spoke it, all right?' he said quietly. 'I asked you whether you understood it. Take a cigarette. Here, light it,' he added, throwing Bill a cheap plastic lighter, 'and keep your mouth shut.'

Bill looked up, a little hurt that his Negro-with-attitude routine was getting such short shrift. But he kept quiet.

'Right,' Harry went on. 'Here's the score. I'm going to be your lawyer. Nod if you have a problem with that. No? Good. First thing that's going to happen is that we're going to fill in a form and you're going to sign it. It's a legal aid form. Nod if you understand what that means. It means you don't have to pay for your legal costs. They're paid for by —'

'Who?'

'You spoke, William.'

'I want to know who is going to pay. I don't owe nothing to no man.'

'Don't worry about it. The British taxpayer will come to your rescue. The government, all right? They pay. And you don't have to pay them back.'

Sweet Bill looked baffled, as if confronted with morris dancing for the first time.

'So,' Harry continued, getting into his stride now, starting to enjoy himself. 'This is how we're going to play it. There's an immigration officer on his way, coming to serve deportation papers on you. They want to kick you out of the country, right? I'm here to stop them doing that. That's the game. If you want to know, our side wins more often than theirs. Our side always wins.'

Sweet Bill, good as gold now, gave him a docile nod.

Harry tapped out a cigarette for himself, not to smoke, just something to play with.

'So they're coming to give you this paper, saying you have to leave the country. You got a passport?'

Bill shook his head.

'Good. That makes it more difficult for them. How did you get in the country? You buy a fake passport?'

Bill nodded.

'OK. You don't tell them that. Understood? You tell them you jumped on the back of a lorry in a strange country, that you paid someone you don't know to bring you here. Whatever questions he asks you, you don't know the answers to any of them. Just play dumb.'

Bill continued to look at Harry, mouth open.

'Shouldn't be too difficult. OK, then, once he arrives and starts talking to you, I'm going to say that you can't go back to . . . where is it?'

'Liberia.'

'Wherever. I'm going to say you can't go back because you are in fear of your life. Say it.'

'Huh?'

'Say it. Say, "I am in fear of my life."'

'I am in fear of my life...' muttered Sweet Bill.

'No. Say it like you mean it.'

'I am in fear of my life?' asked Bill.

'Yeah. Say it as if it's true.'

Sweet Bill sat back, puffed out his chest and planted his hands on the table. 'I AM IN FEAR OF MY LIFE!' he boomed, jutting his chin out for emphasis.

Harry winced at the volume, thinking that the copper down the hall would be able to hear.

'No, no, less of the Idi Amin. Look, here, cock your head to one side.' Harry rushed forward and tipped Bill's head a few degrees like a barber would a young child.

He stepped back. 'Fine. Now open your eyes wide like a puppy, that's it, wider. Now, stick out your bottom lip as if you're about to cry.'

Harry showed him. At first Bill was a little hesitant to compromise his manhood to this extent, but when he heard voices from the corridor outside he was persuaded.

'OK,' said Harry, also aware that time was short. 'Fold your arms across your body and keep rocking, gently rocking. Now, listen. You need to think of a reason why you're in fear, why it's dangerous to go home.'

'I am in fear of my life,' murmured Sweet Bill.

'Something good, like you were beaten up by soldiers.'

Bill came out of character.

'No. I was the soldier.'

'Let's not burden ourselves with the truth here. You went to a demonstration and the soldiers beat you up, OK?'

'OK, chief,' said Bill.

Harry heard footsteps. Quickly, he sat down next to Bill. 'Puppy eyes,' he whispered. 'Bottom lip out. And keep rocking . . .'

5

The duty sergeant handed Sean the fax while he was still shaking the rain out of his hair.

WILLIAM CAMERON – STATELESS
Please note for your records that we are representing the above named in his immigration matter. Our representative will be attending his interview today to take instruction. Please forward any future correspondence to us.

Verma Carter
Associates at Law

Sean sighed, exchanged melancholy smiles with a couple of passing constables.
'How the hell did they find out?'
'He said he got a call from a friend.'
'You've spoken to him?'
'Yeah. He fetched up here, I don't know, half an hour ago.'
'And he's been in to see our boy?'
The sergeant shrugged a *what could I do?*
Now Sean groaned. That meant that Sweet Bill would be claiming political asylum, which in turn rendered the chance of any deportation virtually nil. He had risked a coronary dashing up the High Street for nothing. He still had one ace up his sleeve, though.

'Where is he now?'

'Who, the brief? He's in with your boy.'

'All right. Let's get this over with.'

Sean walked down the corridor, heels rapping against the dried-out lino on the floor. Stopping at the door to the interview room, he snorted in a lungful of air and tried to exorcise all thought of beers and chasers before walking in with his well-practised air of tired authority.

There was Sweet Bill, whom he'd last seen naked, fighting like a bastard with two light-heavyweight coppers. Now he sat quietly in a pair of white overalls, staring into space, tongue hanging out and swaying back and forward hard on his chair. Either he was doped up to the eyeballs or he'd had a stroke. Maybe both.

Sean sat down, paying scant attention to the brief, an Asian bloke dressed like a car salesman, with a ridiculous pair of long, narrow sideburns tapering down his pudgy face. Just what Sean needed. Another fucking spiv lawyer with the gift of the gab and a chip on his shoulder.

Who do these people think they are?

Sean stared at Bill, who had started to dribble from one corner of his mouth.

'All right, Bill,' he said, 'here's how I'm going to—'

At which point the Bombay spiv opened his mouth.

Harry could see he had a right one here. Regular hard-knock, dressed up like some *Kojak* extra. It seemed to Harry that someone had forgotten to tell him and his type that this was a democracy, that people were entitled to legal representation whether they liked it or not. Like they expected to ponce around in their cheap leather jackets, dispensing summary justice left, right and centre. Of course he knew that Harry would have already primed his boy to claim and Harry knew he wasn't going to like it. So what?

I mean, who do these people think they are?

Oh, and another thing. Harry didn't much like being ignored. So when *he* started going on about how he was going to play it, Harry chose to butt in.

'Before we go any further, I think you should be aware that I have taken instruction from my client and that he has expressed a wish to claim political asylum in the United Kingdom.'

'I am in fear of my life,' moaned Sweet Bill, rolling his eyes.

The hard-knock deliberately let his mouth twist into what he imagined was a cynical smile.

'Wonder where he got that idea . . . ?'

Harry resisted the temptation to start mixing it yet, preferred to play the legal eagle for the moment.

'Don't be in any doubt that I will be prepared to report any more injudicious comments to your superiors...'

How do you like that, you bastard? he thought.

'Fear of my life,' gurgled Sweet Bill.

Sean sat back, folded his arms. This one fancied himself, no doubt about it. Now was the time for Sean to play his ace, see how far the spiv was prepared to take it with a piece of work like Sweet Bill, test his mettle . . .

'In that case,' Sean began, 'you may wish to inform your client that when I'm finished with him, my police colleagues are busy compiling a set of charges that includes robbery, indecent assault and, nice one this, attempted rape.'

He slid a form across the desk, put it in front of Bill. Form IS101, Withdrawal of Claim to Asylum.

'If you sign that, William, forget about the asylum business, all that stuff, we might be able to keep the police out of this and even give you a free ride home. How about it?'

Sean rounded this off with a little widening of the eyes, a little tease, letting the spiv know that he was way out of his depth, that this wasn't some Tamil whose biggest crime was washing dishes without permission in a Southall curry house, that he'd touted himself into the path of a real, bona fide toerag. Sean knew enough to know that if the spiv had what it took to play at criminal law, then he wouldn't be in the immigration game to start with.

Sweet Bill, perhaps aware that this, the performance of his life, was going largely unnoticed, started rocking harder, looking frantically at his representative.

'I have fear of my life,' he crooned, unfolding his arms in order to rub his hands maniacally together. 'Fear of life. Fear of life...'

Harry mulled it over.

He stole a glance at Sweet Bill, who was staring back at him, about to rock himself off his chair. The words *attempted rape* had set his teeth on edge.

'I am in f—' Sweet Bill started.

'Shut up,' Harry said.

He rationalised fast. First of all, innocent until proven guilty, right? Another look across at his client served only to confirm his fear that Bill was probably capable of anything. Anyway, immigration was his area. He was an immigration *specialist*. The rest could be handed on later. The officer was setting up a proposition for Sweet Bill. Withdraw the claim to asylum and we might be able to deport you, forget about the charges against you if we boot you out of the country. There were two problems with this. First, Harry doubted if Hard-Knock here had the agreement of the Old Bill. If the police didn't want to let Bill go, he could still do time and then get deported; a double whammy. Second, and more important, no asylum claim, no money for Harry.

I don't think so.

Harry spoke. 'At this point in time I have taken instruction from my client only regarding his immigration matter. If any charges are to be made against him, I will arrange for further instruction to be taken. In the meantime my client wishes to pursue a claim for political asylum.'

Sean smiled. *Nice one*, he thought. *I will arrange* . . . Translation: I'll have my pound of legal aid out of this charlie and hang him out to dry when the time comes.

'That's the way you want to play it,' said Sean.

He served Form IS151A, Notice of Intention to Deport an Illegal Entrant, on Sweet Bill. Then he took the Polaroid out of his case and photographed Bill, eyes wide, tongue sticking out.

'Now,' he sighed, rummaging around for the right paper, 'I'm going to interview you about your asylum claim.'

The spiv opened his mouth again.

Harry didn't want the asylum interview done now and not just because it was knocking on seven o'clock and he'd had enough for the day. He needed time to cobble together some vaguely coherent story for Sweet Bill to give immigration. Once the fiction had been passed on, that would be the end of his interest in Mr Cameron. They'd be wanting to keep him detained and, while Harry knew he was expected to put up a token resistance, the truth was that he thought behind bars was probably the best place for him. The last thing he wanted was Sweet Bill turning up at the office. The tone was low enough there already. But if he broke it up now, and delayed the asylum interview, then he would be able to claim a second dollop of legal aid cash plus expenses for travelling to whichever nick they kept him in. With Bohra breathing down his neck, this was no time to start letting Law Society best practice bugger things up.

'As you can see, my client is clearly physically and mentally distressed. I don't think he's in any state to go over the traumatic events surrounding his persecution in . . . his own country. I request that it be put off until a later date.'

★

Sean was quietly pleased. It was getting close to seven and what with risking his life, throwing up all over himself, chasing a naked illegal through a thunderstorm and being given the run-around by this little shyster, he was ready to knock it on the head and find somewhere to get pissed.

'Fine,' he said. 'You should know that we'll be detaining your client.'

'On what grounds?'

'On the grounds that I don't think he would comply if we released him.'

The spiv shrugged.

'Please register my objections on your file.'

'Whatever you say.' Sean nodded, oddly disappointed that he wasn't kicking up more of a fuss. He suddenly felt edgy, definitely in the mood for a barney.

They both rose, Sweet Bill looking up at them dolefully.

'I'll tell the sergeant we're finished,' said Sean on his way out.

'How'd I do, boss?' Bill asked Harry when it was safe.

Harry looked down. 'You're a fucking star,' he said and started collecting his things. He was already waiting outside, back leaned against the wall, briefcase clutched in both hands, when the constable came back.

'He should be up before the magistrate tomorrow,' said the copper as he led him back to the entrance.

'Tell the duty brief,' said Harry. 'Criminal case got nothing to do with me. Ask him to let me know where they bang him up,' he added, as he opened the door back into the enquiries area and passed through and out, without looking back.

Starting to feel claustrophobic, Sean had got out of the station as soon as he could. He tripped down the steps outside and stood at their foot amid the dank evening air, the rain having stopped only a few minutes before. He took a glance back, saw nobody following him, quickly lunged a hand into his pocket and threw another lithium into his mouth, gulped it down dry. It was becoming a habit now, just as the law of diminishing returns was starting to kick in. He tried to pull back his bent shoulders and rolled his head in a sweeping circle like Maria used to do during her yoga phase. He stared up at the sky, eyes welling up. From the cold.

Why him? So unfair. Just needed something to take it all out on.

At the top of the steps, the old double doors swung open.

Harry saw him, the hard-knock from immigration, at the bottom of the steps, looking strange, as if he'd been crying or something. He went quickly down the steps, hoping to avoid any further trouble. Truth was, he didn't really like confrontation. It drained him. Especially today, with the feeling of that eight hundred still there in his pocket like a lost limb and Bohra's bad breath warming the back of his neck.

He tried to steer a wide path, but he was seen.

'Hey,' said Sean.

Harry kept walking, said nothing.

Sean dropped his case, started to follow. 'I'm talking to you.'

'I'm in a hurry,' said Harry, still moving.

Sean caught up, jogging alongside now, aggressively close. 'Just wanted to say, off the record, just to let you know, that I think you're a fucking disgrace.'

Harry stopped, skidding on his heels, and turned. 'You what?'

'You,' said Sean, jabbing him once in the chest as the rain began to fall again.

'You touch me, that's fucking assault.'

Sean took a step back, his brow furrowed. 'What I want to know is how can you sit in there with that?' He pointed back towards the station. 'Sit there with a straight face and go in to bat for . . . for that. For that slag?'

Harry looked at him, shrugged. 'Come on, man,' he said, allowing a conciliatory note into his voice. 'You get paid to kick them out, I get paid to keep them here. That's the game. I don't make the rules. Just don't ever touch me again. I won't mention it this time. You look a little strung out, mate. We all have bad days.'

'I'm not your fucking mate. Look at you,' Sean raged, scanning Harry's attire. 'Some kind of fucking pimp or something . . .'

'Piss off.'

'Fucking pimp! Touting pimping slag.'

'Yeahyeahyeah,' Harry said as he walked away.

Sean watched him go. He wanted the last word. But, as so often before, it didn't come. He watched as the little spiv bastard, suddenly the manifestation of everything that was conspiring to fuck up his life, just walked away.

Not good enough.

The lithium rattled again in his pocket. Reaching in, he could feel he hadn't screwed the cap on properly and the pills, maybe forty of them, were tumbling loose. He grabbed a couple out and threw them. One landed on the ground in front of the spiv. The other must have made contact because he stopped and put a hand to the back of his neck.

Harry turned in disbelief. At his feet he could see what had struck him, a little pill, blue and red. 'Right,' he said.

Quickly squatting, he opened his case and pulled out the bag of jellybeans. He plunged a hand in and threw a shower of sweets at Sean. An arc of blue/red tablets came flying back at him, attached to a cry of 'wanker'. Harry took a step to the left, dodging the barrage and picked one jellybean, a red one, from a clump in his left hand, choosing to aim at Sean's head. Before it had even reached his target, he let off another then another, then the whole fistful.

He didn't notice the car pull up alongside.

'Are you . . . all right, sir?'

Harry looked across to see a police car on its way back to the station, the passenger window rolled down and a copper, shirt-sleeved, leaning out.

'I . . . er,' said Harry, still standing as if to throw another bean. He glanced ahead, saw that the pill-throwing immigration arsehole had vacated the scene.

'What's that you've got in your hand there, sir?' asked the copper, his colleague behind the wheel sniggering.

Harry put out his palm. 'Sweet,' said Harry. 'Jellybean.'

'Jellybean,' repeated the pig, dry as a bone. 'Put someone's eye out with that. Move along, there's a good lad.'

6

....

Harry drove to Tooting. He managed to get a rare parking space on Topsham Road. Getting out of the car, he walked back on to the High Street past the Bollywood video store and the closed linen shops, dhoti-clad mannequins in the window. Stopping at the familiar grocery store, he went in.

Jay was standing behind the counter, looking down as he read some magazine. He was chewing, as always, some gooey honeyed concoction from the confectioner's next door. An idle hand reached out to grab another piece, which he stuffed into his mouth, ramming it home with the end of his little finger before being wiped down the nasty pale brown shirt that hung out of his trousers and over what had become his hard, round belly.

'All right?' Harry said.

Jay looked up, grunted and pushed the bag of sweetmeats across the counter.

'No, thanks,' said Harry, preferring to grab a bag of jelly-beans from a wire stand next to the drinks fridge.

Jay sighed, pulled out a packet of Silk Cut from his shirt pocket.

'So now it's the Indian food that is not good enough for you, is it?'

Harry ripped open the bag of sweets but didn't reply, not wanting to go down this conversational dead end with his brother. Jay's accent seemed to be getting closer to Peter

Sellers' Indian doctor every time he saw him now. And suddenly, out of nowhere, he'd started giving it the old head shake like in *It Ain't Half Hot, Mum* or something. Jay was three years older than Harry (looked about ten) and, yes, he had been born in India, as he was always quick to remind Harry. But he'd been six months old when the Vermas had upped sticks. Having spoken about five words of Punjabi until the age of eighteen, it was now virtually impossible to get him to speak anything else. He even boasted to having forgotten great chunks of English vocabulary. Harry was the first to agree that if you could make something out of playing the ethnic card, you might as well. But, typically with Jay, his self-conscious attempts to connect with his roots missed the mark spectacularly, ended up making him look like a parody of a Mumbai taxi driver. All this stuff didn't have much to do with India, but it was very, very Jay.

'So how is he?' asked Harry.

Jay, fag in mouth, took a look over his shoulder towards the stairs that led to the flat above.

'Same.'

'Has the doctor been?'

'Popped in. Not for long.'

'Well, what did he say?'

'Usual things.'

Harry sighed, exasperated. 'What did he actually say, Jay?'

'I told you. The usual.'

'That's not what he said, Jay. What does "the usual" mean? A doctor's not just going to say "the usual" and then piss off.'

Jay continued studying his magazine hard, tapping off the end of his fag into an ashtray secreted below the counter top.

'If you come here more than once a week, maybe you know what usual is.'

Harry laughed sourly. 'Yeah, sorry. I've been here a whole minute without having any guilt heaped on me. Cheers for sorting that one out for me.'

'Maybe I'd like the chance to feel some guilt. I got to stay here day in, day out, looking after him while he does nothing but talk shit about you.'

'Not like you to have a chip on your shoulder,' said Harry, walking behind the counter and towards the stairs. 'I'm going up to see him.'

'I'm not stopping you,' said Jay, pulling another cigarette out of the packet. 'Ask him if he wants anything.'

Harry went up, the worn carpet slippy underfoot. On the landing the floorboards creaked, an instant reminder of his childhood in the same cramped little flat. He passed the small kitchen, the dark sitting room, Jay's room, which Harry had shared with him through youth and adolescence, and on to the front of the house, where his father would be in his bed.

Harry stopped at the already open door and looked in. His father lay on his back, looking small, head thrown back on a pile of pillows, eyes closed, mouth open. An open newspaper lay across his body. His white tonsure had grown longer, combining with his beaky nose to give him more than a vague air of the Brahmin. Harry knew Dad wasn't asleep, sensed there was a little conscious play-acting in the mechanical regularity of his wheezing. With a gentle laughing sigh, he walked in.

'Hey,' he said, 'it's me.'

Dad opened one alert eye, closed it again quickly and stretched out a long hand.

'Is that my boy?' he moaned. 'Has my boy come to visit his sick father?'

Harry took his hand, kissed it and sat down on the bed.

'Seems to me you enjoy being sick a bit too much.'

Dad pulled hard on Harry's hand to haul himself up. He grabbed the newspaper, folding it to a quarter size.

'I was just glancing through the legal reports,' he said. 'You've seen them?'

To humour him, Harry took the paper and gave it a cursory glance.

'Yeah, fascinating,' he said, chucking the paper on the floor. The only law reports he paid any attention to these days were to do with Jockey Club suspensions for excessive use of the whip.

'Working on any interesting cases, Harmendra?'

Harry rolled his tongue across the front of his teeth.

'Lot of routine work at the moment.'

'Lots of paperwork, is it?' asked Dad excitedly. Nobody had ever found the prospect of working in an office quite so marvellous.

'Yeah. Paperwork,' agreed Harry. As usual, part of him wanted to blurt out the truth about the professional mire he operated in, just to release him from this distasteful façade of legal respectability. But he couldn't just go and break his dad's heart, especially when it was so close to conking out of its own accord. He stretched and yawned. 'Busy time.'

Dad pursed his mouth a little.

'Too busy to visit your father?'

'I'm here, aren't I?'

'One day you'll turn up and I won't be.'

Harry was almost relieved to hear Jay come up the stairs and into the room.

'What are you bloody doing, man?' barked Dad at him. 'You want us to get robbed, have our livelihoods taken from under our noses?'

Jay managed to look angry and sheepish at the same time. 'What do you think? I locked the door, didn't I?'

'So we are multi-millionaires, we can close the shop early now?'

Jay huffed. 'Look, I just came up to see what you wanted to eat. I was going to go and get a video.'

Dad looked at Harry. 'Too busy to stay?'

'No,' answered Harry, annoyed at the insinuation. 'Of course I'll stay,' he added, turning to look at his brother. 'I can mind the shop if you want.'

Jay looked unhappy, shook his head. 'No. I'll wait until nine. I've got a new till. It's complicated. I don't think you'd be able to understand it.'

Harry laughed as Jay turned away. He liked it when Jay exercised that dry sense of humour. It reminded him of the charming bully he had once worshipped from across their little shared bedroom.

'And listen to me,' Dad was shouting. 'You get a video, make sure none of that Bollywood crap! I want to watch a proper movie. Romantic comedy. Meg Ryan, innit?'

'Yaryaryar,' said Jay, descending.

'He's trying to shove all this Indian rubbish down my throat,' Dad explained. 'Stopping in the middle of a gunfight to have a sing and dance.' A worried look passed over his face. 'Should we have got a courtroom drama?'

'No. Meg Ryan's fine.' He gestured back towards where Jay had gone. 'He's all right?'

Dad gave him a shrug. 'Far as I know. He'll be happier when I'm dead. Then he'll be able to sell his dirty magazines.'

Harry said nothing, just rubbed his temple between forefinger and thumb, hoping it would disguise the shaking of his head.

7

....

The Hole in the Wall stood under a railway bridge opposite the main entrance to Waterloo Station. Its proximity to Waterloo made it a convenient stopping-off point. You'd always find someone from the office there, whatever the time. The back room was a grim, dark parlour panelled with cheap wood and boasting a long, sticky Formica bar.

Sean wasn't sure what had taken him there tonight: perhaps an instinctive desire to belong to the group, more likely a wish not to go back to his flat in Balham. For whatever reason, there he was, keeping quiet, sat in one corner with three others around a table, letting the booze dull the pain in his wrist. He was getting to the stage where they were accepting his presence, although he couldn't be said to be included in the conversation, which was fine by him, the subject under discussion being too close for comfort to his little secret, his *big* problem.

'I can't understand it,' said Dave Carpenter, squeezed into bike leathers, draining another bottle of Newcastle Brown, his fifth, sixth maybe, and resting it in the circle of empties that had gathered around his motorcycle helmet in the centre of the table. 'Why knock it on the head after six months? Six months, for fuck's sake!'

'Yeah, but six months with nothing to show for it, aye?' said Crazy Horse. 'You'd think in six months you could get something to stick to the fucking Bohras. They've got more fucking rackets than Carpenter's got bellies on him.'

Dave belched, a response impossible to interpret.

'Come on,' muttered Jamie Mehta, sipping his lemonade. 'You know the fucking reason, innit?'

They all knew the reason, yet were hesitant to speak its name. Except for Crazy Horse, totally leathered by this point.

'Aye, well, if it's true, if one fucking word of it's true . . . if some little fuckers been giving away our intel . . . I'll tell you what, I don't like working somewhere where I know there's a mole giving the slags all our movements before we know 'em waseels . . .'

Sombre agreement was writ large in the simultaneous downing of drinks. The truth was that someone in the office, someone on the inside, had been feeding the Bohras everything they needed to dodge the full-scale investigation that had been ongoing for the past six months. Every tip, every surprise raid they'd tried to make, every attempt to catch them in the act turning to dust. And the Bohras' numerous sweatshops and brothels, populated by illegals paid less than nothing and blackmailed with threats of being shopped, suddenly disappearing overnight. The thousands of man-hours spent on surveillance, on staking out known associates, all for nothing when the operation had been closed down that week for lack of results and the need for resources elsewhere. It was a serious blow to the department's self-image, and the talk was that, upstairs, heads were set to roll. If, that was, the identity of Bohra's inside man remained a mystery.

'One thing I know,' said Crazy Horse. 'No way it's a senior man. We're looking at someone who hasn't been around that long.'

A silence fell. It took Scan a moment to realise that they were all looking at him. 'What?'

'Just a coincidence, that's all,' said Carpenter, doing Eric's dirty work for him. 'You started around the time the whole operation did, didn't you?'

'Yeah? And?'

'Coincidence, that's all I'm saying. You got back from Lagos around then.'

'Don't be so fucking stupid,' Sean said, which seemed to work. He didn't like the reference to Lagos either, especially as it seemed to stir up Crazy Horse's interest.

'You were Lagos, were you?'

Sean nodded, looked into his empty glass. *Like he doesn't fucking know.*

'Bet you've a few stories to tell...'

'Not as many as you, I'm sure.'

'A few skeletons in the cupboard.'

Sean and Eric stared it out for a moment. The others said nothing. Perhaps they knew what McCleish obviously didn't.

Sean stood up.

'My round,' he said and went to the bar. By the time he got back, the subject had mercifully changed.

It was another ten minutes later that Eric got up, everyone grabbing their drinks as he set the table rocking.

'Right,' he said, grabbing a treble of something and necking it. The others looked on admiringly. 'Nothing to be gained from hanging around with you sorry bastards. Time to pay Letitia a visit. Just in the mood for a shag.'

'You still knocking her off?' asked Jamie.

'Oh, aye,' said Eric. 'She's always happy to oblige a servant of the Crown.'

'You're not still telling her you're going to get her brother a visa, are you?'

Eric shrugged. 'I've got his file out of layby about a year ago. I used to take it round with me, pretend to study it, tell her there were developments imminent. Developments imminent. When I said that, that was time for her to get her knickers off.'

Everyone laughed.

'Now I don't bother taking the file round. She never asks about it. Propping up a wobbly leg on my desk, I think it is. You know,' he added, putting his raincoat on, 'I think she does it now because she likes me. Can you ken that?'

He stopped after a few paces on his way out and turned back. 'By the way, Mrs McLeish rings the pub, I'm down in Stockwell on a job. Tell her not to wait up.'

8

. . . .

They watched the video in the sitting room, Dad with a blanket over his knees enjoying a plate of fish fingers, Jay eating his curry, for some reason, with his nicotine-stained hands rather than a fork, rice falling into his lap and spilling down the sides and back of the chair. Fortunately, Dad didn't notice, so engrossed was he with the movie, to which he added his usual running commentary until he fell asleep about twenty minutes from the end.

'Should we put him to bed?' asked Harry.

Jay shook his head, shutting his eyes. 'He'll wake up soon. Better to leave him.'

Harry waited a few seconds before speaking again. 'Listen, Jay, can I ask you a favour?'

Jay looked over, the flicker of the TV reflected on his cheek. 'You can ask.'

Harry leaned forward on his chair, scratched his leg just above the sock. 'I need to borrow a little money.'

Jay looked back at the screen, snorted a laugh, shook his head once.

'I'll get it back to you straight away,' Harry insisted.

'You wait until he's asleep, yar?'

'I'm asking you, not him. It's embarrassing. I've just wound up a little short.'

'So how much?'

'I was thinking maybe five hundred.'

'What makes you think I've got that much here?'

'What? You mean you've finally opened a bank account?'

'You know what I think of banks. Wouldn't leave anything with those scum.'

'So it's still the shoebox under the bed?'

Jay stood up. 'Maybe. But I've got the money and you don't.'

'Suppose you're right.'

'I want it back.'

'For sure.'

Jay left the sitting room and returned a minute later, ten fifties rolled in his fist.

9

....

Sean stayed until closing. He had drunk heavily but couldn't negotiate himself beyond the state of self-pity he was desperate to escape. He was trying to drink himself elsewhere, where the little secrets, the *big* problems he heaped on himself the rest of the time looked like specks of lint on his sleeve. Alcohol could do that for you. It really could.

But it wasn't working tonight. Maybe that had something to do with the others, irritating him with the fatuous niceties of a conversation that at least purported to make sense long after he had fallen silent. If he'd been alone, he could have been left to just get on with it, to drink himself into an altered state. As it was, his mind had snagged itself on memories. Of Maria . . .

Other people, he thought with a scowl as he forced his key into the lock and opened the door to the flat.

It was the smell that jolted him into recalling his little secret, his *big* problem, the alien scent amid his own ingrained presence. He had managed to forget about her until now; at least the drink had done him that service. As he climbed the stairs to the flat, he could hear the report of the television, muffled voices in unnaturally ordered conversation. She loved television, the window she said it gave her on life here. Sean had scoffed, but then he'd scoffed at everything she had said and done. He had shown her no kindness, except for the one strange act of bringing her here in the first place.

Any flicker of sympathy was quashed as he entered the sitting room and saw her, asleep on the sofa, hair pushed off her face, long slender legs tucked into her belly. A half-empty glass of piss-coloured liquid lay on the coffee table in front. He resented the fact that she drank instant lemon tea. He resented her attempts to 'fit in'. He resented her on his couch, in his life, making it even more fucking messy.

Passing through on his way to the kitchen, he dropped his keys deliberately on the coffee table, rousing her. She offered him a lazy smile and sat up, rubbing her eyes.

'I made some biryani,' she said. 'There's some left if you fancy.'

He sniffed. Over the clawing stench of alcohol in his nose and throat, he detected the smell of curry. Once in the kitchen, he lifted up pan lids, saw that it looked OK. But he hadn't finished with booze for the night.

'We can reheat it tomorrow,' she said.

Sean grabbed the bottle of Absolut jammed into the small freezer compartment of the fridge, smarted at the scalding touch of ice. He rinsed out a glass, filled it a third full of vodka and topped it up from a two-litre plastic bottle of supermarket-brand cola.

He wanted to stay there in the kitchen, not to go back to where she was. Solitude was his right. Even the sight of her made him miserable, and his misery made him angry and his anger made him ashamed. So he responded to her as though she had committed some great offence against him. The only relief from this cocktail of torment nestled at the bottom of his vodka and coke, the cheap mixer pebbledashing his teeth as he swilled and swallowed.

He had found her five days ago, on what was just a routine blag. A Camberwell address had cropped up in the diary of an illegal Bangladeshi chef who'd been arrested for attacking a client at a nearby restaurant. Dixon's haemorrhoids playing up again, Sean had gone to check it out alone. The place, surprise

surprise, was empty, and he'd taken the opportunity to hang around for a minute and enjoy a much-needed shot of vodka from the bottle that fitted nicely into the pocket of his jacket, letting it wash down two of the new pills the doctor had recommended to him as helping to counteract what he described as 'manic intervals'. Sean couldn't remember whether he'd said anything about not boozing on them, but he thought he would have remembered if he had.

That was when the pile of old curtains in the corner started rustling. Pepped up by the vodka, Sean went to check it out, thinking it might be a good story to find a little Tamil shivering under there, cacking himself.

He'd thrown back the curtains to reveal her and it didn't seem very funny any more.

She was scared. He'd never seen anybody so scared. This wasn't the vague, intangible fear of something that *might* happen in a far-off country, the kind of fear that Sean saw in a punter's eyes every day. This was fear of the here, of the now, as she scrambled along the floor on her arse, her legs snarled up in the curtains.

'Don't be afraid,' he said. 'Don't.'

He tried to calm her with the tone of his voice, assuming she spoke no English. He pushed out the palms of his hands in a gesture supposed to induce calm. The truth was that finding her like that had got him panicking as well.

When she said 'Who are you? What are you doing here?', he was surprised. There was an accent there, the slight elongation of the word 'doing' that he picked up on.

'You need to tell me what you are doing at this address,' he said. 'I'm immigration, looking for somebody here.'

'There's nobody here,' she said, still lying below him, looking behind.

'You're here.'

'I am nobody.'

He looked around. 'You can't stay here.'

'Not leaving.'

'What is your name?'

She shook her head. 'No name.'

'You are Indian?'

'And you are genius,' she replied. Sean detected for the first time an edge in her character, a sharpness in her eye, the hint of sarcasm in the corner of her mouth.

'How did you get into the country?'

'I came in through the front door. Now please go and I will leave after a few minutes.'

Sean tasted something metal in his mouth. The doctor had told him the pills could do that.

'You still have your passport?' he asked her, starting to feel a little woozy.

'It was taken from me.'

'It was . . .' he struggled. 'So . . . where is it now?'

'They have it.'

Sean shook his head. 'They? Who are they?'

'The family of my husband. They took everything away from me.'

Sean nodded and blinked, trying to fend off an oncoming headache. Now he got it. 'Arranged marriage?'

She nodded, sad-eyed. He noticed that her underskirt had ridden up, revealing slim legs, her thighs long and lean. 'They . . . trapped me.'

The word 'trapped' stung Sean. He felt it himself; the room had suddenly darkened, it was smaller than he thought, he wanted to get out, had lost his bearings, wasn't sure where the door was . . .

Oh, Maria . . .

'I don't go back,' said the girl. 'They are looking for me. If they find me, they will hurt me. Kill me.'

'Kill you?'

'They are bigshot family. I have disgraced them. They will not live with that.'

'What about your husband?'

'He is . . . weak. His father, uncles, brothers . . .'

'What are they called?'

And she told him. 'Bohra.'

Of course.

Sean really felt out of it now, needed some air. Her own stress was compounding his. Being part of her fear, feeling her fear wasn't something he needed right at that moment. He needed to get out before the walls closed in any further, before he got crushed . . .

'What's your name,' he'd repeated.

'Ranjita,' she'd told him.

'Come with me,' he'd said.

And she had. He put her in the car, took her to his place and said she could stay there.

At the time it had seemed a pretty straightforward decision. Sean knew that if he blagged her, served papers on her and logged her in as an illegal, with her own record and file, she'd be back with the Bohras in five minutes. They had eyes and ears on the inside, and he knew she had real reason to fear them. He wanted that on his conscience? On top of everything else?

Now he wasn't so sure. He didn't know who'd been more stupid: him for suggesting it or her for agreeing to it. But the fact was she'd settled in with an irritating degree of ease and appeared immune to his attempts to suggest his own discomfort. Her self-sufficiency wasn't something he had bargained for or liked. He thought she could at least do him the service of needing him.

The clothes she'd been wearing that day, all she had with her when she'd scarpered, were hopelessly torn and dirty. He'd given her (saying it was a sub) a hundred pounds to get something to wear. Now she was swanning around the flat in a fake pink angora sweater and stone-washed jeans that accentuated her hips and the soft plateau of her stomach.

He'd given her a hundred quid, but she'd been to the market, bought herself two outfits and given him sixty-five back.

'Now it's only thirty-five I owe you,' she'd beamed, this for some reason making him more pissed off. He asked himself why he'd done it, dropped such a bollock. He *pretended* to wonder, but when he cast his mind back to their first meeting he knew what it was. And it boiled down to two words.

Chemical and *imbalance*.

These pills were fucking him up bad. His doctor had given him this photocopied sheet with a list of potential side-effects that would have to be watched out for. The list was a mile long: DTs, the trots, puking, twitching, nystagmus, hyperreflexia, gut pain, seizures, constipation, drying out of skin and hair.

Oh, and impaired judgement.

The fact was that he had the shakes, the runs, a tic and an irritable bowel most of the time anyway, but if you wanted proof of his newly acquired impaired judgement, you only had to take a look at the maharini sprawled out on the couch, baring an acre of naked midriff at him.

He was angry at himself for staring at the stud in her pierced navel.

'Get your feet off the settee,' he said.

'So sorry,' she replied. 'Just that I feel so comfortable here.'

'Yeah, well, don't be getting too comfortable. You can't stay here.'

She fell silent, and again he felt the strange mix of contempt and pity for her. He took a healthy swig of vodka and coke.

'It wouldn't be safe,' he added, inserting a trace of apology into his voice.

She picked up her cold lemon tea with both hands, peered into it but didn't drink. 'It was not my intention to impose. I have—'

'I know,' Sean interrupted with a sigh. 'Let's just not discuss it now.'

She smiled at the chance to change the subject. 'Soon I'll be able to pay you back,' she said, pulling one leg under her body and leaning forward to pick something off the floor. 'I'm going to get a job.'

'Right.'

'No. Seriously. Look.'

She had picked two books off the floor and slid them along the coffee table towards him. One was called *Practical Hairdressing*, the other *The Principles of Cutting Hair*. Both wore dusty plastic covers. Sean picked one of them up and opened it. TOOTING PUBLIC LIBRARY he read from a slip gummed on the first page.

'What the hell is this?'

'Before I came here, I always wanted to have a hairdressing shop . . .'

'No. I mean you got this from the library?'

'Yes.'

'You went out?'

'Just to . . .'

Sean stood up, ran a hand through his hair. 'You fucking went out to the library?'

'You gave me a set of keys,' she said, angry now.

'I gave you a set of keys for emergencies. You can't leave the house. You can't be seen. Don't you fucking understand?'

'I don't have to live like a bloody prisoner!'

'No! Yes! Yes, you do! It's exactly how you . . . you're in hiding, for Christ's sake. You can't go swanning off down Tooting High Street whenever the mood takes you. That's where your family operates. You'll be seen.'

He stopped, struck by a disturbing thought. 'How did you get those books?' he asked.

'I chose them. You get them for free, you know?' she replied acidly. 'You think I stole your money now.'

'You need a card to borrow books.'

'So I got one.'

'You filled in a form?'

'Yes, I filled in a form.'

'You put down your real name?'

'So what?'

'So what?' Sean repeated with a short, gasping laugh. 'Did you give this address? You have to give an address, right?'

She nodded.

'And . . . ?'

She waved a hand in regret. 'I didn't think. Sorry.'

Sean geared himself up to go ballistic, but strangely the explosion didn't come. Instead, he threw himself back down in the chair, rubbing the bridge of his nose between forefinger and thumb.

'If you want to go out there and get yourself . . . get yourself caught by them, then fine. But please—,' he looked at her now '—This is not just about you. I'm taking a risk, a ridiculous risk, by even having you here. You understand how it looks for an immigration officer to be hiding an illegal in his own house?'

'I'm not illegal,' she muttered.

'Don't tell me my job, all right? If you came here as a spouse, that marriage has to be subsisting or else you're in breach of your conditions of entry and liable to deportation.'

'I cannot go back to India. My family would—' for once, she struggled to express herself '—have bezaita.'

'What's that?' he asked, becalmed.

'Forget it. You wouldn't understand.'

'Try me.'

She shook her head, a sweeping curl of jet hair coming to rest on the soft incline below her collarbone.

'It is . . . like shame. Worse than shame.'

Sean laughed once, coldly. 'Then don't worry. I understand bezaita,' he said, getting up for another drink. 'I'm the king of fucking bezaita.'

She was silent when he came back in. Looking down at her, Sean was suddenly reminded of how young she was. Early twenties, if that. Just a girl. For the first time, he noticed the plant that was on the empty bookcase behind the settee.

'I suppose you bought that on your travels, did you?'

She turned to look at it, smiled. 'I thought it might brighten the place up. You . . . don't have many things.'

Sean sat down. 'There's stuff,' he said. 'It's just not here. It's in storage.'

She looked puzzled. 'Don't know storage.'

'It's like in a place where I pay people to look after it.'

'Why this?'

'It's not all my stuff. Most of it belongs to somebody else.'

She looked away, didn't reply. He could sense her trying to retain a neutral demeanour, rein in her natural curiosity. But Sean felt like an ache the incompleteness of what he had said, as if a vacuum around him was pulling more out than he wanted to give up. He stared ahead, glassy-eyed.

'My wife.'

He leaned forward and picked up the remote control for the TV, switching it on.

'We're not together any more,' he added, turning the volume up, cutting off any further conversation at the pass.

10

....

It was close to eleven by the time Harry swung the BMW into the cul-de-sac of a 1960s estate in New Malden, parked and switched off his headlights. He sat, watching the house three doors down, waiting.

Something had stopped him from going back to the poky, characterless flat in a modern development in Wandsworth he was expected to call home. Going there seemed only to raise the spectre of loneliness that he feared perhaps above all else. When he was there, he had to have the television on, or the radio, or both. Otherwise he would just sit there in the sterility of modern comfort and hear himself growing old.

He couldn't face it tonight. So here he was.

He had to wait about another fifteen minutes before there was action at the front door of the house he was watching. The porch light came on and the cheap-looking front door, red paint around frosted glass, opened. A large man tripped out, wearing a yellow tanktop, carrying a plastic lunchbox and a Thermos. A few steps forward and he turned back, speaking casually to someone inside, before carrying on and getting into a black cab parked outside. The porch light died and the cab left.

Harry gave it five minutes before getting out of the car and heading to the same door.

He rang the bell, which chimed naffly in a suburban echo of Big Ben.

A woman answered, tall, dark hair bobbed with green eyes and a sad, sexy mouth. She wore a white shirt that hugged the appealing line of her breasts and hips and a pair of tight denim hipsters that stopped just below the knee.

'Carla,' said Harry.

She eyed him, blinked once in a pantomime of contempt.

'What do you want?'

'I've . . . erm, I've got your wages.'

He pulled out six of Jay's fifties, which he'd separated in the car, and fanned them, holding them towards her, not quite close enough for her to grab. She put both hands on the door and swung out her hip. Harry couldn't resist a glance down at her flat, wide groin.

'Three hundred?' she said. 'You owe me more than that.'

'I know,' said Harry, taking one step forward, keeping the cash just out of her reach. 'I'll get the rest to you straightaway.'

She was looking at him hard, her mouth a little twisted.

'You look great, by the way,' said Harry, offering up his best Latino shrug.

Now she laughed, letting her head fall behind the door, out of view. When she reappeared, it was with a flourish, her hair falling across her eyes. She pushed it back slowly with forefinger and thumb.

'You've got some nerve, coming round here. Darren left, I don't know, ten minutes ago.'

'I know. I watched him go.'

Now she gave him what he was waiting for, that wicked half-smile of hers. He knew he was in.

'You're bad news, Harry Verma,' she said, stepping back and holding the door open for him to come in.

'Bad news,' he agreed ruefully, allowing his hand to brush her as he walked by.

She turned and took the money. 'No waking the baby,' she said.

'I know.'

'And Harry. You're not that irresistible. This is the last time,' she said.

'Always the last time,' he nodded with a grin.

He followed her up the stairs to bed, his fingers strung through the empty belt hooks of her jeans.

It should have been him, of course, and not Darren. A fucking cabby. Christ!

Harry and Carla had been hot for one another from the moment they'd met, which was the moment three years ago she'd put her head round the office door and said she was the girl from the temp agency and where would he like her to start. They had flirted like sumo wrestlers for a week and a half before an after-hours drink to offer her a permanent job turned into a dirty weekend in Ramsgate. It turned out that she'd always had a thing about Asian men (well, black *and* Asian; anyone a bit dark, actually). And it had gone from there, both of them fostering a joint sense of artificial danger by treating each other with charged propriety at work before letting rip out of office hours. It had seemed a perfect arrangement to Harry, who looked back on that time, no doubt mistakenly, as being a happy one.

And then, out of nowhere, there was Darren, with his ubiquitous yellow tanktops and his cabby's badge slung round his neck, coming to pick her up from work, take her out and, before Harry knew it, marry her. An unlikely nemesis.

For Carla, who operated her private life in the same way she organised a stationery cupboard, had given Harry no ultimatum, had caused no scenes. Even with Darren crassly courting her, she and Harry kept shagging, something Harry didn't want to ruin by asking awkward questions about where he stood exactly. Once she got married, he didn't need to ask where he stood, but they still got it on, even resorting to the office by that stage. Her pregnancy had led to an understandable hiatus and six months of terror on Harry's part that she would produce a baby of hue. But Carla was way too methodical for that to happen. The child (Harry realised he didn't even know its name) had come out a brilliant bluey-white, and after a sufficient delay as sanctioned by the medical profession she was quite happy to have her little brown boy between the sheets again, albeit more occasionally now, what with the strain of motherhood, you know.

In so many ways it was an ideal arrangement, so why did Harry, lying on his back, hands clasped behind his head, feel so miserable? Staring up at the plaster swirls on the ceiling, he knew exactly what it was she saw in Darren. It was the cul-de-sac, the semi, the BMX left sprawled on the driveway in a few years time, the big-screen telly, the love of her own children . . .

She kicked him out at about four o'clock.

part two

....

11

....

Immigration Enforcement occupied the first and second floors of Chaucer House, a 1950s construction a stone's throw from Blackfriars Bridge on the south side of the river, all dark wood, clunking radiators and shiny linoleum. Since the upper floors had been condemned for asbestos levels off the scale, they had had the building to themselves. Whether the first and second floors were asbestos-free or whether they'd ever been checked, nobody was sure, but there were those who would always be reluctant to move, even if clumps of asbestos were dropping from the ceiling and into their mugs of tea. Chaucer House was where Enforcement had been based ever since its inception in the late 1960s. It was the spiritual home of the blag.

Sean went in, flashing his warrant to the two security guards, both already well past retirement age, both of whom took pride in their grey uniforms, especially their peaked caps. As usual, they were talking about hypothetical fights.

'No way,' said Leslie, the fatter of the two, an ex-professional wrestler, always the fall guy. 'Ali would take Bruce Lee any day of the week. Take him in two.'

Maltese Frankie disagreed.

'What you talking? Two rounds? What you saying? Bruce Lee would take Ali all the way. Ali wouldn't lay a glove on him. Bruce Lee would be giving it all that jumping, chopping, kicking. Ali wouldn't know what the day was.'

'You didn't say kicking was allowed. That's different.'

Sean climbed the stairs to the first floor, the strange chocolate smell of Chaucer House engulfing him. As he had done
every day for the last half-week, he felt nervous, expecting
someone to suddenly confront him about Ranjita as he walked
the length of the corridor towards the large office where the
enforcement team were based.

He entered a familiar scene. The office was large, open-plan,
windows on both sides, but largely obscured by yellowed net
curtains and row after row of filing cabinets. Two dozen large
desks were scattered around the room, each big enough for two
officers to sit facing one another. On every desk lay a mountain
of files pertaining to the particular area for which they had
responsibility, each roughly equivalent to the nearest police
division. Each file would contain a denunciatory letter, or a
piece of information picked up from an informant about an
absconder or an illegal which needed to be looked into. Most of
them were dead ends. You were expected to deal with them all,
but that was just impossible, so half would get shredded acci-
dentally or just 'lost'.

Around the office, most of Sean's colleagues were in, leafing
through files, telephones clasped between ear and shoulder. In
about an hour, the office would be largely empty as they went
out and set about the day's blagging.

He walked through. One or two people registered his
arrival, offered him a hello, but Sean, with less than a year at
Chaucer, was not really one of the crew yet. Not by a long
stretch.

He sat down at his usual place, opposite Piers Anstruther,
who was on the phone looking distracted. Piers was tall and
angular, with long, narrow limbs usually in some kind of motion
and an unruly treetop of red hair. A band of freckles spread
from cheek to cheek across his nose like spattered war paint. He
didn't notice Sean sit down or if he did he pretended not to. He
was waiting for someone at the other end of the line; his eyes
flickered when they came on.

'Yes,' he interrupted, agitated. 'Is that the visa section? You got my fax? I'd like a reply regarding Miss Natumba's application and I'd like it immediately.'

Piers had been spending a lot of time on Miss Natumba's case over the last year, despite the fact that she wasn't an illegal entrant and not even in the UK. Miss Natumba came to Piers' attention on a holiday to the Gambia, where she accommodated his particular leisure requirements in return for a promise of passage to London. Despite frequent cautions from his superiors for inappropriate behaviour, Piers was persisting in a transparent fury of sexual frustration, firing off faxes and letters of complaint at her repeated visa refusals. Whatever he was hearing down the international exchange, he didn't like it.

'This is an outrage!' he declared, standing up quickly and knocking over a cup of cold tea. The puddle of brown, milky liquid hurried across the desk towards Sean, who picked up a bundle of papers before they were soaked. 'This is nothing short of persecution,' ranted Piers. 'I shall appeal.'

He slammed down the phone. 'Bastard,' he spat.

'Bad news?' asked Sean.

Piers registered his presence for the first time and began to mop up the mess with an old newspaper.

'I can't believe they . . . they seem to think it's like any other case. They don't seem to realise that I'm not just . . . I mean, I spent three years in Islamabad doing marriage interviews. I can spot a duff relationship a mile off, you know . . . they don't . . .'

The cleaning-up only half-done, he stopped and slumped back into the chair, kicking the leg of his desk.

'Carlyle!' roared a voice from across the room. Half-stepping out of his small office set into the corner was Douglas Greatrix, chief immigration officer and Sean's immediate superior, a large man waist-deep in middle age, his hair a suspicious black, his shirt, blue with a white collar, pulled taut over the solid half-orb of his stomach, the badge of the serious drinker.

'A word,' he said, beckoning Sean into his office.

Sean dropped the pile of paper on to his chair and headed across. That kind of minor public school brusqueness was typical of Greatrix, but he naturally feared any discovery of his secretion of the Indian girl. As he entered the office, Greatrix motioned for him to close the door and sit down. His desk was littered with the affectations of a minor functionary: letter opener, fountain pen, ink bottle, blotter. There was something odd about Greatrix, something not quite authentic. Sean half-imagined that there was another man called Greatrix, a small, bespectacled weakling strapped to a ventilator in a home, and that this man was a repertory hack playing him in his absence for Equity minimum.

'Heard about the job yesterday,' he boomed. 'How do you feel it went?'

Sean knew the question was there to set him up. He just shrugged. 'Could have gone better,' he offered.

Greatrix sat down with a groan. 'It could have, Sean. You're right. It could have been handled with a lot more *control*. You're with me?'

Sean nodded.

'You see, Sean, mate, you and me, we're in the *control* business. People ask what I do, I say I'm *in control*, you with me?'

'Yeah. Control,' murmured Sean.

'When you're out there, spinning drums...'

Sean sighed. He hated that expression.

'... you have to retain control . . .'

'Control,' Sean joined in. Greatrix didn't like his singsong tone.

'So a routine blag gets out of *control* and ends up with a chase down the fucking High Street?' bellowed Greatrix, banging a fist off his desk. Like they used to do in *Z Cars*.

Sean shuffled.

'You were just bloody lucky that Eric was there to bail you out.'

A pause.

'I heard you chucked up your guts,' said Greatrix, suddenly quiet, looking down at some paper on his desk.

'I . . . er . . . hadn't been feeling well. Bad pint.'

Greatrix sighed. 'Listen, Sean, mate, you know how it works. I don't care what you're taking, how much you're drinking, where you choose to dip your wick. I don't care about any of that, as long as you keep making the collars. Give me the results. That's all I'm interested in. You give me them and I'll leave you alone. You know that.'

'Right.'

'So it's results I'm going to get?'

'I'll try.'

'That's a good lad. But listen, in the meantime, I've had an idea. Just to tide you over for a little while, until we sort you out another oppo. Doesn't look like Dixon is ever coming back,' he huffed. 'Christ, he must have piles the size of the Isle of Man. The other thing is, I thought maybe this'll be a way that you can learn something, maybe you can learn how we really get results here. How does that sound?'

Sean felt disorientated. Maybe he needed a drink or maybe it was the pills that were doing it to him. Best take another pill to find out.

'If you think . . . what are you thinking of?'

'You might have heard, Eric lost his licence yesterday. Apparently, the bugger burned a hole in the breathalyser.' Greatrix wheezed a laugh at his own joke. Sean smiled weakly, aware of a new light-headedness. 'But there's a man who brings me results,' added Greatrix, instantly serious again. 'No question about it.'

'No question,' said Sean.

'I can't really have Eric stuck in the office. The thought of that nutter being grounded—' he exhaled with puffed cheeks '—doesn't bear thinking about. He needs to be out there, doing what he does best. So I need you to be his driver.'

Sean blinked. 'His driver?'

'Yeah. Driving him around.'

Driving.

Sean knew that Crazy Horse was unique in being licensed to work alone.

Just driving. No flak jackets, no spinning drums. No blagging.

'OK,' said Sean.

He went looking for Eric. Someone pointed him down the corridor, to one of the half-dozen interview rooms that lined it. Through the reinforced glass of the second one he looked in, he saw him standing with one knee bent, foot placed on a desk. Behind the desk sat a West Indian woman, thirties, in a green dress and hat, looking worried. She clutched a handbag to her chest. Eric jabbed his cigarette towards her as he put a question. She answered with a monosyllable and looked down.

Sean tapped on the glass. Eric looked across, pushed his specs back on to the bridge of his nose and came over to the door. 'Aye?' he said.

'Greatrix. He wants me to drive for you.'

Eric looked hard through his thick lenses for a couple of seconds, as if he had no idea what Sean was talking about. Then he nodded. 'Aye, right. That's good.' He beckoned Sean in. 'Come wi' me. You can act as a witness.'

Sean shut the door as he went in and leaned his back against it. Eric turned his attention to the woman.

'Now you're sure about this?' he asked.

She nodded, looked across at Sean with a hint of panic.

'It's what I heard,' she said.

'And where did you hear it?'

'Around,' she said coyly.

'All right,' said Eric. 'I'm going to look into it. If it isna true I'll be wanting this back.'

He reached into his trouser pocket and produced a wallet.

'Right. You watching this?' he said to Sean, who nodded. Eric started pulling notes out. 'Ten, twenty, thirty.' He handed them over. She quickly took them and stuffed them into her bag.

'You never…you never see me here,' she said, getting up and heading to the door. 'I only doing this for my child,' she added quietly.

'See you again,' said Eric, as Sean opened the door for her and let her out.

'She a regular snout?' asked Sean, but Eric didn't answer, distractedly stubbing out his cigarette and reaching for another. Informants were an important element of the blag culture, especially in the murky circles that Eric frequented. There was no official budgetary element that accounted for their payment, but there were ways around that. The most common was to pay the money out of your own pocket, as Eric had done, and then fiddle it back on expenses. Sean, for his part, tried never to get involved with snouts. Just didn't like it, the whole idea of it, particularly as they seemed to spend all their time grassing one another up, trying to leave the field open for themselves.

'So,' said Sean, giving up waiting for a reply. 'You want a lift?'

Eric blew out a throatful of smoke and looked across. 'Yeah.'

He began to busy himself with the contents of his Home Office case. Sean noticed that he wasn't carrying a standard-issue phone, but instead had an ancient specimen, bulky and square with a large flexible rubber aerial.

Sean laughed. 'What's that for?'

'It's a phone,' said Crazy Horse, clipping it to his belt and snapping the box shut. 'What you fucking think it's for?'

'All right, all right,' Sean replied. 'Just trying to be friendly.'

'I've got enough friends. Have you booked out a car?'

'Not yet.'

'We'd better get down there quick, before all the good ones get taken. You're not driving me anywhere if it's in that fucking powder-blue Mondeo. You'll see me in hell first.'

By now he was out in the corridor, heading out. Sean, trotting to keep up, noticed that he didn't have any files with him.

'So where we going?' he asked, catching up.

'I think a little bit of family research is in order.'

12

....

Harry had no choice but to go to Croydon. *I mean*, he was thinking as he drove south, the clock showing just before ten, *if there was a choice, why would anyone go to Croydon?*

But he had no choice. He needed money, and to get money he needed customers. And if Croydon had one resource in abundance other than concrete, customers was it.

He parked the car a fair way away from his ultimate destination and walked. His route took him past the front of East Croydon Station, which was where the trail usually began. He spotted a few of them, a group of half a dozen, late teens, early twenties, dark-haired, sallow-eyed, letting their ethnic distinctiveness manifest itself in a general air of threat. These were Albanians, he was almost certain, although they'd be telling the Home Office that Kosovo was their home, hovering around the outside of a trendy coffee bar built into the station itself, an optimistic but misguided attempt to raise the tone. Harry had represented some Albanians in the past, helped them crib on their Kosovan general knowledge so that they could benefit from the Home Office policy of granting them immediate residency. He and a few others like him had got together and pooled all the standard questions they'd heard immigration officials ask about Kosovo: the colour of the letterboxes, names of local newspapers, registration plate numbers etc., etc. Albanians were easy money, but these boys hadn't just arrived. They'd be lawyered up already and were probably only standing at East Croydon Station today because they'd sussed it was the best place to pick pockets in the area.

Elsewhere, he spotted some others. A lone Turkish male, waiting for someone. Two West Africans, both dressed in garish baggy pants, both carrying mobile phones, shouting and pointing, cackling at whatever the other one said in bastardised French.

A Bangladeshi woman in a cowl.

Harry didn't fancy any of them.

Passing the station, his eye following one of the new trams that led God knows where, he took the familiar right turn, keeping his eyes open for the right kind of punter . . .

'Harry!'

He turned at the sound of his own name. The man who'd invoked it waved, telling him to wait. He was tall, his face drawn but with bright, amused eyes. He was nicely dressed, flash raincoat over a grey, Italian-made suit, expensive slip-on shoes. He wore his black hair pulled back into a ponytail, an exhaust pipe poking from the back of his head.

'Long time, no see,' he said, coming alongside.

'Danny,' said Harry, non-committally. 'All right?'

'Me?' asked Danny, giving the question undue consideration. 'I'm diamond. What you doing here?' He paused and gave Harry a troubled look, baring his teeth. 'Not on the tout, are you, Harry? Please, tell me you're not on the tout.'

Daniel Le Gall (aka Danny Legal) was in the same game as Harry, and they'd met while both working as clerks for Miriam Cooper Associates, one of the best-known immigration firms in London. Danny had been asked to move on a few years back as a result of his abiding devotion to modern chemistry but with the support of his rich French dad had set up on his own. Harry had left a couple of years later, sick of the righteous cant that abounded in Miriam's Camden offices. By that time, Danny's touting days were already over.

'Meeting a client,' said Harry quietly. 'Anyway, what brings the master down here?'

'You'll laugh,' said Danny as they started walking. 'I've got a meeting with the other side.'

'Oh, yeah?'

'It's some bullshit steering group committee. Everything's a steering group with these people. They set up a steering group if they fancy a cup of tea.'

'And they want you on a steering group?'

'Bollocks, isn't it? Immigration Representatives' Best Practice and something something steering group.'

'Sounds like a waste of your valuable time.'

Danny planted a finger on the side of his nose. 'Know thine enemy.'

'Maybe they sussed how dodgy you are.'

Danny ignored this suggestion. 'You want to see them, Harry. They're so scared of us. They're like little mice. You throw in any of the Latin you can remember from school and they all cack themselves.'

'I didn't do Latin at school,' murmured Harry.

'Yeah. Whatever. Of course, Miriam's on the committee, taking it all so fucking seriously.'

'She's spoken to you?'

'Only through the chair, old son. You should have seen her face when I walked in.'

Harry smiled at this.

'Anyway, who's this client of yours, Harry?'

'Refugee. Nothing special.'

This didn't hold Danny's interest long. 'Here, still shafting that secretary of yours?'

'Still shafting that nose of yours?'

'I'm sure I don't know what you mean.'

Danny put a hand on Harry's shoulder. They stopped.

'Listen,' he said. 'You don't want to be bumming around here, touting for peanuts. Why don't you come and work for me?'

Harry shook his head. Every time he saw Danny they got on to this. Yes, Danny was making a mint and running rings around the other side and, yes, he had clients banging down his door for representation . . .

But Danny Legal was a Yardie brief. It was the Yardies who had given him the name (nobody at law school had been clever enough to come up with it). Harry wanted no part of that. Acting for those boys wasn't work; it was a Faustian pact. They didn't just pay you. They owned you.

'Thanks, but no thanks.'

Danny lifted his hands. 'Any time, Harry. You know that.'

'Yeah.'

'Anyway, come on, don't want to be late. I like to get the chair next to Miriam if I can, see if I can drop a rock of crack in her handbag.'

Even if you had no idea where the Immigration and Nationality Headquarters was in relation to the railway station, it wouldn't take long to work it out. All you had to do was follow the stream of human sorrow and self-pity of all colours as it marched towards Wellesley Road, working on their hangdog expressions. These were the latest trail of asylum seekers, people who'd entered the country illegally or had had their six months as a visitor or finished their English course at technical college. Whoever they were, they were following the others to explain that, no, when it boiled down to it they didn't want to go home. After all, they too were in fear of their lives.

Some of them, Harry could see, already had reps with them, scuttling figures, always slightly ahead of the clients, briefcases clutched. There were interpreters too on some cases. Harry didn't like interpreters. Idle, greedy bastards, always full of themselves, always late, always on the make.

Harry kept his eye out as he went, listening to Danny. While he had only a pretty good idea of what he was after, he knew exactly what he wasn't looking for, an elimination process well honed through painful experience and the added pressure of needing money fast.

No young single males, wherever they were from. Chances are they'd have no money with them, and Harry needed to squeeze cash out of somebody pronto.

No Somalis, for much the same reason.

Nobody who looked of average intelligence or above. Not usually a problem.

Definitely no Gippoes. This last one wasn't Harry's own stipulation. He'd had a couple of Czech Roma families and done quite nicely out of them. No, this one had come down from Carla. Ignoring the fact that they were a potentially rich seam, she'd made Harry an ultimatum: any more pikeys and she would leave. This had followed a visit by one family to give instruction during which they had nicked everything that wasn't bolted down with a jackhammer, even stealing a framed photo of Carla's baby that stood proudly on her desk.

So, no Gippoes.

These exclusions accounted for the majority of Harry's market base, so he knew as he turned the corner that he'd have to be able to move quickly when a likely candidate appeared. It wasn't as if he was the only rep on the tout outside Lunar House.

Lunar. An appropriate name for the massive unworldly monolith of stained concrete that housed the Immigration and Nationality Headquarters. With its jagged lines, hundred-foot high tidemarks and the strange sequence of V-shaped concrete struts that adorned its top, Harry always thought it looked more like something that had fallen out of a malevolent 1960s sky than had been built upwards by mankind. Perhaps one day the massive aerial at its peak would pick up a signal from the mother ship and the whole edifice would creak and grind its way up and out of the Croydon skyline, back to the home planet of cardboard cut-out civil servants from whence it had come.

Dwarfed beneath it, the trail of refugee ants Harry had followed from the station suddenly found itself part of a colony outside the doors that led up to the Asylum Screening Unit, or rather a series of small colonies, all easily recognisable. Turks pretending to be Kurds in one corner, Albanians pretending to be Kosovans in another, West Africans, East Africans, North Africans, Bangladeshis, Tamils, Eastern Europeans (Lithuanians, Poles, Ukrainians, Czechs), Middle Eastern Arabs (Lebanese, Iraqis, Iranians, the odd steel-eyed Afghan), South Americans (big new trend, Colombians, Ecuadorians, your occasional Brazilian). Harry looked hard across the goldmine as the sun came out and caressed these restless clusters. Harry knew that most of these weren't applying today, that they were waiting outside while their friends or relations were sweating in the huge queue, ready for their five minutes at a guichet to try to explain how special their case was. Some of the others had already been in, having queued since the crack of dawn. For some, particularly Nigerians, this wouldn't be their first time down there. When one identity became irksome, this was the place to establish another.

Harry preferred to keep clear of Nigerians. A golden rule: never act for anyone who knows the game better than you.

Danny left him outside and went in the edifice through the main foyer. Harry recognised a couple of other briefs there, looking for some action like him, dishing out cards left, right and centre, asking everybody with great care whether they required any assistance. Harry didn't favour the scatter-gun approach – it was just a way of getting lumbered with losers who were more trouble than they were worth, who thought just because you were their lawyer that you had to give a shit about their TB or the fact that half their family were stuck at home and would you help bring them over . . . No, he preferred to bide his time, wait for the right one . . . only a matter of . . .

He spied a minivan, an old one with a dodgy respray, chuff down Wellesley Road. It pulled over on the opposite side of the road and from the back seat two Asian men got out. The first was middle-aged, short, grey beard, his hair hidden under a ratty grey fez. He gestured maniacally at the second man to get out, and he did so reluctantly. He was taller, younger, mid-twenties, dressed in an imitation-leather jacket over a Pakistan one-day cricket shirt, hair and moustache jet black. Everything about his bearing suggested petulant un-interest, particularly when compared with the kinetic excite-ment of the other, who banged the roof of the car hard twice and waved it off.

Harry's ship had come in. He sussed it out quickly. The younger one was here to ask for asylum; the other was a relative, uncle probably, who wanted him to stay around and help with the family business. Perfect for a fast buck. He crossed the road and approached the two as the elder was exhorting the younger to straighten his hunched shoulders.

'Are you Mr Razzaq?' asked Harry.

The short man looked at him irritably. 'Huh?'

'Are you Mr Razzaq?'

'Who is Razzaq?'

'Not you?'

'What are you bloody talking about?'

'So you're not Mr Razzaq?'

'Come on,' he exhorted the younger man.

'I'm sorry,' said Harry. 'I'm meant to be meeting somebody here. A client. Thought it might have been you.'

The man looked distracted, grabbed his junior by the sleeve. 'Somebody else. Not me. Somebody else.'

'Fine,' said Harry. 'I'll wait for him here. My client. I expect you've arranged your own legal representation.'

Harry noticed the man's eyes flicker, saw one corner of his mouth twitch.

'You need lawyer to go in there?' the man asked.

Harry made the face of languid wisdom. 'Need one?' he shrugged. 'You don't *need* one. You don't *have to have* one. But—' he widened his eyes, then glanced at his watch and strained his neck for a glimpse of the imaginary Mr Razzaq '—wouldn't recommend it,' he added quietly.

Harry made to turn but felt a reassuring fist clench the elbow of his suit.

'Why? Why? What do they do?'

'Asylum and immigration,' explained Harry, puffing out his cheeks. 'Minefield. One false move, one wrong answer, one mistake . . . bang, you lose. That lot in there—' he gestured to the door '—they're just looking for anything to stitch you up with. That's their job. That's what they do.'

The elder pulled the younger with him as he followed a slow-moving Harry in the opposite direction.

'My nephew,' he explained. 'Good boy, good lad. Been staying with me. His visit is over, but he cannot return to Pakistan.'

'Of course he can't.'

'He has made bad friends in Lahore. My brother, his father has asked me to try and keep him away, give him a chance in business. I am at a loss, sir.'

Harry bit his lip, looked at his watch again. 'I can't recommend you go in without representation. There are plenty of other . . . where can Mr Razzaq be?'

'Maybe he's not coming?' suggested Uncle hopefully.

Harry looked philosophical. 'He's certainly late. And time is money.'

Harry eyed Uncle closely. He'd used the word 'money' and Abdul here hadn't run a mile. Very good sign.

Harry grabbed his mobile phone from his belt and tapped its own number on the keypad. 'Hi. Yeah. 's me,' he said to the engaged tone. 'Looks like I'm at a loose end. I can cover that habeus corpus at the Old Bailey. Yeah, yeah, that judge loves me . . .'

Harry felt the hand clinging to him once more.

'Let me call you back,' he told the voice telling him that the number was busy and could he call back later.

'Tell me,' said the man. 'You can help me, yes?'

'Well, I mean . . . help? Sure, yeah. I can help. But listen, I represent a professional law body. You see,' he said, handing him a card, one of the better ones, with the embossed printing. The ones he'd had done in the shop.

Uncle read it carefully, tried not to look impressed. 'I want the best for my boy here,' he explained.

Harry nodded sagely. 'You understand there would be a fee?'

'How much?' shouted Uncle, suddenly businesslike, almost before Harry had finished.

Here was the crunch to Harry's little grift. He didn't want to set it too high. After all, this was a little extra, an unofficial top-up to his legal aid allowance.

'Normally, we would charge by the hour. Perhaps in your case . . .'

'How much?'

'Discount for cash?'

'How much money you want?'

'Two hundred and fifty for initial representation.'

'Too much.'

Harry looked at his watch again. 'That's my price. That's the company's price.'

'Too much.'

'I'm sure Mr Razzaq will be along at any moment.'

Uncle mulled it over. 'I want guarantees,' he shouted over a passing vehicle.

Harry gave his best approximation of amused surprise. 'Guarantees? What guarantees?'

'I want guarantees that you keep my nephew here. I pay you two hundred and you guarantee me that he stays here. Absolute guarantee. Or I come after you, get you.'

Harry smiled. *Absolute guarantee?* What Harry knew was that nobody, *virtually* nobody, got deported once they'd claimed asylum, as long as they destroyed their passport beforehand. With the tools of procrastination Harry had at his disposal, the myriad ways of protracting delays from months into years, the lengthy appeals, the avenues for judicial review, the perpetual firing off of new representations, the invention of different compelling compassionate grounds for remaining in the UK, the last resort of a marriage to Essex estate trash – with all that the likelihood was that by the time they finally could get round to deporting him, Pakistan would be a member of the fucking European Union. At heart, it was a question of will. Once somebody like Nephew had his feet on the hallowed soil, the fact was that if he *really* wanted to stay and didn't do anything stupid, he could. The only clients Harry remembered ever getting kicked out were the ones who couldn't hack the weather and were pleased to be getting a free ride home.

So, a guarantee? An *absolute* guarantee?

Safe as houses.

'You have my guarantee that your nephew will be able to stay. And it was two hundred and fifty.'

Harry blinked slowly at the roll of banknotes that Uncle slid out of his trouser pocket. The dexterity with which he peeled off twenty after twenty made Harry smile. He recognised another shoebox-under-the-bed merchant when he saw one.

Harry took the money. 'Right,' he said. 'Let's get cracking,' pulling a pad from his briefcase. 'Name?'

'My name is Anwar,' said Uncle. 'This is my nephew. His name is Baseeq. Good boy. Strong boy. You want to see passport?'

'No. Put it away. Don't show it to them. When they ask for it, say he never had one.'

Anwar cocked his head.

'Look,' said Harry. 'Inside there, they ask questions to get the information they want, which they can use against you. So you give them nothing. OK?'

This was a principle that Anwar clearly did understand.

'Just let me handle it,' added Harry. 'Come on. Let's join the queue.'

In the time he had been grifting Anwar out of half a monkey, the line snaking out from the Asylum Screening Unit had already doubled in length. They took their place behind two Albanians who spent an hour and a half until they reached the front of the queue testing each other on the colour of letterboxes and police registration plates in Kosovo. They were both well up to snuff and would waltz it. Nobody at the Home Office had thought about changing the questions, not even when everybody, without fail, started getting them a hundred per cent right.

Even Harry had to admit to himself, as they shuffled a few inches nearer the line of guichets where Baseeq would be making his application, the twisting line swelling further behind them, that the system was fucked, that it was just too easy for him and the others farming this particular legal patch.

But as he got close enough to see the hatchet faces of the officers behind the glass of the counters, their wilful contempt for everyone who showed up before them writ large across their twisted mouths, his view changed.

After all, it was *their* system, not his. And when you come up with a system as fucked as this, well, you're just asking for it . . .

They reached the front.

13

....

Sean gripped the steering wheel of the powder-blue Mondeo tight. His heart had sunk when they'd gone down to the car pool to find it in splendid isolation. Crazy Horse had given no reaction on seeing it other than to kick the passenger door hard with a Chelsea boot, leaving a nasty looking dent in the bodywork. Looking straight ahead, concentrating on the road, he could sense he was under scrutiny from the passenger seat, where Eric, one foot planted on the dashboard, filled the car with Marlboro smoke. Sean was conscious of his own driving. Eric exuded impatience, even when he was doing nothing.

They were crossing Blackfriars Bridge when Crazy Horse spoke up. 'So, Sean, where've you been?'

Sean dared a glance across. Eric was looking straight ahead.

'Where've I been where?' asked Sean, aware that it didn't make any sense. His own incoherence was starting to bother him regularly now.

'In the service, mate. You been around much?'

'A bit.'

'Where?'

Sean made a face, relaxed a little, almost knocked a scooter on his nearside flying. 'Fuck! Where'd he come from? No, I did twelve years at the airport.'

'Which terminal?'

'I was at One.'

Eric clicked his tongue. 'Fucking picnic, mate. I was at

Terminal 3 for nine years. That's where the work gets done, not just fucking businessmen and bucket-and-spaders.'

'Whatever you say,' Sean answered quietly.

'So, Terminal 1, and then, what? Lagos?'

'Two years.'

'Until when?'

'About a year ago.'

'So how many dodgy visas you take a backhander for?'

Sean didn't reply.

'You were there when the suits were sniffing around, no?'

'Yeah,' sighed Sean, turning a corner. 'I was there.'

'Right,' said Eric, lighting up again. 'But they didn't manage to catch you round the back with a brown-paper parcel?'

'I honestly don't know what you're talking about.'

'Aw, c'mon,' persisted Eric. 'You're telling me you never took a bung for a visa?'

'I was ex . . . they cleared me.'

'Don't fucking worry about me,' said Eric regardless. 'It's no skin off my nose, you taking a few backhanders. Fuck it if you can get away with it, especially when those Foreign Office bastards just accuse us anyway. It's not like there's nobody at Chaucer taking cash or whatever for turning a blind eye. How you think Carpenter afforded that bike of his?'

'How?'

'What do you think? He turns up at a last known address to spin the drum, finds the punter, punter offers him fifty quid, he says make it a hundred and I never saw you. Writes up a report saying he wasn't found. What do you expect after they cut back on overtime. People have to live in the manner they've become accustomed to. His basic just about keeps his wife in Wagon Wheels. You ever met her? Fucking *huge* woman.'

Sean laughed.

'But listen,' said Eric, his voice slowing with curiosity. 'If you're such a saint, how come you didn't see out the three years? You said you only did two.'

'I . . .' Sean stuttered, shaking the gearstick as they waited at a set of lights. 'Something came up.'

'What was that, then?'

The lights changed and Sean moved the car off. He didn't reply. Crazy Horse fell silent for a moment and then looked across. 'You're not the bloke whose . . . ?'

Sean lifted a hand to interrupt him. 'I don't want to get into it,' he said.

Eric let his foot drop from the dashboard and shook his head, looking out of the passenger window.

'Christ,' he muttered. 'Hard to bear.'

They drove up Farringdon Road in silence until Eric told Sean to take a right on to a street with a block of 1960s council flats on one side and a brand-new red-brick building on the other. Sean parked in a bay outside. A sign advertised it as the Family Records Office.

'Is this, like, births, marriages and deaths?' asked Sean.

'Aye,' replied Crazy Horse, inspecting the doorway to the building carefully.

'I thought that was St Catherine's House.'

'They moved it here, further away from our office, so we'd leave the conniving bastards alone.'

Sean shook his head, not having a clue what Eric was talking about.

'So what do we do next?'

'You're going in and getting someone out of there.'

'Who?'

'A wee Jamoke shite called Warren.'

'What's he doing in there?'

Eric looked aghast. 'You never seen *Day of the Jackal*?'

Eric sent Sean in, having given him the full rundown. The guy he was looking for, Warren, had a nice little niche etched out for himself. He spent most of his time here, in the Family Records Office, looking for names of children who'd died in childbirth, then he sold the names on to members of the Jamaican community who would request a birth certificate in that identity. Once they had a birth certificate, you had what you needed to get a passport, or another one to add to your collection. From his time in Lagos, Sean knew that Nigerians were into this in a big way as well. They were masters of the multiple identity. As it was with the Nigerians, so it was with the Jamokes. Identity was a corporeal fact, not a series of names on a pretty form. A name was just a name, easy come, easy go.

But Warren had cornered this particular market. He'd been doing this a while, according to Eric, and so the names he came up with had an inherent value. Sure, you could pop along and find your own dead baby for a name to steal, but chances were that Warren had already sold that name on. If so, the passport checks were stringent enough to know if a second application was being made by a different person. Only Warren knew what names he'd sold on, so doing anything but using him was taking a chance. In the meantime, he also happened to be one of Eric's star snouts.

Which had led Sean to ask why Eric didn't just go in and get him, if he knew what he looked like. Crazy Horse shook his head, told him that down at St Catherine's House, Chaucer had had an almost permanent presence in among the death registers, where a steady stream of illegals would turn up to get their new names. It had been a blagging paradise until one afternoon things got out of hand and a chase had led to three cabinets getting knocked over. The librarians had made an official complaint (hence the reference to conniving bastards), and now anyone from Chaucer was forbidden by order of Greatrix and above to go anywhere near the place, even if it was at a new location.

'Anyone, that is,' Eric had explained, 'that they recognise, which includes me, but not you.'

'How will I know who he is?'

'Just listen out for the sniffing. And when you find him, don't take any shit. Bring him out straight away. I'll be waiting around the side.'

Sean went in, past the small shop in the foyer selling books on genealogy and on to the record library beyond. To the left a queue of people waited their turn to approach a row of post-office-style counters and submit their birth certificate requests. Sean spotted a West African arguing with the clerk behind the glass about something.

'It is for my brother,' he kept saying. 'It is for my brother. He is in hospital. He is dying. I need it to arrange his affairs. You give it to me.'

Sean tuned out just in time to stop the flood of memories of Lagos that he feared. He walked deeper into the room and scanned it. Signs pointed out the three main sections, each of which was distinguishable from the colours of the banks of ledgers: red for births, green for marriages and the inevitable black for deaths. In among them, a surprising number of people were hitting the books frantically, scanning the records as if looking for gold, digging for a nugget that might . . . what? Make them feel like somebody else, grant them a little relief from their familiarity with themselves?

He knew that there would be a record of his marriage to Maria among the green books, an easy one to find as he remembered the date. Somewhere in the red section would be the entry of his birth. It had to be there, but he would never be able to find it. A small sign pointed out the location of the adoptions section. That was where Sean's existence began, when Mr and Mrs Carlyle signed the paper that gave them legal responsibility for an abandoned baby and set about moulding him in their own image, living proof of their sense of civic duty, their sense of moral obligation. And that's how Sean had spent the first eighteen years of his life until he'd walked out, as an obligation, a legal charge, an onerous responsibility . . .

Fists pushed deep into the pockets of his windcheater, he turned and walked towards deaths.

It was hard to miss the sniffing, even over the constant rustling of pages and slamming of books. Sean traced it back to the furthest corner of the room. Looking around the last row of shelves, he saw a small, wiry Caribbean hunched over a desk, his dreadlocks almost scraping the surface of the page. He wore one of those army jackets hanging down to his knees with miniature German flags sewn on the upper arm. Sean watched as he traced a finger down the list of names, sniffing at every one.

Sean walked up and tapped him hard on the shoulder. 'You Warren?'

Warren kept his eyes on the lists. 'No, mate,' he replied in an odd, whiny lisp. 'The name don't mean nuttin' to me.'

Sean moved to his side. 'Funny,' said Sean, doing as McCleish had instructed him. 'The guy said that he was . . . like you.'

Warren kept looking down, but Sean could see he wasn't focusing on the print any more. 'What guy?'

'The bloke who said that he could . . . never mind.'

'What'd he say, the bloke?'

'Why? It's not you.'

'Maybe the bloke, maybe he doesn't know the geezer?'

'What geezer?'

'The bloke you're looking for. The guy.'

'But he told me what he looked like.'

'So what he look like?'

'Who?'

'The guy?'

'Like you.'

'Not that geezer. The bloke who told you what the bloke looked like. What he look like?'

'Dunno. I didn't meet him.'

'So how do you know who you're looking for?'

'My mate. He was the one the bloke talked to.'

'Who's your mate?'

Sean shrugged. 'A bloke.'

'What's he want?'

'To find the bloke the geezer put him on to.'

'And you don't know what the geezer looks like?'

'He looks like you.'

'No. Fucking hell,' Warren muttered. 'The geezer who put your mate on to this bloke.'

Sean shook his head. 'I'm just looking for Warren. My mate needs a favour.'

'Where is he?'

'Outside.'

'Why don't he come in?'

'Chain smoker.'

Warren slammed the ledger he was studying shut and stuffed his notebook into one of his army jacket's myriad pockets. 'Come on, then. Show me where he is.'

Sean faked surprise. 'You Warren, then?'

Warren clicked his tongue. 'Fucking amachurs,' he muttered as they left.

Outside, Sean led him to Eric, who was standing around the corner where the bins were kept, his back to the wall, one knee bent back so that his heel leaned against the brickwork.

Christ, thought Sean. *He thinks he's on telly.*

Crazy Horse threw back his head and offered Warren a cold smile. Warren, realising he'd been conned, threw Sean an eyeful in turn.

'Awright, ya wee shite,' Eric greeted him. 'Managed to scrape you off the wall, did we? Got something for me? I heard say we got a new boy coming from the Yard.'

Warren looked back at him, stooped, mouth open. 'I told you to leave me alone,' he said.

'That's ungrateful, with everything I've done for you.'

'You ain't done nuttin' fo' me, 'cept make my life fuckin' harder dan it already was.'

Crazy Horse pushed himself away from the wall. 'That's harsh,' he said, shaking his head, 'especially when I've got something for you in my pocket.'

Warren sniffed again, ran a sleeve across his face, his eyes flickering contradiction.

'Fuck you,' he muttered, distracted. 'Don't need you, star. I'm sorted.'

'Oh, yeah,' sneered Eric. 'Who's sorting you?'

Sean could detect a change in Eric's voice, a blurring of his normally crisp consonants coupled with a slight drop in key.

Warren pointed at Crazy Horse. 'The Piper going to get you, star. He coming for you. I say the word, you get mashed up, blaahd.'

Eric moved with purpose. He stepped forward and thrust out a whippy arm fast, too fast for Warren, who still had his own outstretched. Eric caught it with his left hand, twisted it, twisted it hard until Warren had no choice but to turn his body away to relieve the pain. He squealed as Eric gripped harder, stepped in behind him, pulling Warren's own arm tight around his neck. Warren spluttered another 'fuck you'. Eric responded by charging him forward into the wall, pushing his face deep into the grain of the brickwork.

'Now you listen to me, *blaaaahd*, your hero Piper . . .' He paused and looked across at Sean, who looked on nervously. 'Raymond Stewart Mackintosh, Jamaican national, street name the Piper.'

Eric nodded and raised his eyebrows.

Sean stared back.

'You got that?' asked Eric, still trying to weld Warren to the wall. 'Raymond Stewart Mackintosh.'

'Street name the Piper,' replied Sean, looking over his shoulder.

'Aye, you got it,' said Eric, pushing his specs back on to his nose with the middle finger of his free hand before returning to Warren.

'Your hero Piper, he was one of my snouts while you were still putting on your mammy's dresses. He coughed so much I thought he had fucking pleurisy.'

Warren demurred. 'Him no squeal, man. You a fuckin' liar!'

Eric pushed harder. 'Just tell me who's coming in, where and when, and you can go back to your dead babies.'

'Fuck you!' said Warren unimaginatively.

Eric sighed a this-is-going-to-hurt-me-more sigh and reached down to his belt. Lifting the flap of his jacket, Sean could see the brickphone, dangling there. Eric seized it.

'You wanted to know . . . ?' Eric reminded him before flashing it towards Warren's head, expertly tanning the back of his neck with the oversized rubber aerial. Warren screamed. Sean suppressed the urge to step in and put a stop to it. He didn't remember any of this from his training course.

Eric reached back to repeat the dose, but Warren signalled a willingness to submit. Eric released some of the pressure, allowing Warren to turn and face him, although he kept a hand firmly pushed against his chest.

'Well?'

'You loco bastard,' said Warren, rubbing the reddening welt on his neck, looking as if he might start crying.

'Who?'

'I nah tell you this t'ing.'

Eric offered him a close-up view of the brickphone, gave it a little shake. 'Who?'

'It be Cougar coming.'

Crazy Horse stamped his foot off the ground, let go of Warren for an instant to clap his hands together. It was almost like, Sean thought, well . . . a celebration.

'I knew it,' he muttered. 'I fucking knew it.' He grabbed

Warren's collar, snuffing out a half-baked attempt to escape. 'Piper's not going to like that.'

'Maybe the Piper don't know.'

Eric smiled. 'Thinking of changing your allegiance, are you?'

'Nobody own me,' Warren insisted.

'Where's this Cougar going to be?'

Warren looked down. 'He's flying in from Kingston.'

'You sorted him for a passport?'

Warren's professional pride made his mouth twitch.

'When?'

Warren allowed his smile to broaden. 'This be the best bit. He arriving 'dis morning. You probably missed him already.'

His little laugh was cut short by a fist to the gut. He slid down the wall like rain, settling in a puddle at Eric's feet. Eric dug something out of his jacket and dropped it by Warren's head.

A plastic bag with a small mound of white dust inside.

'Thanks for the gen,' he said, turning away. Sean followed him, wanting to say something, to at least assert his existence after a period during which he had felt apart, almost invisible. Warren hadn't looked to him for help. He had expected Sean to be just the same.

Sean knew he was way out of his depth. 'What was in the bag?' he asked as they reached the car.

'Warren's a user. Instead of cash, I give him what he wants.'

Eric sensed the discomfort in Sean's silence. 'He's no use to me if he doesn't get a hit. Got to keep 'em sweet.'

'But he didn't want to tell you. You beat him up.'

Eric chortled. 'Ach, it's always the same with him. I always get what I want from him. He just likes to play up a bit. I reckon it makes him feel better about grassing up his mates.'

They got in the car.

'So what now?' asked Sean unhappily. 'The airport?'

'No. We're going for a day out to Alton Towers, ride the fucking ghost train. What you think? And get a move on.'

14

. . . .

Harry led them out of the Asylum Screening Unit. The interview had lasted about ten minutes, during which time Harry had fostered a nice sense of antagonism with the fat bitch in an oversized sweater behind the counter. She was no worse than any of the rest of them, but he knew that pedantry and nit-picking were exactly the kind of things that Anwar expected for his money. When Harry said he would seek a judicial review against any question he felt inappropriate, the old man had almost wet himself with satisfaction. Harry made great play of insisting that his client be issued with an entitlement card which stated that he had made an application for political asylum and could be used to claim benefits while that application was under consideration. When it was duly issued, he even received a complimentary clap on the back from Uncle. By keeping him distracted, Harry hoped he wouldn't notice that they were dishing them out to everyone, whether they kicked up a fuss or not. As with so much else in this game, the reality didn't matter half as much as the appearance.

They shook hands outside, even the surly Baseeq apparently delighted with the performance of his guardian angel.

'It'll take them a while to arrange for a full interview. Months probably before they actually get round to seeing you again. If you have any problems . . . you know,' Harry said routinely, feeling a little tired.

'Of course, sir,' said Anwar. 'We have every confidence. Every confidence.'

Harry offered a weak smile. He needed that coffee now.

Anwar scuttled away, Baseeq shuffling behind. Harry went off at a ninety-degree angle, prepared to take a longer route to avoid them. He felt grimy at having executed such a cheap con, knew that his fatigue was as much to do with that as with his interrupted night's sleep. He blew hard as he breathed out and squeezed the bridge of his nose between thumb and forefinger.

Two hundred and fifty quid. He'd have to pull the same stunt forty times to pay back Bohra, ignoring interest, in the time he had. Sure, there was the legal aid cash which he'd have to claim for, but waiting for that was like waiting for a break in the Croydon concrete on your walk around the back of Lunar House.

It was still morning but the air had started to get heavy, the optimism of a new day already caked with dirt and the breath of dripping exhaust pipes. Harry could feel his skin start to glisten with pollution. Within a minute of coming outside, his sinuses had slopped over and brought down the shutters. Harry stopped his walk to rummage in his briefcase for a packet of paper handkerchiefs.

He blew his nose hard, pushing out with all his might.

He felt something inside give, a tiny pop.

With the hanky still to his face, he saw a people-carrier on the opposite side of the road, travelling abnormally slowly. Approaching him, it virtually came to a stop and signalled to come over to his side of the road.

Harry felt something trickling down the inside of his left nostril. He held out the handkerchief.

Blood.

He tasted salt, dabbed a finger on his tongue.

More of it.

Bending over, he watched as scarlet drops fell from out of sight and danced in splashes on his shoes and the pavement around them.

'Fuck,' he muttered, searching for another snotrag.

The people-carrier crossed over the dividing line and swung into a position directly adjacent to him. Harry looked up as it halted, saw there was a huge gobbet of blood perched on the end of his nose in the mirrored window. He threw his head back and staunched any more with a bullet of toilet paper up each nostril.

The side door of the vehicle snapped back. Harry saw a giant shape shift within. He knew what was coming.

'Hello, Mr Rumpole,' said a low, strangulated voice, followed by an annoying staccato laugh.

Bohra always laughed at his own jokes. 'What's the matter?' he asked.

'Dust a dosebleed,' Harry explained.

'Come on,' said the voice. 'Hop in.'

Harry gingerly put his head in and stepped up. There sat Bohra in the middle of the three rows of seats, lay rather, swimming in his own immense girth, rustling in a silver and purple shell-suit. He looked uncomfortable, struggling with human limbs on what was basically a seal's body. The hair was black, matted in complicated swirls. Although clean-shaven, there was a patch of grey stubble under his chin, which rasped against the man-made collar. Despite the darkened glass of the windows, he was wearing large sunglasses.

Behind him, on the back row, in attendance as ever, were the twins, the Bohras junior, looking back at Harry with studied uninterest, both moustached, both wearing Manchester United shirts over track pants. They flanked another young man with the same jet-black hair, one Harry didn't recognise, not that he could see the face with him hunched forward, anorak zipped up, eyes down.

Harry sat, perched on the edge of the small space allotted to him next to Bohra who, Harry saw, was spending a lot of time fiddling with his genitals through the cloth of his shell-suit.

'You like the motor?' Bohra asked.

'Yeah. Nice.' Harry thought he noticed an incongruous tear appearing from behind the dark glasses, slithering down his cheek.

'New today. Only thing I don't like is what they call them. People-carrier makes it sound like a bloody hearse, innit?'

He cackled again, scratching and pulling at his dick. Harry tried to smile, but he felt the blood inside his nose starting to encrust. He motioned to pull at one of the paper plugs.

'Ah, ah, ah,' said Bohra, waving a fat finger then patting the upholstery. 'New today. Like my trainers.' He lifted a foot to show Harry the blinding white of his new shoes. 'So no blood on the seats. Not unless it's really necessary.'

He stopped to laugh again. Unlike before, the twins joined in a little this time.

'Drive,' said the patriarch.

'Where to?' asked the man behind the wheel. Harry recognised the leather jacket he saw through the toilet door at the bookie's.

'We can give you a lift?' asked Bohra, shoving his hand into his pants.

'I've got my car around the corner,' said Harry, throwing his head back, feeling a thickness sliding down the back of his throat.

Bohra mulled over his reply for several seconds. 'Around the block,' he shouted.

The van jumped out spastically towards the middle of the road.

'What the hell are you doing?' shouted Bohra, clinging on to the handle above the passenger window.

'Clutch,' came the explanation. 'Shallow clutch.'

'Bollocks,' replied the owner before diverting his attention back to Harry. 'How's your father?' he asked.

Harry didn't much care for the question. He changed the subject. 'Look, Mr Bohra, if it's about the money . . .'

'If it's about the money?' repeated Bohra. 'If it's about the money?'

'I'll get it back to you very soon. You have my guarantee.'

'Guarantee?'

'Guarantee.'

Suddenly, the people-carrier swung hard to the left, Bohra's weight almost for a moment threatening to tip it over on its side. He let rip a tirade of Punjabi abuse, wiping away another tear spilling from behind his shades.

'You said around the block,' complained Leather Jacket.

'You want to get us all killed?'

'I don't know. There's something wrong with the steering.'

They moved again, after a brief grinding of gears.

'You should never give your guarantee, Harry. Thirty years in business and I never guaranteed nothing to no man,' he explained proudly.

'But what I'm saying, Mr Bohra, is that you have no need to worry. I've got the work. I'm in a growth industry,' Harry went on, gasping for air through his mouth as he spoke. 'I mean, just as an example, I've only just come away from a job with a new client.'

'You mean them Pakis? I saw you with them Pakis. What you doing, helping them? We're supposed to be at war with them, man. Kashmir-nicking bastards.'

'Doesn't mean they can't be exploited,' said Harry, hoping to hit the right spot.

Bohra did chuckle. 'Well, as long as you promise me you're exploiting them.'

He laughed long again, expecting Harry to join in. Fortunately, the car came to an immediate stop, the body nearly lurching off the chassis with the force. Harry was sent flying off the edge of the seat, his face ground into the back of the seat ahead, dislodging one of his nose plugs. He hurriedly reinserted it.

'Bastard,' bellowed Bohra, who was furious, despite being unmoved.

There was a shrug from up front.

'Heavy brakes, Mr Bohra.'

'Pull over.'

'I'm just getting the hang—'

'Pull over!'

Leather Jacket obeyed.

'Let me drive, Dad,' said one of the twins. The one on the left.

'Shut up,' replied his father, turning his attention back to Harry, who committed himself to telling him what he wanted to hear.

'You owe me a lot of money, Harry.'

'I know, Mr Bohra.'

''Cos you're a good Indian boy, I treat you well. I could be killing you with interest payments by now. But no, I say to myself, he's a bright boy in a good job. In a *profession*. Who knows, I might need a lawyer myself one day, when I wind up in the Old Bailey.'

This must have been a joke, for Bohra laughed.

'Not my area, I'm afraid,' said Harry.

'No. You're too busy being friendly with the bloody Pakis, who should all be deported, all fucking terrorist bastards.'

Harry shrugged apologetically. Bohra made an effort to pull himself up a little.

'The fact is, Harry, that there is something you can do for me. A little thing.'

Harry swallowed, began to rub the crown of his nose.

'There's money in it for you,' added Bohra.

'How much?' asked Harry.

Bohra didn't answer that one. 'I need you to find me a person.'

'A person.'

'Girl.'

'Well, that narrows it down.'

'It's an urgent situation. I need her found. We'd do it ourselves, but it would be a little awkward for me . . . for us. You understand?'

Harry didn't.

'I'm trusting you to keep this a private màtter.'

'So who is she?' Harry asked, starting to feel a little light-headed.

'Her name is Ranjita. She owes me something. Like you, Harry.'

'Do you have a picture?'

An envelope was handed over from behind and on to Harry.

'The picture's inside,' said Bohra. 'All you have to do is find her and bring her to me.'

'Where do I start?'

Bohra nodded. He clicked his fingers in the direction of the youth who sat between the twins. A hand grabbed the back of his collar and pulled it, drawing the head back. Harry saw a face trapped in adolescence, acne around the mouth. He could just make out the eyes behind the flop of hair, was unnerved at the way they stayed rooted to the ceiling of the vehicle.

'Where will she be?' Bohra asked him.

'Don't know. Don't know,' he sang rather than spoke.

Harry noticed him flinch at an invisible blow from one of the twins, possibly a kick.

Bohra growled his low rage. 'No son of mine,' he spat back. 'Try the common,' he told Harry. 'Try everywhere. Just bring her back to me.'

The man behind sat forward, grabbed the headrests on the seats in front. 'Don't know. Don't know!'

He was cut short by another blow, one Harry saw this time, a row of knuckles planted hard above the elbow, giving him a dead arm. The other twin spoke to him, affecting an odd lisp.

'Hit his a family ish-yoo,' he commented, dealing another slap on the head with the flat of his hand. 'Show some ris-peck.'

Harry got it now. 'OK,' he said. 'But for how much?'

'If you find me the girl within a week, then I will consider your debt to me paid.'

'The whole lot?'

'In full.'

Harry gave it a second. 'Deal.'

Bohra lunged forward to grab his hand, clasping it in his own. 'You shake hands, that's your guarantee.'

Harry laughed carefully. 'I'm not going to say no to an offer like that. The only thing . . . I mean, what if she's . . .? What if I can't find her?'

'We have a deal now. I have your guarantee.'

'But, I mean . . .'

'One week. The money or the girl,' Bohra said, pointing to the door.

Harry got out and set about cleaning up the mess in his nasal passages. Alongside him, the people-carrier bunny-hopped away.

He was relieved that the flow of blood had been staunched. He cursed the fact that Bohra had shown up at just that moment. Somehow the fat bastard had a knack for seeking Harry out at moments of embarrassment or vulnerability. Or maybe it was just that his proximity brought on nosebleeds.

Still, at least now Harry had learned more than Bohra would have wanted him to know. Firstly, that he had a third son, a bit backward maybe, who he'd airbrushed out of the family album. And, more important, that his daughter-in-law had done a runner. Bohra had tried to keep this part from Harry, but family tension, like murder, will always out. Hence Bohra's exhortation to keep the matter secret. He would feel the disgrace of a runaway bride in the family sharply. To go looking for her himself meant an admittance of what had happened. Hard to imagine anyone in that shell-suit feeling disgrace at anything, but there was no accounting for taste. But then Harry wasn't complaining, even if the money he owed seemed way over the top as compensation for finding her. He sniffed hard, satisfied that the torrent had dried up, dragged what was in there back up into his mouth and gobbed it out. Of course, he knew that he had no hope of finding her, that she was probably long gone, being groped by a bunch of rugmunchers in some women's refuge or,

God help her, in Bradford. But it bought him a little time. And time was indeed money.

He did his sums quickly. Still had two hundred from the money Jay had given him last night and Anwar's two hundred and fifty. More than enough.

He went into the first newsagent he passed and bought a copy of *The Racing Post*. He drove to Tooting, parked and went straight to his regular bookie's, surprised at having to dodge a brace of workmen who had planted themselves on the dozen stairs leading down into the shop.

'What's all that?' he asked Tommy, who was sitting cross-legged in his regular corner chair. Harry was reminded of the fact that he'd never seen Tommy come in or go out of the bookie's, only ever seen him downstairs.

'They're building a stairlift, so that even if you lose both your legs to the fags and/or the booze, not to mention a serious accident, you will still be able to savour the Sporting Life and fritter away your sick money accordingly. I'll tell you this, though,' he added, raising his voice for the benefit of Donna behind the counter. 'This place becomes a magnet to amputees and the deformed, I'll be finding somewhere else to invest my savings.'

'Promises, promises,' cooed Donna, without looking up from whatever she was doing.

'All I'm saying is, any action has consequences, unforeseen consequences. That action, putting that thing up them stairs, changes everything.'

'Look,' said Harry, checking the paper. 'There's a horse called Chaos Theory in the 2.20.'

'I'm serious,' implored Tommy. 'That thing there changes the balance. By putting it there, it makes the possibility of us having to use it increase. It's a premonition of doom. You might as well put a sign up saying "amputees welcome."'

'What's with the amputees?' Harry asked with a pained expression, starting to look at the form.

Tommy relit his roll-up and shrugged.

'It's an Irish thing,' he said, suddenly waking up and doing the jabbing thing with his roll-up. 'Part of my cultural heritage, just like your seven-armed fellers. So you'll show some respect.'

15

....

Eric filled Sean in on the way to the airport as they raced along the outside lane.

'Leslie Philip Montgomery. Street name Cougar,' he explained. 'You got that?'

Sean nodded.

'Wanted in Kingston and Toronto for armed robbery, kidnapping, more assaults than you can shake a dildo at. A real tasty bastard. Can't wait to meet him.'

Sean just kept driving. He was aware of the time and how long he had before this shift would be over.

'Here's how I see it,' Eric went on. 'You've got a big market in London for your average Yardie, but we're not in the top league yet. That's the States, mainly eastern seaboard, not so much West Coast where the gooks have it pretty well sewn up. Now you're talking tasty. Hack up their own children for a poke of chips, those motherfuckers.'

Sean tried to disguise the involuntary shaking of his head. Crazy Horse had been watching too many movies. Or maybe he'd been in too many movies.

'No, but the Yardies prefer it out east. But like I'm saying, London is like one rung off the top of the ladder, it's like the first division compared with the premier league. But in the premier league, once you make it, you've got an easier life, you know what I'm saying? You've got time to step on the ball and look up, whereas down in the first division every match is a pitched battle. You have to prove yourself in the first division in order to get up, right? Well that's what London is for these people. It's the chance for promotion, but you have to be able to prove that you have what it takes. So this is where they fight it out. This,' said Eric, barely able to suppress his pride, 'is the place to be . . . You see them on their way up while they're here. Some of them get stronger and make the move. Some of them get their wings clipped, you know what I mean? It's like watching fucking Darwin in action,' he purred. 'Darwin in fucking action.'

He stopped and pondered his own exegesis, smoke everywhere. Then he started again. 'What we got here, now, today, is Leslie Philip Montgomery, street name?'

'Erm . . . Cougar.'

'He's coming to make his play. That's what he's up to. Everything I've heard about him, and I've heard plenty, makes me think he's got what it takes, by the way. The others are all spaced out, too deep into that Rastafari shit to be effective. Doped up morning and night, hanging around with public schoolboys, for Christ's sake.' He sounded almost outraged. 'It's crying out for one guy to step in. This Cougar thinks it's him. But he didn't reckon with me.'

Sean realised he was keen to help with this blag. He wanted to do something that would erase the memory of Warren's beating up or at least make it seem worth while. If they tagged Cougar before he reached Immigration, where he could be arrested and kicked straight out, then he'd feel better about the whole business, the ends justifying the means. Although why not just call the immigration office at Terminal 3? That was just Eric's way, mused Sean. Eric the glory hound.

'We're going to make it in time?'

Crazy Horse glanced at the digital clock on the dashboard.

'Oh, aye. The Royal Caribbean's never on time. Plus there's the walk from the gate and the baggage waiting time. No worries.'

Sean weaved lanes to get across for the Terminal 3 turn-off.

As they drew into the airport proper, Sean signalled to turn into the main multi-storey car park.

'What you doing?' asked Eric.

'Parking.'

Crazy Horse leaned across and grabbed the wheel, the car veering across two lanes.

'Go to Arrivals,' he said.

'All right, all right,' said Sean, wresting control back. 'Jesus.'

As they hit the slow-moving lines of airport traffic, Eric started to get anxious. He was leaning over again, pushing down on the horn, urging Sean to make impossibly tight manoeuvres, pressing the horn some more. Lowering the window, he thrust his warrant out to halt a van in the next lane so that Sean could squeeze out in a switch that bought them about two seconds.

Sean's nerves were pleading for lithium by the time he pulled the car around to the first large revolving door for the Arrivals area.

'Just stay here,' said Eric, who had opened the door with the car still in motion and jumped out.

'I can't stay here,' said Sean, annoyed at not being asked to help in Cougar's apprehension. 'I'm blocking half the road. They'll move me along.'

'Show 'em your warrant,' shouted Crazy Horse, quickly lost in the crowd.

Sean sat and waited. He was learning quickly that however much he chose to tell you, you were never really going to know what went on in Eric's mind. Inevitably, a sour-faced hag knocking on fifty in a BAA uniform, carrying a walkie-talkie, approached. He tried to deflect her meddling by raising his warrant to the driver's side window.

She wasn't impressed and tapped on the window with her radio. Looking straight ahead, Sean re-flashed the warrant but she just tapped again.

He turned down the window. 'Yes?'

'I'm sorry,' she said, the sheer weight of her lipstick restricting her mouth movement. 'But I'll be having to ask you to move along there, love.'

Sean pushed the warrant at her a third time. 'Immigration,' he said.

'Yes, I can read, but this is a no-parking area. There are no exceptions, other than for vehicles of the emergency services. If you could just see your way to moving along, sir . . .'

'I'm in the middle of a job here.'

'No, sir,' she spat back. 'You're in the middle of the road.'

'This is a matter of national security,' he hissed, but without conviction. The truth was he was struggling to work out why Eric had wanted him to park here. There was something that didn't quite make sense. Something he'd said . . .

'Are you going to move?' shouted the airport harpy.

'Are you going to fuck off?' retorted Sean, distracted as he went looking for his lithium. He was suddenly aware of planes flying perilously close overhead.

'What did you say?' she asked.

'I said . . .' Sean struggled, fighting the urge to go and hide. He had that claustrophobic thing again, wanted to punch a hole through the car roof. 'I said that I wouldn't be long.'

'You told me to fuck off, you cocksucker. I'm taking down your number and reporting this to the police.'

Sean located a couple of pills rolling loose among the fluff in his jacket pocket. He made a face at her and wound up the window, leaning forward to wipe the tablets clean and knock them back. Looking up, she was upfront, as good as her word, writing down his registration number. She looked through the windscreen at him, threw him a V-sign and walked off, quickly obscured by an arriving passenger pushing a trolley piled high with luggage . . .

Luggage.

That was what Eric had said, the thing that Sean realised had been nagging him. He'd said that they'd be in time because you had to allow for him to *collect his luggage*. But if you were there to intercept and blag him, it had to be before he picked up his luggage, while he was still in the immigration area . . .

Sean got the metal taste in his mouth again, the one that spelled trouble.

And then Crazy Horse appeared. Not alone. Dwarfing him was a black Caribbean male, six-four maybe, dressed in jeans and a buttoned-up denim jacket, baseball cap and sunglasses, not too happy at being shoved along by Eric, who stepped around him to open the back door.

'Get in.'

The invitee hesitated.

'Fucking get in, Leslie,' snarled Eric. 'Or we'll be marching straight back through to Immigration. You want that?'

He got in.

'Not on the seat,' said Eric, following him in.

'What you talking 'bout, star?'

'Get down on the fucking floor, where you belong.'

Eric, his strength never ceasing to amaze Sean, grabbed him by the collar and threw him down.

'I'm this fucking close to taking you back in there,' he hissed.

'You don' know what you dealing with, star,' came the voice, followed by a grunt of pain as Eric twisted something.

'Ditto, pal.'

Sean threw a look over his shoulders. All he could see was Crazy Horse, teeth gritted, forcing something out of sight down. And a pair of denim knees.

'What you fucking looking at?' asked Eric. 'Get a fucking move on.'

'Where?'

'The way we came!'

Sean put the car into gear and drove off, riding the speed bumps hard, each one recorded by the grunts of the reluctant passenger eating carpet in the back.

Eric said nothing until they were off the airport site. Sean was watching him in the rear-view mirror, looking around frantically, tongue sticking out, issuing the odd wordless reminder for his charge to lie still. Only as Sean pulled the car on to the inside lane of the motorway leading back into London did Eric feel relaxed enough to jab a Marlboro in his gob and push back his specs.

'Well, who would have thought it? Guess who we've got as a passenger. How you doing down there, Leslie?'

'Me name's *Cou*-gar.'

'Not to me, sunshine. I've read your police record. To me you are plain old Leslie. Back-door Leslie.'

'Me name's *Cou*-gar. You dem seh it.'

'Listen, I understand ya. If my name was Leslie, I'd want to change it also.'

It was there again, Sean was sure of it. That alteration in accent and stress that Eric had adopted with Warren. But it was more marked now, the vowels longer, the bass more growling.

'But hear the news, man,' Eric carried on. 'I wan call ya Leslie, dat how it gwan be.'

Oh, Christ, thought Sean. He tried to work out what the hell Eric was playing at. This guy, this bloke lying on the floor of the car, was *the guy*, the public enemy number one they'd gone to the airport to blag and send back, the one currently getting a free cab ride up the M4, albeit in the cheap seats.

But even more worrying than the obscurity of Crazy Horse's motives was the fact that now the mad bastard was *fucking talking like one of them!*

Eric was going native on him.

'So, listen deh, Les-*lie*. You and I got bid'ness.'

Cougar laughed. 'I ga nah bid'ness wiff no Snowflake, think him niggah.'

Cougar's appraisal of Eric, however accurate, brought immediate recrimination. In the rear-view mirror Sean caught a fleeting view of the brickphone on a sharp descent. There was impact and a dull grunt. When Eric spoke again, it was much nearer to his familiar patois. Sean sensed that his pride had been injured.

'You wanna watch your mouth, ya wee bastard.'

'I have breddahs waiting for me,' said Cougar firmly, although there was a recognition in the voice of Eric's unpredictability. 'They come looking fe me.'

'Oh, yeah? Who might that be? Jeremy Carlton Green, street name Head. Clive Lloyd Richardson, street name: Bangman. You getting these?' He looked up at Sean.

Now Cougar sounded genuinely perturbed.

'How deh ya know dem t'ings? You pol-iss?'

'Worse,' said Eric. 'Immigration. I got powers the pol-iss never dreamed of. I can kick you out any time I want. I can have you locked up for ever without a charge and no fucking magistrate for you to go crying to. I—' he added with a little belch— 'can do anything I want. And I've been waiting for you a long time, *me breddah*.'

Sean noticed that Cougar, Leslie, whatever the fuck this bloke was called, let Eric's latest slip into the vernacular go unmentioned. His tone was more measured when he spoke again.

'I heard of you, man,' he said.

Eric didn't seem particularly surprised. 'What do they say?'

'Dem say you fucking crazy, man.'

'Believe it,' said Eric, happy as Larry now, sitting back, doing up the buttons on his jacket.

'Dem say you know more about boys from the Yard than demselves do.'

Eric tapped his own temple. 'All in here. Photographic memory. Never forget a face or a name. It's a gift.'

'Can I sit up, skipper?'

Eric's good humour wasn't stretching that far. 'Stay where you are,' he said coolly. 'It's time for business.'

'No bid'ness, man,' Cougar protested. 'I'm here for a holiday.'

'And I'm Haile Selassie.'

'Yeah,' Sean was impressed that Cougar still had the sang-
froid to snort a laugh. 'Him were mad fucker too.'

'I know what you're doing here, pal. You're knocking on that
door, *Les-lie*. The street's in a state, pal. They're all too busy
mashing each other up. Time's right for a boy like you.'

'And you gwan help me?'

'No. That would be immoral. Sacking offence.' He grinned,
looking up towards Sean, who avoided his look in the rear-view
and stared at the road, thinking *not happening, not happening*,
then thinking *beer and chaser, beer and chaser.* 'No,' continued
Eric. 'I'm no going to help you. You going to help me.'

'So what you want?'

Eric shrugged. 'Names, addresses. Who's coming, who's
going, who's scoring what off who . . .'

'I ain't no fuckin' snitch, star!'

Crazy Horse took a deep breath in through his nose.

'Listen to me, pal. This is my fucking country, OK? There's
no way I'm going to let you black bastards run riot in my fucking town!'

My town? Sean could have scoffed.

'You shitkickers have to be *controlled*,' Eric was explaining. 'But
listen, I'm a pragmatist. I know there's no way to do that without
help from the inside. So I let you become a big fish and you help
me keep the pond small. It's a question of—' Eric paused,
brought both hands to his chest, palms facing up '—balance.
That, or we turn this motor around and I wrap you up and send
you with a compliment slip back to my friend Inspector Reece in
Kingston. Take the turn-off for the Chiswick roundabout,' he
instructed Sean.

Sean thought he heard Cougar smart at the name Eric had
cited. He pulled the car into the nearside lane and signalled to
come off the motorway. Eric looked down again.

'You've got one turn around the roundabout to make your
mind up or we're straight back to the airport.'

Sean hurried the car down on to the slip road, eyes dancing as he tried to hear Cougar's response.

'Wha'cha asking, to snitch me breddahs, it's a low t'ing.'

Eric didn't reply. Sean heard the faint crackling of another Marlboro being lit.

He's not going to do it, thought Sean, privately elated. He wanted to take the scrote back, erase this whole fucked-up journey. They could still make amends.

'You ask plenty, mistah.'

Again, no response. Sean turned on to the short stretch of road that led to the roundabout, rammed the car through the gears quickly, pushed his foot down hard.

Make that turn, make that turn . . .

'I risk losing respect if they know seh I squeal to you . . .' added Leslie, businesslike.

'Reckon so,' replied Eric. 'That's if anyone found out, which they won't.'

Sean could see the roundabout ahead. The lights leading on to it were giving him green. He charged them . . .

'What, you saying we keep dis t'ing a secret?'

'Soul of discretion, pal.'

A hundred yards away, the lights turned amber. Sean hunched forward, willing the car on . . .

'You pay me?'

Red light! Too late to brake. Sean swung the car wide and lunged it on to the roundabout. It shaved the bumpers of two cars coming at him from the right. Sean gritted his teeth at the horns of outrage.

'Pay you? Maybe.'

'How much?'

Sean had to brake hard to dodge a female cyclist. Amid the tight lanes of the miniature circular, he got stuck behind her . . .

'Depends what you give me. Fifty quid a week plus whatever I think you're worth.'

Sean had got around and veered across lanes to make the exit, straight in front of him. Then it was gone, as a furniture lorry rolled across him. He had no choice but to brake hard, hitting the horn. He got a summary two fingers from the driver's window.

'I've turned around. I'm heading back to the airport,' he announced, aware that his own voice was a little scratchy. 'I've made the turn. It's too late,' he said, looking back and down. 'You've had your chance.'

He saw Cougar's head appear in the rear-view. He was looking forward, over Sean's shoulder, taking hurried stock.

Sean saw him turn to Crazy Horse. 'Got yoursel' a deal,' he said.

Eric handed him a card. 'There's a pub in Balham called the Spatchcock. Nobody you know will be there. Most people don't even know it exists. You'll be there every Tuesday and Thursday at opening time, in the back bar, next to the jukebox.'

'It's too late,' asserted Sean. 'It's . . .'

The furniture van's engines snorted and it trickled forward. Sean caught a fresh glimpse of the sliproad back up to the motorway.

'If you're not there,' Eric whispered to Cougar. 'I'll come looking for you, not before I've told ever breddah you've ever had about this conversation.'

The furniture van inched forward. If Sean could get around it. He dragged the car out left to get past, but a black cab was trying the same thing and he ended up wedged between the two other vehicles.

'Fuck,' he whelped. 'It's too late. It's too fucking late.'

And then he heard it. The sound of the car door opening, like a gun breech being pulled back. And then the slam as it closed, the shot to the heart.

Eric had let him go. Sean sat still for a moment, aware of the cascade of horns in the background as belonging to a different sphere, the other world he saw but couldn't fathom. Only he was sane.

Eric leaned forward and jabbed him hard on the shoulder. He was pointing at something. 'Pull over there,' he was saying. Sean saw that he was indicating a filling station on the round-about. 'I could murder an Irn Bru.'

Sean sat in the forecourt and watched him buying the pop, not a can as he had expected, oh, no – with Crazy Horse it had to be a two-litre bottle, and a packet of Marlboro. Watching him talk to the Tamil working in the shop, Sean half-expected him to leap over the counter and spin his drum there and then.

Inspecting him at a distance through two panes of glass gave Sean a new-found objectivity. While he was pleased at being able to reach a rational conclusion, it was still a troubling epiphany as its subject headed back to the car.

Eric was one loose fucking cannon. A regular two-litre headcase.

He got back in, planting his feet on the dashboard, unscrewing the bottle. 'Want some?'

Sean declined.

'Your loss. Caledonian nectar,' he explained, swigging it back with both hands. 'This,' he added after swallowing, 'is a national institution. Do you know that? Irn Bru is very important to me.'

Sean was non-committal.

'Ah, what the fuck do you know about culture?' Eric went on, turning himself to snap open his Home Office box lying on the passenger seat and pull a small bottle from it, with a cloudy viscous liquid inside. 'You English are all the same. Where is it you come from?'

'I'm from here,' Sean said pointedly.

McCleish paid no attention. 'Where were you born? Where did you grow up?'

'I was born . . . somewhere else, but I grew up in Tonbridge.'

'Tonbridge?' whooped Eric. 'There you are, then. You're from the Home Counties, where having an identity is frowned on.' He produced the sweet tin he had shown Sean the other day and took out a fat ready-rolled cigarette from it. 'Christ, Tonbridge. You're in deep there. Full of people who make one trip a year on the train into London and start complaining about how dirty it is by Clapham Junction, then scuttle back again after their matinée of The Lion King.' He lit the joint and bit on it, sucking in hard between clenched teeth, then taking the smoke down deep. 'There is a point, you know, at which people become so middle class they evaporate into a blue rinse. Tonbridge. Christ.' He coughed and released a hanging cloud of familiar sweet-smelling smoke, then set about unscrewing the top of the bottle.

'What's in there?' Sean asked.

'Rum. Not that Bacardi shite. The real stuff. Want a try?'

Sean was tempted by the thought of a drink, but he didn't want to give anything away to McCleish. Plus the whiff of battery acid coming from the bottle was less than inviting. He watched Eric's eyes water as he took a shot, having to reach for the Irn Bru straight after.

'Anyway, I just grew up there. I haven't lived there for nearly twenty years. Haven't even been there.'

'Do me a favour,' responded Eric, chucking the bottle into the glove compartment, making a tight face as he pulled again on the spliff. 'Look, where I grew up people were proud of what they were, proud of belonging. That's what we had. What has Tonbridge got?'

'I don't know. Brands Hatch? The motor-racing track?'

Eric threw his head back and laughed. 'Formula One? Oh, I rest my case. I rest my fucking case right there.'

A gap in the traffic let Sean off the forecourt and back on to the roundabout. 'Which way?' he asked, with a sigh.

Crazy Horse had found a tape in his pocket and shoved it into the car stereo, giving the volume knob a healthy swing. A thunderclap of bass and drums signalled the throb of hard-core reggae.

'I feel like celebrating,' screamed Eric, his eyes traced with red from the dope. 'We gwan to Brix-ton.'

'Brixton?'

'Get something to eat. It's on me. Everyt'ing coooool . . .'

16

. . . .

Harry walked the muddy path, teeth gritted as he went over it, as he relived it, race by race. It was incredible, *impossible* to believe that he, who could now look back on it with detachment, was the same person who had, only an hour before, been in a frenzy of excitement and frustration, heart thrumming at the chance of winning, and the fact of losing.

He had started well, that's what made it worse. An each-way long shot had actually come in, but it was a bet made on the back of research: a modest field, a stable in good form, a horse on the upgrade which performed at the trip and liked the ground, which was well weighted and carried an apprentice jockey whose allowance brought the burden on the beast's back down even further. Harry knew the satisfaction of a job well done as it took up the running half a furlong out and won by a handy two lengths, the kind of satisfaction that work could never afford him. So what perversity of nature had led him to abandon the method from thereon? Hubris made him assume that a winner would jump out at him from the twenty-five runners in the next, a five-furlong dash that nobody in their right mind would bet a fiver on, never mind the hundred that Harry wagered. And things disintegrated further as Harry, this strange Harry he could barely recognise, gave up reason and let instinct run free as he tried to chase his losses, backing anything that had won last time out, then picking on a favoured jockey before (sin of all sins) choosing a horse with a name he gave an arbitrary significance. Carla's Lad had trotted in second last. Added to a steady dribble of losing dogs at Oxford and Sunderland, it was only with less than fifty quid left that Harry awoke, as if from a dream, his manic alter ego dispersed.

He had left immediately, not even saying goodbye to Tommy and walked angrily to Tooting Bec, from where he had headed to the common, breathing heavily to relieve the clump of anguish nestling behind his solar plexus, wincing at the squeals of self-hatred ringing in his ears, urging him to step off the kerb in front of a passing double-decker.

In truth, Harry feared the inevitable self-analysis as much as the haemorrhaging of money that preceded it. He understood why he gambled. It wasn't rocket science. He gambled because gambling was straightforward, there would be one of two outcomes, excluding a withdrawal or a dead heat. Or a Rule 4. But generally you knew where you stood. You either won or you lost, lost, lost. He gambled for some element of directness in his life. He needed cheap thrills to counter the sophistry of an average working day. Nobody, not even his own family, really knew how it worked, how a one-man band doing immigration work operated, nobody on the outside would understand the required blend of chicanery and bogus outrage that had gradually sucked the very life out of him. Virtually all his old friendships had withered and were slowly biodegrading, simply requiring more energy to survive than Harry had left to give.

He tried not to think about the money. He'd always been mortgaged up to the hilt and maxed on the plastic, but there was a time when Harry would have marched into the bank, demanded more money, bandied threats about race relations litigation if they hadn't offered him double what he wanted. But somewhere he'd lost his bottle and fatally gone all apologetic with his numerous institutional creditors. Now he couldn't bear to go in and face the Spanish Inquisition he got every time he went to see the junior assistant Business Manager or whoever the hell he'd been relegated to next, the ink barely dry on the fucking HND certificate framed on the wall behind him. Fearing that one day he'd be summoned in to discuss another overdraft extension with the guy who cleaned the Barclays staff toilets, he'd followed the path of least resistance and given in to Bohra's persistent offers of a 'community loan', kidding himself that he would use the cash to diversify and begin the process of getting out of the immigration game for good. He'd borrowed the ten grand only to piss the lot away on knacker's yard fodder. An interesting definition of diversification.

As he walked, he realised that he'd covered this stretch of the common before. He looked down at the passport photograph of the sad girl in his palm, the faded orange backdrop, a man's hand caught over her head in the frame, surreal and oddly threatening. He slipped it back in his wallet. The only people he'd seen were retired folk walking their dogs or, famously for Tooting Common, furtive gentlemen sitting on park benches hoping for an assignation with their like-minded brethren.

But he hadn't seen her, as he knew he wouldn't.

'Stupid,' he said to himself, and gave up looking.

17

....

Sean twisted the fork in his curried goat. It wasn't bad, but he didn't really feel hungry. He had no more lithium and felt the stirrings of panic, not helped by the astringent strip lighting in the restaurant on Coldharbour Lane where they ate, trains rumbling by outside. To call it a restaurant was misleading. Basically, they had adopted one of the two Formica tables at the back of a takeaway. As Eric ate and Sean played with his curry, the odd local came and left with polystyrene boxes of food. Eric had insisted that he sit facing the door, and every time the bell attached to the door tinkled he was looking up and over Sean's shoulder, clocking faces.

'These blokes, these—' Eric leaned forward to whisper '—Jamokes, Yardies, whatever you want to call them, they've got the right idea, if you ask me. They play up to it, they like being tough. But that's honest. Being tough is what really matters, like when you're at school. Nobody cares how well you play the piano or how many languages you speak. The harder you are, the more important you are. And that's true. It's not in question. That's the way life really is. That's what *we* used to be like. They're not interested in how it looks to other people, just as long as it scares them. But they know, if it wasn't them, it would be somebody else. That fat cunt Bohra, you think 'cos he's Indian that really he's a nicer person than them? Don't kid yourself. The stories I've heard about Bohra, the things he does to those young girls he pimps for, make you go grey. In the meantime, he's talking shit about the community sticking together. And him, he spends half his life cacking himself about the Turks muscling in where he operates. You didn't know that? It's common knowledge. He's paranoid about Turks.'

Sean looked down, uneasy with the subject of Bohra. But Eric didn't linger there.

'They're all looking over their shoulders. At least with my boys here, at least they throw themselves into it. If they're going to be crooks, they go the whole hog. If they roll a seven, at least they lived a while. They're not interested in respectability. They're interested in money and feeling good and black girls. I don't blame them. And I'll tell you something else about them. They get blagged, they don't start bleating for fucking asylum. That would be . . . disgraceful. They're not interested in *society*, here or at home.' He bit the word off like the unwanted end of a cheap cigar. 'They don't recognise the idea. They don't care about your homeless moaning bastards or respect for your war dead. They take their blagging like men, get deported and try to come back. They're free men. Fuck it, I like them. I *like* their culture. It's for me,' added Eric, swigging from a can of Black Stripe he had secreted in a plastic bag, the premises having no licence.

'You live fast, you die young,' said Sean quietly. *Tired*, he thought. *Talking in clichés*, he thought. Eric didn't seem to mind. Clichés did it for him.

'If they can catch you. But you're right. These fuckers are all on a short fuse. They burn out. Like our friend Leslie. He's just the same. That's why I have to make use of them while I can. If we're going to keep the blagging figures up.'

Sean looked down at his food. He was sitting, listening to a mad Jock explaining the need to facilitate the illegal entry of Jamaican criminals into the country to help with departmental statistics. One economic migrant playing a warped game with a bunch of others, with South London as their piss-stained sand-pit. Today had been some fucking education.

'You don't think,' he proffered, 'that there's a possibility that you . . . that we've lost sight of our original aim here?'

Eric shrugged, stuck out his bottom lip and blinked slowly. 'You mean that things are out of hand?' he asked. Sean watched him smile, a chink appearing between those thin lips, revealing a line of shoddy teeth set at irregular angles like gravestones after an earthquake. 'Fucking great, isn't it?'

Crazy Horse got up to pay. From his back pocket he pulled a numbered receipt book and, licking his fingers, began counting through until he met a virgin page. He approached the counter where a large Caribbean woman was slinging hash. 'How much?'

She eyed him with a knowing ill ease, as she had when they had come in and ordered. They obviously knew Eric in these parts, maybe even feared him a little.

She told him the price. Seven quid. Peanuts, really. He handed her the book.

'Do us a favour, Grace,' he said with a wink. 'Fill one of them out for us, will you? Make it for twenty-five.'

This was classic expenses-fiddling. With no official budget for informers, this was how Eric and others acquired the money to pay their snouts. But Grace wasn't happy. She shook her head defiantly. 'I don't want to break the law no more, Mr McLeish.'

Eric planted one hand on the counter, the other on his hip. 'Come on, Grace. I thought we had an understanding here. If you're so worried about the law, maybe a tour of the kitchens might be in order. Everybody got permission to work, have they? I bet half of them haven't even got permission to breathe in this country. I'd hate to have to close you down, love. Where would I come for me curried goat then? Just fill in the fucking receipt, there's a good girl.'

She did as she was told. Sean could see from the manner in which she set her jaw that she wanted to say more. Eric grabbed the completed receipt book and put it away. The door rattled and the bell rang as two giant young men entered, creaking in pristine leather jackets. Eric gestured for Sean to leave with him.

'Bye, Grace. See you again, darling.'

The tone of this last comment inspired Grace to speak up. 'I don' want you coming here no more. You coming here is bad for my bid'ness.'

Eric turned. 'You what?'

'You scare off me udder customers. You are bad for bid'ness.'

Eric took this as a personal affront, marching back to the counter with purpose. Sean had a high-pitched ringing in his ears, the unerring sign of impending doom.

'Now you listen to me, you dozy bitch, one phone call from me and you could have half the Met rummaging through your knicker drawer. I fucking own this place. I own you, and don't you forget it!'

One of the two new customers had stepped forward and tapped Eric hard on the shoulder. 'Don't be making no threats at the lady,' he suggested slowly.

Eric turned, amazement and contempt reaching some kind of half-baked compromise in his eyes. He said nothing as he scanned them deliberately, head to toe. The humming in Sean's ears was reaching dog-whistle frequency.

'What'cha looking a', raas?' asked the other man. The bigger one. Huge bastard.

Eric scanned him slowly, head to toe. 'Wha'am I looking at?' replied Crazy Horse. 'Something I scraped off my shoe, that's what.'

'You got some fucking mouth on you, star. Maybe I seal it up so it's nice and tight for your boyfriend there?'

Sean felt his own tongue slide out of his mouth and grip his top lip. He would have preferred to be left out of the conversation. Moving forward, he took Eric's arm. 'Let's go, mate.'

Eric shook him off, still staring it out with the two others.

'Come on,' hissed Sean, starting to feel a little anger streak into his fear. 'We're leaving.'

Eric took a promising step forward but stopped there. 'I want your names,' he said to the two men, holding up his warrant at them.

Sean groaned.

'You fucking see that? Give me your fucking names.'

The two men glanced at each other and then burst into sniggering laughter. Their amusement was a lightning flash of common sense, the objective expression of Eric's patent absurdity. It would have been funny, thought Sean, if it weren't so fucked. But Eric wasn't ready for such revelations. Sean's initial relief was tempered when he looked again at Crazy Horse, who was livid, approaching meltdown.

As the two men made to walk on to the tables at the back of the shop, he dropped quickly to one knee, pulled up a trouser leg and pulled a small white rectangle from within his boot. He was up again in an instant, arm outstretched.

There was a click and a snap of metal as the blade of his spring-knife shot out.

The two men stopped and looked on from a good six feet away as Eric waved the steel around.

'You want cutting?' he asked, backing towards the door. 'Is that what you want? You want cutting?'

As he reached the door, Grace decided to speak again. 'Don't be coming back here!' she said.

'I wouldne' come back to this shithole. Not even if me hat blew in! And your curried goat is shite, *by the way.*'

Sean glanced apologetically at the others as he followed Eric out. They both ran across the street to the car.

'Tight fucking squeeze,' said Crazy Horse as they got away. 'Bit tasty, them two,' he added, pushing his specs back on to his nose.

Sean looked in the rear-view. There was no sign of anyone following them.

'Don't do that again,' he said quietly.

'Eh?'

'Don't ever pull that out again.'

Eric looked out of the window. 'I need it for protection.'

'I'm not talking about the knife. The knife was ridiculous. The knife was . . . I'm talking about your warrant. Don't get your fucking warrant out like that in public. Not when I'm around. Please.'

'You don't want people to see the badge?'

'We were just having something to eat. You waving your warrant around . . . What was . . . ?'

'What is it? You don't want anyone to see the badge, that it? You don't want to be identified? Is that it, Tonbridge? Afraid of getting your hands dirty? Ashamed, are you?'

Sean bit his lip and looked at the dashboard clock. 'My shift's finished,' he said. 'Where do you want dropping off?'

18

....

Harry was surprised to see Dad down in the shop, where he kept his appearances to an absolute minimum. This was explained by the additional presence of a couple of his High Street cronies. As Harry entered, he acknowledged him, but there was none of the affectionate display of the day before. Not in front of the neighbours. He was sat on a high stool behind the till wearing an old coat with a sheepskin collar, a scarf folded under his neck. Jay had taken the opportunity to pop out while the old men gossiped in their usual pick 'n' mix of languages.

As he had entered the shop, Dad was jabbing a copy of the free local newspaper on the counter in front of them. His outrage at whatever he had read was being shared by Mr Chettin, who owned the dry-cleaner's over the road, and Mr Butt, the confectioner next door whom Jay single-handedly kept afloat.

'Disgrace,' said Mr Chettin.

'Worrying,' said Mr Butt.

'Bloody scum,' said Dad. 'Here, Harry, you seen this?'

Dad held up the paper. REFUGEE BEGGARS SWARM TOOTING it read.

'Refugee beggars swarm Tooting,' explained Dad. 'There it is, all there.'

'No news to me,' said Mr Chettin. 'You just have to look out of the shop window. You can see them, these women, all wearing scarves around heads, holding their babies, stopping people in the street, asking them for money. They are frightening people. Dirty. They chase them down the road. I've seen it.'

'It says here,' said Dad, 'that they are busing these people in. Bloody racket, man. We don't want them here. And what do the police do? I'll tell you. Nothing. Bloody disgrace. What's bloody poll tax for? Refugees, eh? Makes me sick, you know. People like us work hard to keep our families and then these bloody . . . Gypsies, innit? They're running up and down, terrorising honest people.'

'And you know,' piped up Mr Butt. 'They already getting money, houses. Soon as they get here. Not like when we came here. Then they start begging where we live and work.'

'I'll tell you what it is,' Dad went on. 'This country, we're too bloody soft. That's what it is. They should come here, be put straight in the camps. Beg off each other there. You going to pay for them sweets?' he asked Harry.

'Sure,' Harry replied over a mouthful of jellybeans.

'Nothing you can do about this?' asked Dad, referring back to the newspaper.

Harry felt a slight disorientation. Why was he making a connection between him and swarming refugee beggars? 'What's it got to do with me?'

'You're in the law,' said Dad. Harry noticed him flashing a look at the other two as he said this. 'There must be some way of stopping this.'

'I'm not sure that begging is an offence if it's done without menaces. Not really my area.'

Dad huffed impatiently. 'I don't mean the begging. I mean there must be a way of kicking these bastards out. It's not right that they come here. It's not right. Should be against the law.'

'And they get legal aid. Taxpayer pays for it all,' chimed in Mr Chettin. 'Taking our money to pay lawyers to help them so they can come and beg in front of our shops.'

'You know any of those lawyers, Harry?' asked Mr Butt.

Dad answered before Harry could. 'Harry doesn't involve himself in anything like that. You wouldn't have anything to do with people like that, isn't that right? People like that, don't know how they can look at themselves in the mirror.'

Harry rammed another handful of jellybeans into his mouth and bit on them hard. 'Everybody has a right to representation,' he garbled in English.

'You're comparing us with them?' asked Mr Butt.

'No,' said Harry.

'Not the same. Totally different thing. Amin would have killed us all. We were fleeing for our lives.'

'I'm just saying, from a legal standpoint . . .'

'The legal mind sees things differently,' Dad explained, glad at the chance to patronise the others. 'But sometimes it doesn't see how things are in the real world.'

Harry was happy to be painted as some kind of ascetic abstract thinker, as long as it got them off the subject. Jay came in at that moment. He clearly had none of the awkwardness Harry felt in this company. He was carrying a plastic bag from Butt's Cakeshop and a couple of videos under his arm.

'Where've you been?' snapped Dad.

'Just went down the library,' he said cheerfully, waving the videos. 'They've got a big Bollywood collection there. Bloody cheap.'

Messrs Chettin and Butt expressed an interest.

'Bloody rubbish,' insisted Dad. 'Nothing wrong with Sandra Bullock.'

Jay saw Harry, and his attitude reverted to the disgruntlement of yesterday.

'Bloody hell,' he said. 'Twice here in two days. What's the matter? Infestation of cockroaches at home, is it?'

'I was in the area,' Harry said.

'We are most honoured, oh great one,' answered Jay, moving behind the counter with that old bully's grin. Harry vetoed the idea of asking to borrow any more cash. He could tell that Jay was relishing having Harry in his debt. His concomitant smugness was more than Harry could bear. As the conversation reverted to swarming beggars once more, he headed to the door.

'I'll be off, then,' he announced.

'You're going?' asked Dad.

'Got to. Just popped in to say hi, really.'

Looking back, he felt the stab of hurt in Dad's eyes. His self-contempt rose three notches.

'Always on the go,' said Dad to the assembled company with a smile, but Harry sensed that he was meant to interpret it as a charged comment.

'I'll be around again soon,' said Harry, grabbing the handle. 'It's just that I've got . . . paperwork.'

The invocation of this petty deity at least softened the old man's stare a little as the shop door gave its familiar ring.

'Watch out for scrounging bastards!' he shouted.

'I'll keep an eye out,' said Harry as he left.

19

. . . .

Sean sat in the pool car. He was cold, with his jacket zip pulled right up to his neck. Somehow, movement seemed impossible. He had searched every inch of the car, under the seats, in among the tapes, in the glove compartment where Eric had left his killer rum, for any of the little blue and red pills on which he pinned his hopes, but without success. Worse still, the search of the glove compartment had led to contact with the 501 Spanish verbs book, and the memory, the one memory, had been triggered . . .

Don't get out of the car . . .

Funny how you recall moments from a third person's point of view, so that you become a character in your own recomposition of events.

And so Sean watches himself, in close-up first. Just his own face, staring ahead. He looks older than was the reality, older than he is now, in fact. But this older Sean looks pretty good, certainly thinner. There are lines of experience around his eyes – he is a man who has been through good and bad times, this Sean, who laughs with the best of them but has known heartache. He has lived but has come through it all. There is confidence in his eyes, which have changed colour from brown to blue.

The camera pulls back. He is sitting on a beach. The sand is warm on his bare feet. The simple clothes he wears, shorts and a dark cashmere sweater, calmly declare opulence. In truth, Sean has never owned a cashmere sweater. He tried one on in a shop but found it irritated his skin.

The view turns ninety degrees, moving behind Sean. The sea appears, waves roaring silently in. The sun is out, yet the sky is dark. In the distance a dark landmass can be made out through a haze. The waves, just gentle shifts in the water, are the subjects of Sean's gaze, the windsurfers, dozens of them, bisecting each other's wake as they weave the ocean.

The camera doesn't stop but carries on around Sean, coming to rest in front of him. Over his shoulder, a wooden beach hut sells drinks. From within it a woman emerges, small and dark-haired, carrying two bottles of beer. She wears a white T-shirt, which clings to her narrow, full-breasted body, and a sarong, sometimes red but as often blue, as it is today. Inside it, Sean knows her legs are slimmer than was actually the truth. The gentle wind pushes her hair into her eyes, causing her to stop and throw her head back. Her face is perfect, but then it always was . . .

Suddenly, Sean sees her feet and her blue sarong and simultaneously feels her hand brush the back of his neck . . .

He looks up, and they share a smile of absolute, eternal understanding.

Maria . . .

That moment.

That moment . . .

Gone.

Don't get out of the car . . .

Then he felt the blunter memory of his day with McLeish. Strangely, the more he thought he should feel outrage at the afternoon's professional aberrations, the less it bothered him. What did Sean care for the reputation of the immigration service after everything they'd put him through with their bullshit investigation in Lagos? Searching their home, hauling him in for interrogation, even interviewing Maria, putting the wind right up her. That was what had made her leave.

So what did Sean care for their reputation? Fuck them. Anyway, Sean knew that Crazy Horse was the symptom, not the cause, and that as long as Greatrix was getting his beloved results Eric had carte blanche. Nothing Sean said would put a stop to that, so best to say nothing. Tomorrow he'd ask Greatrix to find another driver for him.

What was really niggling at Sean was what Eric had said about him, about Tonbridge. The accuracy of it stung like ice. It hurt to hear from a mouth like that the truth you've been spending your whole life trying to subvert. He had always been aware of the force of inertia that came with the curse of a solid Home Counties, middle-class background. It had been in sharp relief today, his placidity as he had stood by and watched McCleish get on with it, first with Warren and then Cougar. Why hadn't he tried to stop him? Or why hadn't he joined in and got some for himself? It didn't matter which. But doing nothing, just letting it happen . . .

He'd once thought Maria would be the answer. What could be more exotic, what could go against the grain more than an Italian wife? He'd met her when he hadn't long been at Terminal 1 and while she was studying English in Richmond. He'd pursued her avidly, worn her down, dreaming of other places to call home. And yet, too late, he discovered what she, one of a family of seven sharing a third-storey flat in Verona, wanted. She wanted him for everything that he already was and wanted to be free of. She wanted the semi-detached, the spare bedroom for guests, the kitchen gadgets, her own little run-about, a garden, how she wanted a garden . . . She thought the suburban south-east was paradise.

Funny, really. That, of course, was the reason why she hadn't wanted to go with him to Lagos. She was excited about it for a little while, when it didn't seem real, but as time had gone on and the fact of it had seeped in, he knew it wasn't what she wanted. But he had insisted, selfishly trying to follow his own bliss at the expense of hers, even if it was only going to be for three years. *Only* three years. He remembered their day of arrival and being shown their quarters, being introduced to their servants. She'd liked the idea of having domestics to order around, but when it came to the part where they were shown the security arrangements, how you were meant to run into the bathroom in the event of an intruder and bring down the iron shutters to protect yourself, he saw the sadness and fear in her eyes. God, he'd felt sorry for her then, at that moment, like he'd never felt sorry for anybody in his life before. Except himself . . .

Something distracted him. There, over on the passenger side, in the furthest corner. Sean sat up straighter to get a better view. In the crevice where the windscreen met the top of the dashboard, a speck of blue plastic.

Licking the end of his middle finger with the little saliva he had, he reached across, straining to get it. He was just able to touch it, and as he lifted his hand it came with him, stuck to his fingertip.

A lithium pill.

But as he brought it to him, the suction failed and it fell, bouncing off his knee and on to the floor at his feet. In a lunge of panic, he dealt the steering wheel a crashing blow with his forehead. He groaned but, undaunted, pushed back the driver's seat and searched for the pill. Somehow it had rolled under the plastic mat beneath the pedals. When he picked it up again, it was covered in dark matter and fluff. He rubbed it hard once on his jacket and took it, gagging on a hair that was still attached.

As soon as he swallowed, he felt better. Then, about a second further on, came the shame, then the anger, then the self-pity and the shame again, and on and on, the cycle quickening until it was a blur. He was starting to navigate the one-way system to nervous breakdown with increasing efficiency.

Don't get out of the car . . .

Checking the clock, he realised he'd been parked outside his own flat for an hour and a half.

20

....

Harry went back to the office, ostensibly to fill out a few legal aid applications. Carla was putting on her coat to leave as he came in.

'Can you make sure the bins are emptied?' she said.

'Eh?'

'It's five o'clock and you've just got here, so you must be the cleaner. Am I right?' she said with a dark look behind a sarcastic smile.

He tried to laugh it off. 'I was busy. Glad I caught you.'

She wasn't in the mood. 'What's going on, Harry?' she asked. 'I've got half of fucking Somalia here trying to talk to you, every immigration office in London wants a Crown Office Reference or Appeal Grounds, and you've disappeared off the face of the earth. Not to mention bloody Miss Sharma for five hours, threatening to sit on me if I don't pull you out of a hat. You've got your phone switched off—'

'Have I?' He checked. The battery was dead.

'—And you still owe me money.'

'Soon. I've just got a backlog.'

'Listen, Harry, Darren's spending half his time circling secretarial jobs in the paper and shoving them under my nose.'

Harry took a step towards her and tried to brush her face with his hand. 'You wouldn't . . .'

She slapped his hand away. He tried to put it on her shoulder and she shrugged out from under him. 'Try me, Harry. My patience is wearing thin. I don't know what's happening to you,' she added quietly, clicking her handbag shut. She pointed to a pile of papers on her desk. 'These are for your urgent attention.'

'You can't leave me,' he said. 'I couldn't . . . I need you.'

'There are other secretaries, Harry,' she said, closing the door behind her. He listened to her footsteps click away.

'That's not what I meant,' he said to the door.

He sat down at his desk and started to go through the papers, rubbing his forehead with the heel of his hand. The first was a memo in Carla's big, childish hand. FIND MISS SHARMA A FUCKING HUSBAND!!!! it read. The truth was that Harry had alienated enough of his acquaintances by suggesting they help out foreign uglies in marriages of convenience. The 'agency' he used to refer people to, basically a bedsit above a tattoo parlour in Elephant and Castle, had ceased operating after its founder and proprietor, a Liverpudlian named Mandy, was sentenced to five years for fraud and six counts of bigamy. Any potential husband for Miss Sharma would probably want more than she could afford. He took Carla's memo and put it to the bottom of the file.

Next up was a file about Farah Saad, one of Harry's many Somali clients. He'd arrived on the Eurostar from Paris a month before, saying he'd left his homeland only the day before and, yes, he was in fear of his life. Home Office enquiries had discovered that he had in fact been living in Holland for the last three years. Under an inter-governmental agreement, the Dutch authorities had agreed that he should be returned to them to have an asylum claim considered. With no right of appeal, Harry had done what every other immigration lawyer was doing and had asked for a judicial review on the basis that Holland was an unsafe country for his client. There were thousands of cases like these ongoing, with refugees moving from one European country to another apparently on a whim. *Asylum shopping*, the Home Office called it. As so often, legislation intended to speed things up and cut the number of applicants had failed and actually produced more than ever, with the backlog now reaching the kind of proportions where an amnesty for all such cases was starting to get sniffed on the wind. Harry and the others weren't complaining, although even he had difficulty keeping a straight face arguing that a country where nobody nicked the communal bikes was less safe than, say, a trip on the Northern Line.

But as he read over the file, he heard the echo of Dad's comments in the shop. Yes, Harry silently admitted, it must be hard for him to look on and see how things were changing, how the faces were changing. Late-afternoon ennui started gnawing at Harry. He felt himself puny and pathetic, a cheap lowlife helping out the toerags and a leech on the genuine refugees, taking them for a ride, prolonging their agony.

The more he thought about it, the more sick he felt.

He pulled at the top drawer of his desk. It rolled out. They were still there, the pile of green forms, dozens of them, Sweet Bills, Baseeqs, Miss Sharmas all in there, all filled out, never sent to the Legal Aid Board, many of them probably too old now for him to claim. Probably enough there to pay Bohra off, but Harry wasn't going to send them, his self-destructive lethargy an insurmountable blockade. They seemed strangely . . . abstract. All he was interested in was instant gratification, cash in his pocket and tomorrow's runners and riders at Market Rasen. So they sat in his drawer, as a reminder. Of something.

The phone rang. He picked it up on the second ring, realising too soon that it might be the dreaded Miss Sharma. It was a male voice, however, that spoke.

'Harry boy?'

'Who's that?' said Harry, sitting back, stretching his free arm.

'Bohra speaking.'

Harry tugged at his tie, opened his collar. 'Mr Bohra? How are you?'

'You found her yet?'

'Erm,' Harry started with a laugh. 'I might need a little more time. I do have other things I need to be getting on with. I'll be giving it my full attention as soon—'

'Give it full attention now,' came the curt reply.

'No, I mean, absolutely . . .'

'You want to get your priorities right, man. I ask you for some-thing, Harry boy, not some fucking Paki or Turk here. I'm one of yours, Harry, not a bloody Turkish bastard.'

Harry leaned forward, wrote down the word 'Turk' and started doodling around it. 'Actually, I was thinking of calling you about it.'

'You found out where she is?'

'No, not yet. It was actually . . . I was more thinking that you might be better off using somebody else. I don't think that my tal-ents lie in that area. You see what I mean?'

A pause followed. It was broken by a hissing intake of breath. 'I can't say I like what I'm hearing, Harry boy. I thought better of you. What would your old man say if I go round, tell him you don't pay your debts?'

Harry scribbled hard on the pad in front of him. He felt his teeth grit. 'I'd prefer it if you didn't bring him into it. It has noth-ing to do with my family.'

'No. We wouldn't want to upset them, eh, Harry Boy? Not with them being so proud of their lawyer boy, helping all Pakis and Turks, innit?'

'You've got absolutely no reason—'

'I charge a limb for every thousand unpaid. Those are my terms. That's going to leave me with an extra six thousand to take back at my discretion.'

'You know I don't intend it to come to that.'

'Nothing else should be occupying your time. Just find the little slut and bring her to me.'

'What are you going to do with her?' asked Harry, but Bohra had already hung up. Slowly, gently, Harry replaced the receiver, then picked up the whole phone apparatus and launched it across the room.

21

....

.

Sean went up to the flat. It was quiet, no TV raging. At first he thought she might be out, parading herself up and down Tooting High Street on a float or something. But no, she was there, on the settee, dressed in the tight jeans she'd bought at the market and a painstakingly ironed white shirt with a high collar inside which her hair had fallen. Bare-footed, legs outstretched, she was avidly reading one of the books about hairdressing.

'Hello,' he said.

'Hi,' she replied. 'Early for you to be back.'

'Yeah,' Sean said unsurely. 'It is,' he added with a weak smile. He felt uncomfortable, but in a novel way, for it came with the realisation that this was virtually the first time he had spoken to her sober. 'Have you . . . erm . . . been out at all?'

She looked worried. 'I had to go out, very quickly mind you, because there was no food here. I bought a few things and then came back down the sidestreets. Nobody followed me.'

He nodded, aware that he was dodging eye contact, sneaking looks at her.

'You're hungry?' she asked.

He shook his head, the curried goat still with him. 'Maybe later.'

He looked at her and she held his gaze, smiling at him, smiling at him with a suggestion of something shared, something understood that didn't need corrupting by being said out loud. He just didn't know what it was.

She was smiling at him.

Oh, Maria . . .

She swung her legs around and stood up, gracefully freeing her hair from within her collar and drawing it across the other shoulder. Blinking slowly, he noted the dip of her neck as it blended into narrow collarbone and the gathering of her waist beneath the shirt. Looking at her, she seemed impossibly delicate to him, an inevitable victim.

'Guess what I bought today?' she asked him.

He shook his head.

She picked up a paper bag from the top of the television. 'I saw them in the market and couldn't resist. They weren't very expensive, so I thought . . .'

She extracted a box with a clear plastic top and showed Harry the contents. Inside it were two pairs of long scissors and three combs of various sizes. COIFFEUR SET was written along the sides.

'My first set,' she said, adding, 'I've read both books twice now.'

'That's good,' Sean replied.

'They both say that men's hair is more straightforward to cut.'

'That would figure,' replied Sean, his eyes darting around the room.

'Are you looking for something?' she asked.

'What? No, it's not here,' he said, scratching his forehead hard. He wondered whether there might be some lithium tablets still lying on the ground outside the nick where he'd thrown them the night before, whether it was worth a trip to go and see.

She frowned. 'Are you all right?' she asked, cocking her head in that way he'd noticed before. He brushed past her towards the kitchen.

'It's been a bit of a hard day,' he said, realising he was shouting as he did so. 'A strange day.'

'You need to relax,' she called after him.

He lunged for the freezer compartment, only to find that his bad dream had been a drunken reality. No vodka. From his haunches he stared inside, willing a bottle to appear from a secret compartment in a haze of dry ice like in a television commercial, until the chill air made his eyes water. With regret, he pulled Eric's bottle of rum from his pocket and unscrewed the top, summoning up the courage to take a swig.

Behind him, he was dimly aware of activity. He turned and watched her through the doorway as she disembowelled the local paper and lay sheets of it on the floor. A headline on the front page caught his eye. REFUGEE BEGGARS SWARM TOOTING it said. Shock fucking horror, thought Sean. He watched her, patting the paper down flat.

'You make yourself a drink and I've got a little surprise for you,' she said, still looking down, not aware that he was watching, blinking every second.

The fumes from the rum had drilled their way into his nostrils, enough to make him screw the top back on without drinking. He rose and secreted the bottle at the back of the food cupboard.

When she had lain down six sheets, she disappeared briefly out of view, returning with one of the two upright chairs from the table, which she placed in the centre of the paper. On the chair was a white towel, folded neatly.

'Sean,' she said, 'are you ready?'

Slowly he walked out. The scissors, combs and one of the books, open, lay on the table next to her. She pointed to the chair. 'You can be my first customer,' she told him.

His mouth twisted.

'Please?' she asked.

He sat down.

'Take off your jacket,' she said.

He did so, handing it to her. She draped it over her narrow, almost tubular arm and went to hang it over the back of the other chair.

'This is a way for me to repay you,' she said as she tugged at his shirt collar, then drew the towel across his torso and up around his neck. 'Did you not want a drink?'

'It doesn't matter. There's none left.'

She shook her head. 'I bought some,' she said. 'Just stay there, relax. I'm going to look after you.'

In dull anguish, he shut his eyes. He listened to his own breathing, short and shallow. His wrist throbbed. And then, haunting himself, the darkness ahead of him gave way to the strange light of his memory, the *one* memory . . .

And he's there on the beach, staring out, watching the wind-surfers as they lean back, hands free, trusting the breeze, letting it silently pull them away. Behind him a wooden beach hut sells drinks. A woman emerges, carrying two bottles of beer. She wears a white shirt and jeans. He feels a presence alongside him and looks up . . .

Ranjita stood over him, a bottle of beer between her long, beautiful fingers. 'For you,' she said.

He stared up, mouth open.

Maria . . .

He took the bottle.

Maria . . .

From far off he heard the squeak as she tried out her cheap scissors on thin air.

Forgive me . . .

Maria . . .

The moment he felt her fingertips brush the back of his neck, he choked on his own guilt. A sob tore through him. 'Forgive me . . .'

'What's the matter?' she asked. 'Did I hurt you?'

He put both hands up to his face and leaned forward but felt her carefully peeling them away, finger by finger. When he saw her again, she was on her knees, close to him, gently shaking her head.

'Sean,' she said. 'Sean, Sean. You saved me. You saved me. You saved me.'

She kissed him gently on the lips once and rested his head, letting him weep into her long dark hair.

Later, as they lay on his bed together, still clothed, Sean feeling the puffiness around his eyes and cheeks start to subside, she told him some of what they had done to her. Or at least he guessed there was more than the ostracising, the locking her away in cupboards, the hair-pulling. She told him about the time she had gone out unescorted and as a punishment Bohra had made her eat curry with half a pound of salt in it and then stood over her while she was sick, pleading for water.

'They wanted a country girl, someone who wouldn't rock the boat. But Bohra hadn't been to India for ages. He didn't know how young people there have changed. Of course, it's different for my father's generation. When he sees this fat slob come back to the district where his own father was born, waving his British passport, offering him the chance to unload one of his daughters . . . he's just a farmer, my father, you can't expect . . . If I went back, the shame would kill him. Of course, it's partly my own fault. I was so desperate to get away that I didn't think much about it. I had a choice. My father wouldn't have sent me away against my will. You understand that?'

Sean nodded, put his hand on her waist, wanting to silence the voice in his own head that she was protesting too much.

'The day we were married was the first time I met him. By then it was too late.'

'What do you mean?'

She blinked. 'Nothing. They exclude him. His own mother, even. He only has a tiny bedroom, away at the top of the house. He hides away there, on his computer all the time. But,' she

added, speaking quickly now, 'he was funny sometimes. I liked
to spend time with him. Whenever he was away from the others, he was better. Different, you know? He could impersonate
the other ones so well. He could hear a sound and actually
make it himself. It was like a gift.' She seemed to stop herself.
'One time we were supposed to go away together, the two of us,
to Frankfurt, to visit one of his cousins. We got the visas and
everything but the fat pig stopped us going, even when he knew
it looked funny to the rest of the family.'

'He wouldn't move away?'

She shook her head. 'You don't move away from the Bohras.
He couldn't. Like I said, he just stayed in his cupboard at the
top.'

'How did you share it with him?'

'I didn't.'

'He's your husband.'

She struggled. 'That wasn't . . .' She took a deep breath. 'A
woman cannot have two husbands.'

He took his hand off her. 'Who?'

She pulled the pillow tighter under her head.

'Bohra?' Sean asked, praying he was wrong.

She nodded. 'The fat pig wanted me for himself. But I
always refused. Then he started to threaten, say he would make
me one of his whores. He showed me photos of them, all pos-
ing for sex. Still I said no . . . until the last time, when he waited
until there was nobody else in the house and my shouting
wouldn't alert them. He found me in the kitchen and was very
nice to me. But when he started touching me, asking me
whether I liked the photos and I said no to him again, that was
when he attacked me. He tore my clothes and tried to—' she
closed her eyes momentarily '—fuck me. On the table.'

Sean saw that she was intent on not crying, but still he kept
his hand off her.

'It was Ranji who heard us, he had forgotten about Ranji. It
was Ranji who tried to pull him off me. I managed to get a hand

free. There was a jar of chilli on the table. I threw it in his eyes. And then, when he fell back, all over his dick. That would hurt, wouldn't it?'

Sean nodded, wide-eyed. 'Oh, yeah. That's going to hurt,' he confirmed.

'Good.' She smiled quickly. 'That was when I ran away, straight after. I knew that if I went to the police they would send me back to him. He always boasted about how he paid them to work for him. I had an address that another girl who had left the village gave me. I sent her some letters but she never replied. When I got there I realised that it was deserted but at least I was away from him. I was too scared to leave. The next thing was you saved me.'

Sean waited before speaking. 'Maybe we shouldn't be here, doing this, you and me.'

She furrowed her brow, looked hurt. 'You think I'm damaged goods? You don't want me because I'm on the rebound?'

He almost laughed at her choice of expression. 'No, no. It's just that I don't want you to think I'm . . . that I'm like . . . That I would use you, just because . . .'

'I don't think.'

'My wife, her name was Maria, she died.'

'I know. You have been in denial. Now you come here.'

As they kissed, a thought struck Sean. 'You said you went to Germany?'

'No,' said Ranjita, rolling him on to his back and beginning to unbutton his shirt. 'Didn't go. Were supposed to go but didn't. Don't you listen to what I say?'

'But you said you got the visas?'

'Yes.'

'How long ago?'

'I don't know. It was less than a year, maybe nine months ago.'

'You used your passport?'

'No,' she said, tugging his shirt from inside his trousers, 'I drew one in crayon. Of course I used my passport.'

'And you had a visa?'

She made a face. 'Yes, I had a visa. Like any other person.' The thought made her stop what she was doing and strike a defiant pose. 'It's not fair. I have passport, visa, everything. Why cannot I live my own life here?'

Sean nodded his sympathy. 'Yeah, but you came as Ranji's wife. If you leave him after so short a time, you'd have to re-apply to stay in the country. Otherwise you're illegal.'

'So I apply?'

'No, no. They'd try to deport you unless you agreed to go back to Bohra's. Social services, the same. Your UK visa is useless now but not your German one. That still counts.'

She fell silent, although unimpressed.

'That visa?' Sean went on, conscious of approaching the issue carefully. 'You remember if it was for any other countries? For France and Germany? Belgium and Germany?'

She nodded.

'I think it was for all the European countries. We were thinking of going home a different route, so we thought it would be easier to get one for all the European countries.'

'A Schengen visa,' said Sean. 'It covers the lot.'

'Right. Lift your legs.'

She rolled off the bed to pull his trousers off.

'And how long was it valid for?' he demanded.

'I can't . . . no, hold on, I remember. A year. He got them for a year because we were going to go back because his cousin was due to get married. But it never happened. He wouldn't leave his girlfriend. She's Turkish. Can you imagine what they made of that?' She slid out of her jeans, hips wriggling.

'Where's your passport now?' Sean asked, peeking down at the evidence of his own arousal, pleasantly surprised at its totality.

'The fat pig took it as soon as we got back. He's got it.'

She lay back on the bed in her white shirt and knickers, legs slightly apart, arms by her side.

'Come on,' she said.

'What?'

'I'm not doing everything myself,' she told him, exasperated. 'Undress me.'

Sean sat up, scanned the length of her body, pursed his mouth as if to speak but said nothing as his brow furrowed.

'What's wrong? You don't like me?'

'No, no. It's just . . . how far do you . . . ?'

She rolled her eyes. 'I want you to undress me and then have sex with me. I've read enough about it. I want to know what it feels like.'

part three

·····························

22

....

Harry stood, a few yards from the edge of the pool, watching the nutters at the other end rubbing themselves down with liniment and then throwing themselves into the water. It was a chilly day. As they jumped in concert into the water of Tooting Lido, Harry half-expected to hear the crack of breaking ice.

The man he'd spoken to, dressed in the green overalls of a council employee, came back out from the small brick building at the entrance to the lido.

'Sorry, mate,' he said, handing the little photo back to Harry. 'Nobody's seen her here.'

They both turned to watch as the swimmers, having done half a width of the pool and turned back, got out, their flesh wobbling with shivers, and embraced giant towels.

'She doesn't look barmy enough to be around here,' the caretaker commented. Harry nodded and left.

Three days and no sign. Nothing. He'd spent so much time walking around Tooting Common that he was starting to get looks, suspicious or knowing, from people who'd seen him more than once. He'd learned the name of Conrad, the resident tramp, whom he'd passed a dozen times, exchanging pleasantries. If he'd had a bit more cash he could have delegated the job, found some dole wallah to waste his time. Meanwhile, he was trying to run the firm from the end of the phone. He'd explained the situation roughly to Carla, gone over his last intact credit card limit again to mollify her with a fraction of what he owed her in back pay and promised her that he was going to find Miss Sharma a husband if it was the last thing he did. But if he couldn't find this girl . . .

He looked down at the photo again, studied the face more closely. Even Harry, who'd never really gone for your Indian girls, thought she was a looker, although the shawl left a lot to the imagination. She had those sad eyes he always associated with his mother, although in the latter's case it was the result of half a decade of the agony of stomach cancer. Harry's mother had got her release, but this girl, if he found her and took her back to Bohra, how long would her hell last? What would her punishment be?

Harry put the photo back in his wallet with a shiver of his own. He couldn't think of it like that. Life was shit for everybody, and he needed to get Bohra off his back. In truth, Miss Sharma's fate was a more pressing consideration. If she sat on you, literally pressing.

His mobile rang. 'Yes?'

'Lawyer?'

'This is Harry Verma. Who's that?'

'Anwar speaking.'

Harry racked his brains.

'I paid you at Croydon.'

'Oh, right.' Harry remembered his neat little squeeze outside the Asylum Screening Unit. 'How are you?'

Anwar cut to the chase. 'Baseeq arrested by immigration.'

Harry froze. 'Arrested by immigration? Not possible. We regularised his stay while his claim to asylum is being considered. His papers will be at Croydon for months.'

'Croydon, no. Not Croydon. Arrested at Heathrow.'

'What was he doing there?'

'I told him not to go. Now he's arrested.'

Harry put two and two together. Baseeq had tried a classic scam, not a new one but one that the authorities were only just

starting to get wise to. You buy a cheap one-way ticket to somewhere, anywhere, show your real passport at check-in, then
when you get airside, you rip up your passport and head back
around to Arrivals, saying you've just arrived from the dangerous country of your choice and, yes, you are in fear of your life.
Harry knew it was a speciality of Pakistanis who pull it in order
to come back as Afghans, always from the same town on the
border where they speak Urdu rather than Pushtu, the point
being that Afghans get permission to stay and all the perks
immediately, while Pakistanis will get refused. Lots of Albanians
try it too, returning five minutes later as Kosovans. It's a great
ruse if you're an illegal or in trouble with the Old Bill because
you can, of course, give yourself a new name and a new income
support book. But if, as with Baseeq, you get rumbled, you're
up shit creek. A fraudulent second claim to asylum gets put in
the fast lane and detention is axiomatic.

'Where are they keeping him?'

'Rochester Prison they got him. They interview him today,
asking about asylum. I tried calling you.'

Shit, thought Harry. That *was* quick.

'Look, I'm not going to be able to get down to Rochester.
Maybe you should think about hiring another . . .'

Anwar wigged out. 'Fuck off! You think I'm paying you two
hundred and fifty to lift my own boxes? You get him out of
there! I got boxes everywhere!'

'If I'd known he was going to go and do something so stupid . . .'

'Guarantee I've got! Your guarantee! You get him out!'

End of conversation.

'Great,' muttered Harry. 'Just great.'

He went to get something to eat, and ten minutes later he
was in the Fried Chicken Bar, only a stone's throw from the
family shop. He didn't sit in the window, not wanting to be seen
if Jay or, highly unlikely, Dad saw him there. He struggled with
the motives for his reluctance in going in and making them one

bag of jelly beans lighter. He was aware of always seeming to stir things up when he turned up, provoking Dad to persist with pointless comparisons between his two sons and Jay to dig himself further into his morose personality crisis. Despite having spent part of the last three days nearby on the common, the memory of the atmosphere on his last visit was an uncomfortable one. And yet there he was, on the other side of the road, dipping his chips into his coleslaw, killing time, mulling it over.

His mobile rang again. Wiping his greasy hand on the Formica table top, he put it to his ear. 'Uh-huh,' he said.

'Harry?' Funny thing. It was Jay.

'You all right?'

'Where are you?'

'Erm . . . Close, as it happens. I'm close.'

'You need to come round.' Harry could hear the tightness in Jay's throat.

'Everything all right?'

'Just come. *Bohra's here*,' he hissed.

'Eh?'

'He's here, looking for you. They're all here, Harry. Where are you?'

'On my way.'

He was out of the door, throwing his coat on as he left the chicken house. Up a sidestreet he spotted the people-carrier and his hurried step warmed up to a trot. Pausing briefly outside the shop, he breathed hard, wanting to calm down, just be cool.

He charged in, the bell tinkling.

Jay was hunched over the counter, smoking fast, keeping a nervous eye on the Bohra goon he recognised from the driver's seat of the people-carrier, who was browsing through the small collection of faded greeting cards on a spinning rack, one of his less successful ventures. He looked surprised at Harry's arrival.

'I was close. I said,' Harry explained, almost apologetically.

Jay's eyes darkened as he flashed glances between the leather jacket and Harry.

'They're looking for you,' he said in a cold whisper to Harry. He sounded strange, strangled.

'Oh, yeah?' Harry asked, furrowing his brow as he walked to the counter.

Leather Jacket looked up at him, coughing a laugh at Harry's gormless look of surprise. Jay spotted it and hissed out a mouthful of breath.

'Is this your fault?' he whispered again.

Harry waved a not-the-time hand, rubbing the other palm across his mouth. 'Where are they?' he asked.

Jay didn't answer straight away, preferring to look down into his packet of Silk Cut and extract another fag. 'His room,' he told Harry, sheepishly.

Harry gasped. 'And you're down here?'

'Fuck off,' hissed Jay. 'Someone has to . . . What am I supposed to do? Three of them against me? How could I stop them?'

Harry could see he was close to tears. He heard the sound of Bohra's voice from upstairs. It sounded uncomfortably measured, his businessman voice, his pillar of the community voice. Trouble.

'All right, all right. Stay here.'

'This is your fault,' Jay reminded him, struggling to light his Silk Cut. 'He's an old man.'

Harry took the stairs two at a time, almost slipping and falling halfway up on the worn patch of carpet. Reaching the landing, he saw the door to Dad's room open. He stopped for a moment to calm down, slow down his step, not wanting Dad to see him flustered. He hoped at least to surprise Bohra with the speed of his arrival, but as he stepped forward the old creaking floorboard gave him away. The voice from Dad's bedroom stopped.

He walked in.

Dad was sitting stiffly up in bed, knees drawn towards his body, hands clasped together on his lap. The panic in his eyes was like a fireworks display. Harry winced at the sight of it. Bohra was sitting side-saddle on the bed, unnaturally close to Dad, dressed in a black puffer jacket and a pair of grey track pants. The shades had gone, but a redness around his eyes was detectable. Beyond him, the twins stood near the bay window to the front, each wearing baseball jackets advertising an American college, each absorbed in the fascias of their respective mobile phones.

Dad saw Harry. 'Harry,' he said, only his eyes and mouth moving. 'Mr Bohra's here.'

Harry took a step further into the room. He opened his mouth to speak but was interrupted by an electronic burst of the *William Tell Overture*.

'Sorry,' sniggered the twin on the left, baring a set of sharp teeth. 'It's got a choice of fifty different ringing tones.'

Bohra smiled indulgently, but not without irritation. 'We were just talking about communication, weren't we?' he said, looking at Dad. Dad, however, was just sitting, staring across at Harry, pleading for help with his look. 'How important it is for families to communic—'

He was cut short by a burst of noise from the other twin's mobile.

'What was that?' asked his sibling.

'*Ode to Joy*,' he read back.

'Bollocks, that one.'

'Fucking shut them fucking things off!' shouted Bohra. Harry saw Dad flinch. He hated the f-word. 'What it is,' Bohra went on, his composure regained, 'I've just bought new mobile phones for everybody.' He raised his hand to show another one clasped within. 'So as we can all be in touch. That's family, the way I see it. Family has to stick together, isn't that so, Mr Verma?'

Dad nodded.

'Family and community,' Bohra went on, turning to Harry. 'Helping each other out. Otherwise we've got no community, just be overrun by the bloody Turks. Imagine that? I was just saying to your father, Harry, I was just pointing out how much we rely on community to protect ourselves from the outside. A shop like your father's, think about it. Businesses like that rely on community, isn't it? If the community doesn't support it, what would happen to it? You'd have your windows broken, imagine that, windows smashed, stuff getting nicked, people just walking in and taking stuff. Maybe even a fire, the whole place set on fire. Could you imagine? All because some people don't play their part, Harry, some people don't want to be part of the *community*. Even when they've got no choice. Even when they're born into it.'

Bohra looked back to Dad.

'Makes a lot of sense,' Dad said, looking down at his hands.

'Uplifting stuff, Mr Bohra,' Harry said. 'Was that what you came round for, to share your wisdom with us?'

He kept his eye on Bohra, who was unmoved, but sensed the increase in the twins' interest level.

Bohra stood. Harry's eyes were drawn to another pristine pair of trainers.

'I heard your father was not well. I came to pay my respects on the way to the temple.'

'Oh, you're a good man, Mr Bohra. Everybody in the community knows your reputation.'

Bohra shrugged. 'What can I say? What you see, you get.' He turned once more to Dad. 'I'm not one for secrets. Do you think Harry has any secrets, Mr Verma?'

'He can't tell me everything,' Dad said. 'Lawyer–client privilege, they call it.'

'You can see he's tired,' Harry said. 'Thank you for your visit. I'll show you out.'

Bohra motioned for the twins to go first. They left, the second catching Harry a blow on the shoulder with his own as he passed.

'Goodbye, Mr Verma,' Bohra said. 'Another visit soon, maybe?'

Harry followed him out on to the landing, shutting the door behind him. Bohra seemed intent on leaving, but Harry grabbed his coat and he turned.

'You have no right. This is not the way to get what you want.'

'I'll be the judge of that, Harry boy. You got the message? You're lucky he's too gaga to know what fucking day it is.'

From the shop Harry heard an uncomfortable sliding noise, followed by a heavy crash.

'What the fuck . . . ?' Harry said, moving past Bohra to get downstairs. Now it was his turn to be held back.

'Think of it as an interest payment on what I'm taking if you don't come up with the bitch.'

'What's the matter with you? I can't find her. She can't be found. She's gone.'

'Where?'

'I don't know. I can't find her.'

'Look harder.'

'It's not poss—'

'The bitch by Monday,' said Bohra, moving down the narrow stairs.

'Or the money,' said Harry.

Bohra just laughed, shaking his head.

'I want it seen to by Monday. Or the shop's unprotected.'

Harry stood frozen at the top of the stairs as Bohra descended. There was another crash, not as loud as before, then the shop door opened and closed again a few seconds later. A can of pop rolled across the floor to the bottom of the stairs.

'Harry!' shouted Jay.

Harry rushed back to the bedroom. Dad was standing by the window, dressed in the thermals he wore to bed, peering out of the curtains down to the street below.

'Dad,' said Harry. 'You all right?'

Dad kept his eye on the High Street until they were out of view. He looked back at Harry seriously. 'Coward,' he said.

Harry felt winded. 'Look, Dad, I . . .'

'Bloody coward,' Dad interrupted him, 'coming up here with those two thugs in tow. Not man enough to face me by himself.'

He means Bohra, thought Harry. *Thank fuck*. 'I'm sorry,' he said. 'I didn't mean for that to happen . . .'

'*Harry!*' he heard Jay shouting from downstairs.

'Comes here,' Dad went on, getting back into bed, 'talking community this, community that, making threats. I'm not going to be intimidated, in my own bloody home and all.'

'But listen, Dad . . .'

'Harry!' Another shout from downstairs.

Dad stopped him with a hand. 'Harmendra. I'm not stupid, you know. I know what's going on. I know exactly what's going on.'

Harry fell silent.

'He's trying to intimidate you,' Dad explained. 'But you mustn't give in to the likes of him. You must see it through.'

Harry's eyes danced. 'See what through?'

'The court case. You're suing him on behalf of a client, aren't you? I'm not stupid. I can see what he's trying to do, coming here, making threats. You have your day in court and beat him, Harmendra. There'll be plenty of people who'll thank you for it.'

Harry put a hand to his mouth, rubbed his top lip to disguise the gesture. His mixture of guilt and love for Dad threatened to make his knees buckle.

'*Harry! Harry!*' redoubled the shouts from the shop.

'Better go down, see what they've done,' Dad said with a patriarchal nod.

Harry tripped down the stairs and on into the shop. The greeting card stand had been flung across the shop into a shelf that had previously held tinned fruit. They had knocked the drinks fridge over, sending cans and bottles all across the floor. The lottery machine had been pushed off the far end of the counter and lay on its side, issuing a melancholy bleep. Nearby, on the stool in the corner behind the counter, sat Jay, hunched, eyes wide, staring ahead into space, arms wrapped hard around his chest, right hand squeezing left elbow hard.

'Better call an ambulance,' he said quietly as Harry came in.

Harry shook his head. 'Don't worry. He's OK.'

Jay remained impassive. 'Not for him. For me. I think I'm having a heart attack.'

23

....

Sean was nervous entering Chaucer House, even on this, the third day since he'd chauffeured McLeish. He'd gone in the next morning with the intention of telling Greatrix that it wasn't working out but had found a note in his pigeonhole saying somebody else 'more suitable' had already been found. The slight was, of course, intended, and Sean knew he had been the subject of unofficial briefings by Eric and others. His isolation from the core of Chaucer, where Eric was a figure of totemistic importance, was complete. At least he had Ranjita now, three days without a drink or a pill and the almost physical sense of being hauled back from the brink.

Everything seemed normal enough as he passed the security men, deep in a debate over 'Iron' Mike Tyson's chances against Giant Haystacks.

'Technically a diamond wrestler,' Leslie insisted. 'Very gifted, technically.'

'What you talking?' Maltese Frankie demurred. 'Tyson in three.'

Since his demotion, Sean had been back to routine work, pulling West Africans out of burger kitchens by the hair and paying home visits on dodgy marriage candidates, who were never in. Today, he was starting late and working on-call. If the police anywhere in Chaucer's region arrested someone they suspected of being an illegal, it was Sean's job to get down to the nick and serve papers. Some days that could mean feet up reading two-week-old papers left lying around, but with his luck Sean had the feeling he was in for a busy night.

He'd thought about calling in sick, but knew that he needed time to think things out away from their bed, away from Ranjita and her constant barrage of questions about her immigration status and suggestions for improving it. Her apparent belief that the UK was a country where right would always prevail over wrong was touching but potentially suicidal. He'd spat out a mouthful of tea when she pronounced she was thinking of going to the newspapers because the English press was 'interested in the truth'.

Stepping into the main office, he was still a little conscious of his spartan new haircut, a salvage job after the wreckage of Ranjita's attempt to cut his hair. 'Whoever did this,' the barber had told him, picking up the number-one clippers, 'they wanna go back to piano-tuning.'

His edginess reminded him of the bare bones of his situation. He was still harbouring an illegal immigrant, one who was in hiding from a vicious criminal family his own colleagues had been investigating. It was a real fucking mess. He needed to come up with a way out of it, one that would work. So they could stay together. That, at least, was understood between them. They had no time for a candlelit melding of minds, for getting to know one another. One another was all they had.

Sean stepped out of the office into the corridor to get a coffee from the machine. Piers Anstruther approached him, equally preoccupied.

'Can I have a word?' he asked.

He led Sean around the side of the machine.

'I just had a little question for you. You know I'm helping a friend of mine with an application to come over here?'

'Yes,' Sean replied unsurely. He couldn't remember the name of the hooker Piers had met on holiday.

'The thing is, the people at the High Commission in Gambia . . . well, they're just being a bunch of fucking arseholes about it, you know?'

'Right.'

'I just wanted to ask your advice about something. You were in Lagos for a while, am I right?'

Sean said nothing.

'I just wondered whether, if Dolores, if Miss Natumba, were to pop on a plane to Nigeria, whether she'd have more chance of getting a visa over there.'

Sean shook his head. 'I don't understand what you mean. She can apply anywhere. As I think you know,' he added tartly.

'No, I know, but what I mean is, would she stand a better chance? Is there anyone there she can talk to?' He leaned forward and whispered. 'Is there anyone there who would help her? For a price?'

Sean's eyes narrowed. 'You're talking about bribing someone in Lagos?'

'I'm talking about an arrangement. You're not trying to tell me it doesn't go on. I heard you might know something about it.'

'You heard wrong.'

Piers laughed awkwardly. 'Come on. No smoke without fire. Look, I can make it worth your while. I'm not saying you had anything to do with it. I'm just saying you might know who would.'

Sean lunged at him, pinning him to the wall with a hand pushed hard into his chest. 'I went through hell and back for six months because of pricks like you believing every lie they heard. I had nothing to do with it, whatever it was. I wasn't suspended for one day, not one fucking day, and I have to live with this shit everywhere I go. I'm tired of it. If you're that desperate for a blow-job, why don't you hire a lorry and drive her in yourself?'

He let go with a glare. Back in the office, the phone on the on-call desk was ringing. It was the duty sergeant at Kennington Police Station. They'd picked up an illegal immigrant for indecent exposure in the park.

24

. . . .

The junior doctor, hair cropped, yawned. 'Sorry,' he said. 'Look, it may seem an odd thing to say about a man your brother's age, but he was lucky that it wasn't a much more serious attack. I'm having his cholesterol chart framed and stuck on my fridge door.'

Harry pinched the bridge of his nose and tried to make his laugh sound like a sigh.

'I'm not going to give him or you any lectures about Asian diet, Mr Verma, but I've told him that the levels of fat and carbohydrate he's consuming, along with the fags . . .' He stopped to scratch his head and yawn again. '. . .You know what I mean.'

Harry nodded.

'The way he's going, he's in a high-risk category all of his own. People don't always like to hear that kind of thing from doctors. Maybe it'd be a good idea if you tried to explain it to him.'

Harry smiled. 'You haven't got a brother, have you, doctor?'

His quizzical laugh gave the doctor another chance to yawn. 'How did you know?'

'Because if you had you would never have made that suggestion.'

'Fair enough,' groaned the doc, rubbing his hands down his face two or three times.

Harry frowned. 'Tell me something. How long have you been on duty?'

The medic made a face. 'I've just come on,' he said. 'But I'll tell you what. This is definitely the last time I go clubbing before a shift.'

Harry went in carefully, a little worried by what change he might see since they'd wheeled Jay in to the ambulance three hours before.

He was sitting up, staring up at the opposite wall, dressed in a shortsleeved tunic, a drip piercing his right arm. In a white room, with white sheets wrapping him, he looked . . . cleaner.

He didn't register Harry's entrance, his attention retained by whatever it was. As he moved further into the room, pulling up a chair to sit by the bed, he saw it was a TV on a high shelf. There was cricket on.

'Cricket?' asked Harry.

'On Sky,' said Jay coldly. 'Private healthcare. This is where the money goes.'

'Who's playing?'

'India, Australia.'

'Oh, yeah?' said Harry. 'How's Tendulkar doing?' he asked, seeing the little wizard tapping down the wicket.

'Just come in. Hit a couple of boundaries.'

Harry gave a little imaginary forward defensive, made a click of the tongue to suggest ball on bat. 'Bloody genius, Tendulkar,' he said.

Jay shuffled. 'Big India fan now, are we?'

'I remember being the one who used to drag you down to the Oval. You would never have seen Gavaskar bat if it hadn't been for me.'

'All right, you're such a big India fan, you tell me who Tendulkar's batting with.'

Harry peered up, hoping it would be someone he recognised. But it wasn't. It was a young guy, probably playing in his first test. 'No. Who is he?'

Jay scoffed. 'Big India fan,' he muttered.

'Jay, do you think we might be able to have a conversation which isn't about who watched more episodes of *Mahabahrat*. You know, you're my brother . . .'

'Shot!' shouted Jay, as half way across the world Tendulkar stood on his toes and whipped a wide one through square on the offside for four.

'You're lying in hospital here, Jay. You could be dead, for Christ's sake. Can we just let it be normal, just this once?'

Jay was quiet, eyes still trained on the box.

'I've spoken to the doctor, Jay. You're going to have to ch . . . you're going to have to make alterations to your lifestyle, what you eat. And the cigarettes.'

'Bullshit,' muttered Jay.

'How can it be bullshit?' Harry pleaded. 'You're lying in hospital with a drip in your arm. You just had a heart attack.'

'Of course, that has nothing to do with the fact that the shop was just ransacked!' said Jay, voice raised.

Harry said nothing, waiting for him to calm down.

'I'm here because of you,' Jay said. 'You put me here. It's your fault,' he added, not responding as Tendulkar glanced one off his legs with perfect timing down to the fine leg boundary. 'Who's going to look after the shop?'

Harry shuffled. 'I would, you know that . . .'

'Fuck off, Harry. Don't want you going anywhere near it.'

'I'll find someone. I promise.'

'Least you can bloody do, after putting me here.'

'I had no idea they would do something like that. I was paying Bohra back, but he wanted—'

Jay raised his left arm to stop him. 'Pay him back? Pay him back what?'

Harry's eyes glazed over. 'I borrowed . . .'

Jay groaned, slid further into the bed. 'From Bohra? Are you a fucking lunatic? And now you can't pay him back?'

'I'm working on it.'

'Go to hell, Harry. Bohra? Unbelievable. You remember Sammy, in my class at school? His house burned down with him and his baby in it. That was Bohra. Sammy owed him money, Harry.'

Harry felt something drop inside him. He stared up, eyes glistening, as Tendulkar went on the back foot to a ball short of a length and edged it neatly into the hands of second slip. 'Out,' he whispered, signalling a few seconds of mourning.

'You needed money, you didn't come to me?' said Jay eventually.

'I didn't want to . . .'

'How much?'

Harry pursed his lips. 'Fifteen thousand. Plus interest.'

'How much?'

'Call it sixteen. You don't have to . . .'

'I wouldn't be doing it for you. I'd be doing it to keep the shop. We make an arrangement, contracts, everything, for you to pay it back monthly. And I add my own interest.'

Harry swallowed, shrugged. 'Whatever. You've got that much?'

Jay shrugged. 'It's a big shoebox. So you write me out an IOU now.'

'Now? I haven't got any paper. How about on the back of a business card?'

Jay nodded. Harry took out his wallet and rooted around for a card, one of the good ones. He found one, half-wedged into the wallet's stitching, had to pull hard to get it out. As he did, some of the other contents, a few receipts, plastic cards, went with it, landing on Jay's lap.

'I've got one here,' said Harry, clicking out the end of his ballpoint pen. 'What do you want me to write. Just IOU?'

Jay was studying something. 'Who's this?' he asked, holding up the little photo of the girl, Bohra's daughter-in-law.

'It's, erm . . . just a girl. I'm supposed to be looking for her. I'm not going to find her.'

Jay looked at it hard. 'I've seen her.'

'You sure?'

Jay nodded. 'H'm. Saw her today.'

'Where?'

Jay had to think. 'Library,' he said. 'Yeah, at the library, in the video section. She was dressed differently, but it was definitely her.'

Harry breathed out hard through his nose. 'You didn't see which direction she went in?'

Jay shook his head. 'No. But she'll be at the library tomorrow.'

'How do you know that?'

'Video rental's only for one night. She'll have to drop it back off. Or there'll be a fine.'

25

....

Sean took a break and went to make a cup of tea in the police station tearoom. Checking the time by the clock on the wall, he calculated that he'd been there, at Kennington nick, for five hours. In that time he'd served papers on more than a dozen illegals the Old Bill had brought in: two Polish prostitutes, three Albanians and an Algerian done for illegal hot dog vending, three Malaysian kitchen workers who'd been arrested following an investigation into a spate of disappearing cats, and one vagrant from the Democratic Republic of Congo. The rest, inevitably, were illegals of all flags driving unlicensed, uninsured taxis. The Old Bill were always turning up at the scene of a prang to find a London cabby sitting on some poor Tamil or Nigerian, insisting they be deported the same evening. There was one in particular who took a perverse pleasure in it, a right nutter, always wore a yellow tanktop.

Strictly speaking, most of these punters shouldn't have been brought down to Kennington, but experience had taught Sean that word got around quickly. Every surrounding station would send their illegals straight down to wherever there was an immigration officer out on-call, in the hope that a quick heave-ho might be in the offing. But the Albanians, the Algerians and the Congolese all claimed asylum the second Sean started talking to them, all said they'd come in on a lorry, all gave the stock answers, which meant they got a slap on the wrist and kicked straight out, with instructions to report for an interview in three months' time. The Polish hookers and the Malaysian cat killers could be deported, though, and Sean set up their detention before their flights home. They didn't take it too bad. For one of the Polish girls, this was the third time she'd been blagged and deported from London and probably not the last. She'd spent their whole interview together winking at him and expertly realigning her fishnet stockings.

'You let me go, I give you free one,' she had offered. 'Faggot!' she said in a less conciliatory tone when he declined. 'Last time you guys found me, I met a more understanding officer.'

Sean looked up from the documents he was preparing in her name.

'We came to an agreement,' she added, puckering her lips around a Superking.

'Balding? Glasses?' asked Sean.

She shrugged. 'I no remember.' She jabbed her cigarette at him. 'But he was real gentleman, not sick little homo.'

As Sean stirred sugar into his tea, he could already hear the duty sergeant lining up more Albanians for him. He was starting to run out of Notice to Deport forms. Exiting the tearoom to find out where the photocopier was, he saw a family of South Americans, mother and two young sons, being brought in.

'You immigration?' asked the copper, holding the door open for somebody else to come in from the van outside.

Sean nodded.

'Say they're from Ecuador. I caught them stealing buskers' money at Leicester Square. Any chance of kicking them out?'

'Speak English?'

The copper shrugged. 'Any of you knackers speak English?' he barked.

They weren't admitting to it, the two children hiding behind their mother's legs. Meanwhile, a sinewy African man, topless, wearing ripped knee-length jeans, sandals and a trilby, shuffled in.

'Who's he?' Sean asked.

'Him? He was the busker. Says he's from Chad.'

A second constable came in and handed the man his bongo.

'We're going to need an interpreter,' Sean said glumly. 'Photocopier?'

He was directed to a small annexe off the room behind the duty sergeant's desk. The rate this was going, he thought as the photocopier churned out more of the pointless papers, he would be there until two in the morning. A week ago it wouldn't have worried him; he would have been relieved at the chance to keep busy. But now he ached to get away, back to Ranjita, back to the divine exile of her smile. Maybe he should have called in sick. Maybe he should go for a medical retirement, cultivate his haemorrhoids like Dixon . . .

He picked up the copies he'd made from the tray at the side of the machine and headed out of the small office. The door that led back to the rest of the station was ajar. Sean could see through it that there was a bit of bother. His instincts of self-preservation kept him where he was for the moment. He heard grunts as a struggle ensued, caught sight of a constable's helmet as it flew across his view, bouncing once off the desk and away. White-shirted rozzers appeared from their hiding places to get a little action. Sean moved to his right and saw a black man, his face obscured by the duty sergeant's body, being forcibly pushed down on to the desk by three coppers while his arms were pulled back and his wrists handcuffed together.

'Right, sergeant,' said a breathless constable, both hands planted on the handcuffed man's head, keeping it forced down on the counter top. 'I have arrested this gentleman on suspicion of possession of prohibited substances, intent to supply prohibited substances, grievous bodily harm, indecent assault, resisting arrest and injuring a police officer. He's high as a fucking kite, sarge. And he's cut Barney bad.'

Sean leaned across further and saw another copper receiving first aid for a nasty-looking cut not far below the eye. Blood everywhere.

The duty sergeant nodded. 'Get Barney a fucking ambulance,' he told someone. 'Name?' he asked the man sprawled out in front of him, still writhing.

No response.

'Do you understand the charges against you?'

Sean saw the duty sergeant step back from a bullet of spit fired in his direction.

'I'll take that as a yes,' he said. 'Take him away. Possible self-harmer. Fifteen-minute watch.'

Sean moved towards the door, thinking it would be just about safe to come out now. As he did, he saw two restraining coppers step back and pull their charge back up on to his feet.

Sean almost shat when he saw the face.

It was Cougar. Leslie. Cougar, the pupils of his eyes tiny, teeth bared like a crazed cat.

Sean ducked back behind the door, dropped down to his haunches, ran a hand through the stubble on top of his head.

Christ!

He tried to think. Cougar hadn't seen him, he was pretty sure. Even if he had, the state he was in, he might not have recognised him. Anyway, Sean had been driving the car and Cougar had been stuck on the floor with McCleish's boot on his face. It was unlikely that he'd caught a really good view of him. Maybe it was going to be all right. He hadn't heard them say anything about an immigration involvement. It might remain a strictly police matter. They probably assumed he was British at this point. Presumably, that's how he'd got in the country, with a UK passport provided with Warren's help. Even so, he was struggling to swallow and a band of cold sweat sprang up, tracing the line of his spine. Events were giving him the signal to what he already knew. It was time to get out. And he needed to find Eric.

'You all right, mate?'

Sean rose quickly at the sound of the desk sergeant's voice, leaving himself dizzy. 'Erm . . . not really. I just felt a bit sick. I've had something, you know. Thought I'd kicked it, but it looks like . . . I'm sorry, I'll have to go,' said Sean, walking by.

He collected his stuff and left, the Ecuadorian family watching him ruefully from the seats by the exit, the percussionist from Chad more absorbed in practising his paradiddles.

Eric wasn't in the Hole in the Wall, but Dave Carpenter was, drinking alone, dressed in his bike leathers and pissed into a state of maudlin surrealism.

'Eric? Eric the Red? Eric the Half a Bee? Eric's cleaning the streets,' he explained, chugging three-quarters of a pint with one flex of his Adam's apple, 'doing good works. Washing feet,' he added, bursting into a spurt of cold mirth. 'Washing plates, mate,' he was barely able to add. 'Drying the cutlery. Drying everyone's fucking cutlery in public. Ooh,' he added, holding up an invisible prop. 'A dirty fork.'

'I just want to know where he is,' said Sean through gritted teeth.

'Eric? Different fucking planet, guv. Great bloke, don't get me wrong, but different planet.' He put his hand sloppily to his head in an approximation of a salute. 'Born to blag, sah!'

The hand dropped, incidentally slapping Carpenter's giant thigh on the way down. 'Fuck knows what Crazy Horse'll do when they shut us down. Fucking suits,' he burbled.

With the hard core at Chaucer, there was no group held in more contempt than the mandarins of Lunar House, aka the Gasworks on account of its architectural charm. Sean agreed it was hard to take lectures on how to behave in the field from a bunch of polyester-shirted, four-eyed desk jockeys who by any other civil service standard were grade-A failures, but he presumed Dave's intimations of doom were the malt and hops talking.

'Just hope you stashed enough of that Lagos money away for a rainy day,' said Dave, contemplating the feasibility of standing up to get to the bar.

Sean chose not to rise to the bait. 'Yeah, right. Whatever you say.'

Dave made a strange face, eyes closed, lips pursed.

'All I want is to find out where Eric is.'

Dave stood up unsurely, waving his arm for balance. 'What are you, his anal worm?'

'Where is he, Dave?'

Dave paused to think. 'What day is it?'

'Tuesday.'

'Tuesday night? He'll be at the Annie.'

The Queen Anne's Head, all its downstairs windows blacked out, stood alone like a haunted house in the middle of an estate of brown-brick boxes, only a few hundred yards behind the railway lines that came and went from Vauxhall Cross. Sean had never been, but he knew about it, knew what it was. It was a regular haunt with the boys from Chaucer, but he had always baled out when the wind steered an evening on to that course. He knew it was something to do with Maria. Now she was dead, the thought of her disapproval was more potent than it had been before.

Taking a short cut over the field that led to the pub, the wind welding his shirt to his back, he entered by a pair of double doors at the pub's corner.

It consisted of one large room, although the deep dank brown of the walls made the discernment of a particular shape almost impossible. In the opposite corner to the door began the long bar, above which hung dozens of dated photographs showing fat white boxers. Directly opposite it, away to Sean's left, was a large rostrum three feet off the ground, a masterpiece of unadorned chipboard sculpture. Brass poles, one in each corner of the imperfect square, rose upwards and into the ceiling, and around each of its four sides a shelf was nailed at the perfect height for a seated man to rest his drink. There was no spare room in the round tonight, as they crammed themselves in on low stools, cheering and clapping as a naked woman, clutching a few shreds of clothing she had picked up off the floor, scurried off the stage on precarious high heels. As she disappeared behind a door held open for her by a white-haired, flat-nosed man whose younger likeness may well have hung over the bar, the audience scattered.

Still sitting there, alone, was McCleish.

Sean swerved bodies to get through to him, managing to grab himself a perch ahead of one or two others hopeful of a front-row seat.

'Eric,' said Sean. 'Glad I caught you.'

Crazy Horse looked at him slowly, blinking once. 'Your mammy know you're here?'

'I need to talk to you.'

Eric looked at him, inscrutable through his thick glasses.

They were joined by a third presence. Looking up, Sean saw a woman, redhead, early thirties, a backless gold-lamé dress squashing her breasts under her armpits and hugging the gentle pot of her stomach. She held out a pint glass, half-full of change.

'I'll be performing next,' she said.

Sean was a little slow to move to his pocket. She rattled the glass right under his nose. 'You're expected to pay for the privilege, darling.'

Sean dropped a pound coin in the glass.

Eric stood up and gave the girl a smile, putting an arm around her shoulder and turning her away from Sean to whisper something in her ear. Sean saw her nod. When she turned again and waddled away towards the corner, an incongruous brown note nestled in her glass among the twenty-pence pieces. Eric sat down and Sean pulled his stool a little closer.

'Look, I've just come out of Kennington nick,' he said to the back of Eric's head. 'They've just brought your friend Leslie in.'

The corner of McCleish's mouth turned up, but not in a smile. 'What's he done? Pissing on a street corner? Just the pol-iss, marking their territory. Don't worry your little head 'bout it.'

'Drugs. Serious, Eric. Drugs. And he cut up a copper.'

McLeish didn't reply, barely even responded, but Sean thought there was a hint of discomfort in the mouthful of smoke he hissed out between pursed lips.

'I came to find you,' Sean went on. 'He's your boy, Eric.'

This got Crazy Horse's attention, big time. He spun on his stool and looked Sean up and down. Sean, a little intimidated, shook his head. 'Your mess, Eric. Not mine.'

Their stare-out was broken up as the faint grumblings of the jukebox gave way to the thumping beat of some soft rock classic and a crowd gathered. Looking across the stage, Sean saw the golden dress shift as its occupant climbed the steps and began to move to the music. There was no way you could call it dancing.

'Eric?' Sean pleaded. 'Do you understand what I'm telling you?'

But Eric was engrossed, watching the show as the gold dress was peeled down, releasing the giant breasts from captivity. Looking around, Sean watched the other men (lot of Chinese, he noticed) watching the fat stripper with the intensity of chess grandmasters thinking ten moves ahead. He had to admit there was something hypnotic about those tits as they swayed on the off-beats.

'Eric,' he said, managing to look away as the dress hit the floor and she struggled to bend over provocatively in the black G-string that remained.

'What if he talks? What are we going to do?' he gulped. 'It's got nothing to do with me. I didn't ask—'

A cheer went up as the G-string was pushed down and kicked away, revealing of bush that matched the colour atop her head.

'Hoy, ginna!' came the shout from a stag outing at the back.

'Ooh, you think of that all by yourself?' shouted back the woman, clinging to one of the brass poles and striving to lift one leg at right angles to her body. 'Who's a clever boy, then?'

Crazy Horse's intransigence was driving Sean to distraction.

'Fucking hell, Eric, this is serious.' He was aware of high heels on the stage clumping in his direction. 'You're going to have to do something. What if—'

He was cut off by a scream, shrill and long.

'Don't you touch me, you dirty cunt!' wailed the stripper. 'He touched me!' she shouted at the bar. 'The little shit tried to touch me!'

Sean looked to see who had offended and stood up, knocking his stool back, when he saw she was pointing directly at him.

'Him! That sick bastard there!'

From nowhere, giant hands seized him by the arms and he was moving.

'I didn't do anything,' he pleaded. 'I didn't touch her. I swear . . . Eric! Tell them!'

But all Sean could see was Eric's back as he turned to signal to the bar for another drink.

Of course, he thought as he hit the pavement outside, feeling his bad wrist again on impact. *Nobody gives a stripper a tenner without a good reason.*

26

The atmosphere in the main office at Chaucer was different, subdued, the normal buzz of insults and in-jokes dampened. Sean sat at his usual desk, blankly staring down at an open file, opposite an edgy Piers Anstruther, scrupulously avoiding eye contact. While everybody else was consumed with the presence in Greatrix's office of some new troubleshooter sent down from the Gasworks, Crazy Horse was dominating Sean's thoughts. There'd been no sign of him today, no general swell of interest as he came in with some new anecdote or morsel of gossip. Maybe Sean hadn't handled it too well the night before. Maybe he should have been cooler, not steamed in like that. It had obviously been news to Eric, Cougar's arrest, and the seriousness of the charge wouldn't be lost on him. Sean consoled himself with the thought that McCleish would have to do something about it, not for Sean's sake but for his own.

The door to Greatrix's office rattled and the chief immigration officer stepped out, led by his big gut.

'Carlyle,' he barked. 'A word.'

Sean stood up, sending Piers rooting in one of his desk drawers for something. As before, images of being confronted with Ranjita's existence tightened his jaw.

He knocked once and went in.

Greatrix had scurried back behind his desk. Sean's entrance didn't distract him from a conversation he was having with a man seated on a low armless chair in the corner of the room, bespectacled, pinstriped, thin.

'Yes,' Greatrix was saying, 'I knew him from when I was down at Dover. Could drink you under the table. Then he turned up in Accra, I remember, when Derek Borthwicke . . . Did you know Derek . . . ?'

'No,' said the man slowly.

'Derek left,' asserted Greatrix. 'Trouble with her indoors. Drinker, she was, that's what I heard. But Roger came out as temporary cover, ended up staying a year and a half.' He laughed. 'Bloody good bloke. Did you ever play golf with him?'

'Golf?' said the man with an undertaker's reverence. 'No.'

'Hell of a golfer. Think he liked the nineteenth hole the best, though. Hell of a drinker. Bloody character,' added Greatrix, tapping his desk for emphasis. 'Good at the bloody job as well.'

The man in the corner nodded. 'Well, as I said, I only met him on a two-day security seminar. He was taken ill on the second morning.'

Greatrix huffed. 'Sit down, won't you. Sean?' he said.

Sean sat. 'Who's this?' he asked, gesturing behind him.

'This is Peter Childerstone. The new commissioner of enforcement.'

Sean looked over his shoulder. 'I hope you know what you're getting yourself into.'

Childerstone smiled knowingly. 'After fifteen years at the tax office, I think I'm pretty unshockable.'

Sean turned back trying not to laugh. *Tax office*, he mouthed at Greatrix, who didn't respond. Sean suddenly felt uncomfortable.

'Peter's here to help me get to the bottom of a particular matter. I'm hoping you can help us out.'

Sean shuffled. 'I'll try.'

Greatrix slipped on his pince-nez. A bad sign. 'You left them in the lurch at Kennington last night, aye?'

Involuntarily, Sean looked down.

'Another bad pint?' Greatrix asked.

'I . . . personal matter,' Sean heard in a strangled version of his own voice.

'It's embarrassing when we display that kind of unprofessionalism. It doesn't reflect well, Sean. We're lucky there was somebody else to get down there, tidy up your mess.'

'It won't happen again,' said Sean.

Greatrix paused before continuing, the silence broken only by Childerstone's heavy nasal breathing. 'They had an interesting guest at Kennington last night. One—' he checked a thin file in front of him '—Leslie Philip Montgomery.'

'Right,' said Sean, shrugging in ignorance.

'Jamaican national.'

'Jamoke. Right,' Sean answered with a nod, putting his hand to his mouth to cough.

'Arrested last night, bailed this morning.'

'Bailed?' Sean repeated.

'That's what I said. Bailed. Smartarse lawyer with a pigtail argued that they had the wrong man, name in the wrong order or something. Eric knows him, says he's a regular Yardie brief. What it is, apparently this . . . Montgomery asked to speak to an immigration officer last night but you'd disappeared by this time with your . . . personal matter.'

'Sorry. Couldn't really be avoided.'

Sean heard the scratching as Childerstone crossed his long legs.

'Mr Montgomery had a story he wanted to share. Frankly, it's hardly credible, but I wanted to run it by you.'

Sean nodded again, breathed deeply. 'OK,' he said with a feeble smile, hands together now on his lap.

'He told the officer who got down there a story regarding his entry to the United Kingdom. He seems to think that the immigration service had full knowledge he was entering the country illegally.'

'How's that possible?'

'You might well ask. You might well ask . . . The thing is, Sean, he says he was helped. By one of us.'

Sean shook his head. Privately, he thought he saw his way out. If he had to grass Eric up, then so be it. 'Seriously?'

Greatrix shut the file. 'He says it was you, Sean.'

Sean gagged. 'No fucking way . . .'

'He described the car you drove him away from the airport in. The powder-blue Mondeo. It stands out, that one. I checked. It was signed out to you, Sean.'

'No fucking way. That was the day I drove McCleish around.'

'We've got a statement from a BAA employee at Heathrow who says she had an altercation with you on that day. She says you were in the car, alone—'

'He was already inside. It was McLeish. He was already inside—'

Greatrix cut him off. 'Don't make a bad situation worse for yourself, Sean. We've already spoken to Eric. He told us what really happened.'

'What? What did he say? What line of shit did he give you?'

'He said that you were on your way to make the intercept, that you started an argument, kicked him out of the car and drove off without him.'

Sean got up off his seat. 'No! He's a fucking liar!'

Greatrix rose to face him. 'Listen to me. You want to put yourself up against Eric McCleish, it's not a contest. I trust him, do you understand?'

Sean tried a different tack. 'Why? Why would I do it? Don't you see? It doesn't make any sense. What would I gain?'

'Mr Montgomery stated that you told him you'd make sure he was deported if he didn't pay you regularly. For money,' added Greatrix, matter-of-factly. 'What else? It's not like you haven't got previous.'

'And what exactly is that supposed to mean?'

'Let's not piss around. Everyone knows you were in up to your neck in Lagos.'

'Go on, keep going. I'll sue you. You know damned well I was exonerated.'

Childerstone took his moment to join the others in standing. 'If I might interject. What you say isn't strictly correct. I've viewed the detailed report on the matter, the weight of circumstantial evidence against you, and in truth it was, as you know . . . unfortunate circumstance that led to a suspension of the investigation and your departure from the visa section in Lagos on compassionate grounds. The charges were neither confirmed nor rebutted.'

'So I'm innocent until proven guilty.'

Greatrix clicked his tongue. 'Do us a favour, Sean,' he growled. 'I've spoken to Carpenter. He told me you more or less admitted it to him last night. You're just going to make it harder on yourself.'

Sean gasped in sour amusement. 'Carpenter could hardly stand up last night. I'm sick of these lies. You're all in on it, aren't you? It's the same as Lagos. Just make him an outsider and then hang him out to dry whenever you need it. Eric McCleish is out of fucking control, but I'm getting stitched up to keep him happy. What's it going to take before you wake up? You have to wait until he kills someone?'

Greatrix turned to Childerstone. 'Eric McCleish is one of our most respected and successful officers. He gets results. And I,' he continued, back to Sean, 'am not going to listen to work of his quality being undermined by troublemakers who've been here five minutes.' He sat down again, visibly trying to regain his temper.

'And who, I wonder, who made it down to cover for me at Kennington last night? Someone maybe who had no way of knowing he was needed down there, someone who wasn't even on fucking duty. Who was it, huh?'

'That's not relevant.'

'Crazy Horse?'

Greatrix sat down, seeking refuge from the question in a file before him. 'Mr Childerstone has authorised your immediate suspension while this matter is looked into further. Your warrant?'

Sean pulled it out of his back pocket and threw it from his waist, sending it skidding across Greatrix's desk and on to his lap. He left the office and walked straight out of the building, past the security guards, who were discussing the number of rounds Sugar Ray Leonard would have needed to knock out a polar bear.

Sean got outside, gasping for air.

Now or never, he told himself.

27

....

Harry sat among the sleepy pensioners on a leather bench, flicking through his umpteenth magazine, never letting his eyes off the issues desk for more than a few seconds. He was into his fifth hour of what he laughably told himself was surveillance. Surveillance sounded better, less passive, than just hanging around, waiting. He was dreading the entrance of someone he knew.

He glanced down at the copy of *Which HiFi?* on his lap. Blinking hard, he realised that he'd read the same integrated amplifier review for the third time. It wasn't as if he had a clue what an integrated amplifier was. Sniffing hard, he got a noseful of his fusty-smelling neighbour on the bench, long asleep, dribbling over a copy of *Country Life*. Harry got up and threw the magazine back on the low table where he'd found it before stuffing his face with a fistful of jellybeans. He winced as they tugged at his fillings. His tongue not strong enough to dislodge them, he had to resort to picking them off with his fingers.

Of course, that was the moment his mobile phone went off, when he had his hand halfway down his throat. He tried reaching the phone in his right side pocket with his left hand, but this only sent him spinning round himself like a dog chasing its own tail. It also cost him two more piercing rings and the hissed hostility of the waking crumblies.

He skidded down into British History and finally got his finger on the keypad. 'What?' he whispered.

'Lawyer?'

It was Mad Anwar, the one he'd skinned in Croydon. Harry grimaced as he remembered Baseeq, still banged up in Rochester, something he had done nothing about.

'Listen,' Harry said. 'Slightly difficult time . . .'

'No,' bellowed Anwar. 'Now. Where are you? Why not at Rochester? Your guarantee, your guarantee. My money, boxes everywhere . . .'

'All right, all right,' Harry tried.

'Not all good. All fucked up. They send Baseeq home tomorrow.'

'Eh?'

'Asylum refused. Plane tomorrow. You do nothing.'

Christ, thought Harry. *That was quick. That* was *quick.* He sneaked to the edge of British History and poked his head round.

'OK, let me assure you, I—'

He stopped at the first sight of the issues desk. There, turning to leave, was the girl. He was certain it was her, despite the dark glasses, the weird pink sweater and the jeans.

'Call you back,' he told Mad Anwar and set off, silencing a wail of fury with his thumb on the OFF button.

Outside, he had to look both ways before seeing she'd gone right, towards the Broadway. Harry wondered what the hell she was doing, dressed up like a fucking mascot, like she wanted to get caught. He scuttled after her, keeping a little distance, choosing to play a waiting game. He didn't want to risk a scene in too public a situation. He just followed, keeping his gaze trained on the pink sweater. Watching her on her progress down Upper Tooting Road, so close, Harry remembered his disgust at Bohra and his hypocrisy, felt it like a branding iron hovering at his shoulder, ready to scorch him. Did he want Bohra's mark on him for ever?

She took a turn towards the covered market. Harry echoed her movement, stepping to his right and coming to a halt a few feet away as she stopped to inspect a pair of silk panties hanging outside a stall. Harry's momentary twinge of voyeuristic excitement was cut short by a nasty nip to his upper arm. He turned to see a headscarved woman, small, sun-dried, a bundle cradled in one arm.

She gave him a gold-filled smile and put out her palm.

'Please. Baby. Please.'

This was the one-woman swarm of refugee beggars. Harry pegged her as a Czech Roma, probably cradling a bottle of Teachers.

He shook his head.

She nipped him again. 'For baby,' she repeated, less friendly.

'Piss off.'

'Money, money,' she insisted.

Harry stared down at her in outrage, glared her away. When he looked back across at the market entrance, the girl was gone. 'Shit.'

He went in under the corrugated iron of the market roof. Shouldn't be that hard to spot, he assumed.

But suddenly he was seeing pink everywhere. On the linen stalls, the flower displays, in the unnatural colours of the pick 'n' mix sweet concession, but not on the girl's back. He was pulled further into the market in his search for her, gradually immersed in the warm odour of the spice shops that always reminded him of his mother, his eyes flickering with the bustle of the shoppers crisscrossing before him. When his eyes finally settled, it was on what was, to say the least, an unwelcome sight.

The Bohra twins were difficult to miss, both dressed in white knee-length puffer jackets, standing unnaturally close to the owner of a pet supplies stall, who was giving them money with apparently nothing in return. Having counted it and patted the worried-looking shopkeeper on the head, they moved out into the stream of shoppers. Harry moved in behind them, still looking around frantically for the tell-tale flash of pink angora . . .

There! Away to the left, heading across his eyeline, on a crash course with the twins, who were at that moment engaged in a game of knocking each other's baseball caps off.

Harry made his move, stepping forward and tapping both brothers hard on the shoulder. 'Boys.'

They spun around with a hint of menace.

'What's happening?' Harry asked, bobbing his shoulders in an attempt at streetwise enthusiasm.

They looked at one another. Harry had a second to glance over their shoulders and see the girl, oblivious to the danger, waltz past them . . . only to stop at a haberdashery stand right in front of him.

'Haven't you got a job to do?' said one of them. The lisping one.

'Just taking a break,' offered Harry.

'You haven't found her?'

Harry struggled to hold his eye. He didn't want either of them looking over their shoulder.

'Getting close. Matter of time.'

'You'd better make it a short break, then.'

'Yeah,' said the other. 'You'd better find her. She needs disciplining.'

Again the twins looked at each other, each smiling in a way that Harry didn't like.

'Yeah,' said the lisper. 'She needs a real man to sort her out. She needs some hard loving,' he added in little more than a whisper, making his brother snigger.

They bounced fists.

'Still, man, if you don't find her, I'm looking forward to fucking your old man's shop.'

Harry bristled. Something dangerous, almost self-destructive, triggered itself within him. 'Sorry to disappoint. Not going to happen.'

'Then you'd better find her, my friend.'

'Maybe I already have,' Harry said, setting his jaw into a cocky smile.

This got their attention.

'Say what?'

'Maybe I found her already.'

'Maybe you're full of shit.'

Harry laughed. 'Maybe she's standing right behind you and you're both too fucking stupid to even see her.'

Suddenly, they were strangely edgy.

'Of course,' Harry went on, 'if you looked around and she wasn't there, that would make you look pretty fucking stupid as well. But go on,' he teased them, widening his eyes, 'have a look. Right behind you.'

Harry looked between them and saw the girl turn as if to head towards them. Seeing the brace of puffer jackets, she halted, frozen.

'Look,' said Harry to the twins, 'I'm waving to her,' he said, wafting his hand. He started gesturing with his head for her to get away. 'Look,' he added, 'I'm telling her to get away before you see her.'

The lisper stepped right into Harry's face. 'Hey. Fuck you and your mind games. The only reason I don't break your fucking legs now is that—'

'Well,' asked Harry with a sigh. 'What's the reason?'

Lisper's eyes danced. ''Cos it'll be more fun later.'

Harry rolled his eyes. 'Oh, good reason.' He made to walk past them. 'Seen the time? Schools'll be out now. Haven't you got some kids to sell drugs to?'

A few steps past them and he shouted back, 'Say hello to your brother for me. You know, your brother! Your brother!'

They heard him, everyone in the market heard him, but they didn't look back. With a sour satisfaction at scoring what he knew was a direct hit, he set off after the girl, taking the turn in the direction she'd disappeared. Rounding the corner, though, she was nowhere to be seen. He proceeded slowly, looking carefully around and behind him to make sure the twins weren't after him. Ten minutes later, he'd reached the furthest point of the market without finding her. Working his way back, he stopped at the sweet stall to buy some more jellybeans. As he poured his third plastic scoop into the paper bag, he noticed a platinum blonde in a black T-shirt come uncomfortably close and pick up a tube of Love Hearts.

'Don't look up,' she said.

Harry snapped out of a momentary reverie, where he was imagining working behind the counter in Dad's shop with Carla by his side.

'Sorry?' he said.

'Don't look at me.'

Looking down, Harry saw her open a plastic bag to show him a pink angora sweater. 'You can buy anything here,' said Ranjita. 'I've always wanted to be a blonde.'

'That's unlucky,' said Harry, suddenly tired.

'I have to thank you.'

'In that case,' said Harry, pouring a full scoop of jellybeans into a paper bag and handing it to her, 'you can pay for these.'

28

....

Sean heard voices as he entered, not the shrill voices of TV, but quiet, concerned voices that stopped as his footfall on the stairs grew louder.

Ranjita wasn't alone. Sitting hunched forward on the armchair, clutching a mug in both hands, a blend of embarrassment and defiance in the strange angle of his mouth, was a man. A blonde wig lay like a dead mammal on the coffee table. Sean looked at it but didn't ask. He didn't want to know.

They recognised each other. The Bombay spiv laughed in disbelief when he saw Sean.

'What do you know?' said Sean.

'Promise you won't throw any more suppositories at me.'

Ranjita stood. 'You know each other?'

'What's he doing here? Touting for business, are you?' he taunted Harry.

'Good to see you too,' said Harry.

'He helped me, Sean. He spent days looking for me. He went to the lido,' she added surreally, giving Harry a little smile. 'He came to warn me.'

'Oh, yeah? Has he charged you yet?'

She moved to him and took his hand, bringing him nearer to the sofa. Perched on its arm, she explained what had happened in the market.

Sean listened, staring at the spiv, occasionally glancing down at the syrup of fig on the table.

'So you see,' she rounded off, sitting next to him, brushing his temple with the palm of her hand. 'You see?'

Sean leaned forward and picked up a business card lying on the coffee table.

'Verma Carter Associates at Law,' he read. 'You're Verma, right?'

'Good guess.'

'And where's Carter? He out, doing the touting while you're saving the world?'

Harry rubbed a knuckle under his nose. 'There is no Carter.'

Sean splurted. 'A lie?'

'I just thought it sounded better . . . Some people are more comfortable if they see a name like Carter. Just facing facts.'

Sean shook his head and smiled. 'Might as well start as you mean to go on.'

Harry sat back. 'Here we go. You can't help yourself, can you?'

'So how's Sweet Bill?'

'How should I know?'

'You're his brief, aren't you? You're the one standing up for his constitutional right to be a scrote.'

Harry just laughed. 'That's so fucking typical. You're just a bunch of regular blokes, just doing your job, but we're not. We're a bunch of monsters; we never sleep, feeding off human flesh.'

'You said it.'

Harry started to warm up. 'Checks and balances, that's how it works. Get you and the size of your egos. Like we shouldn't exist and you morons are just left to get on with it, unchecked. Can you imagine the carnage?'

Sean lowered his eyes for a moment. He didn't need to imagine.

'Anyway,' Harry added with a wave of his hand. 'Fuck knows why I'm defending it to you. Why I'm defending it at all.'

That much was true. For a man who spent most of the time despairing at what he did for a living, he seemed suddenly keen to justify it, get into the tired old face-off so they could both knee-jerk their way to an impasse.

'Think of it this way,' he concluded. 'At least it gives no-marks like us the chance to play at cowboys and Indians.'

Sean put out a hand and slapped its wrist with the other.

'Native Americans, surely?'

Harry flashed him a sour smile.

Sean sat forward again.

'How did you know who she was?' he asked Harry. 'Why would you happen to be there at that time, at that place? How would you know who she was?'

Harry nodded gently at the question, stared down at the floor for a moment before looking up at Ranjita and holding out his mug.

'Any more coffee?' he asked.

'Four sugars again?' she asked.

'Sweet tooth,' said Harry, mildly embarrassed.

'I'll have a cup too,' Sean said, looking up at her as she rose, unable to stop himself gently caressing her flank as she stood.

Harry and Sean waited for her to go into the kitchen.

'You two,' Harry said with a sniff. 'You're . . .'

'You got a problem with that? Does that offend your ethnic sensibilities?'

Harry laughed. 'No. I mean, obviously she's . . . Indian girls.' He made a face. 'It's just that you and her . . . she has to get away, you understand that?'

'Why don't you just answer my question? How did you know who she was?'

'I was carrying a photograph of her. Bohra gave me it. He wanted me to find her and take her back.'

'You work for Bohra? You're his lawyer?' Sean asked, turning it into a rhetorical question.

Harry shook his head. 'I owed him money. This was how I was supposed to pay him back.'

'How much?'

'How much money?'

'Yes.'

Harry shrugged. 'About ten grand.'

Sean thought about it. 'But you brought her back here?'

'Looks that way.'

'You want money?'

Harry hissed his dry amusement. 'A fucking thank you will do.'

Sean put a placatory hand out. 'I'd like to know why you did it.'

'I did it . . .' Harry struggled, pulled up by the guilt accompanying the thought that if Jay hadn't given him the money, he may not have been so charitable. 'I suppose I didn't want it on my CV.'

There was a pause, a moment of revelation, when what they had both been thinking with the security of independence suddenly became tangible because the other knew it to be true. A moment of uncertainty too, the pause for thought before a step into uncharted territory.

Harry licked his lips and tried to say it. 'If he finds her . . .'

Sean nodded.

'She stays here, it's only a matter of time,' Harry added.

'I'm working on it.'

'Where are you thinking of going?'

'I'm working on it,' Sean snapped back. And in truth, he was. An idea that had been tugging on him feebly had been building muscle for the past few days. With today's events at Chaucer, it had become plan A. But it was only now that he'd been offered a chance to actually put it into action. Problem was, it would need the Bombay spiv to do him a favour.

'I'll just give a hand with the coffees,' he said, getting up and heading into the kitchen. He closed the door, saw that Ranjita was pouring water from the kettle.

'Which one's his?' he asked in a whisper.

She pointed to a white mug with MIND THE GAP written on its side. 'Why?'

'Nothing. You go through. I'll bring them in a minute.'

She gave him the look, but he stood firm.

'Thanks,' he insisted.

She went through. He heard the spiv say something about her having to leave. Sean opened the cupboard over the sink.

He feared his plan was pretty far fetched and knew it was potentially dangerous. If he was going to get the spiv to go along with it, he'd have to loosen him up first.

Just a hunch, but Sean guessed he didn't hold his booze too well.

He reached back into the cupboard and felt for the unlabelled bottle of rum that Crazy Horse had left in the glove compartment. He poured a generous slug into Harry's coffee and then stirred in an extra half-spoonful of instant coffee and two sugars.

He went back in.

They were talking about the possibility of going to Scotland, which had somehow got her on to the Edinburgh Military Tattoo.

'I like all that history,' she said. 'Maybe we should go there.'

Sean shook his head. 'Not Scotland,' he said, thinking of McCleish.

'I go with Sean,' she stated.

Sean, almost as if to snub her, didn't respond, but handed Harry his mug. 'Here,' he said. 'Hope you like it strong.'

'Whatever. You've got a better idea of somewhere to go?'

'A few. Cheers.'

Sean sipped at his unadulterated drink, watching Harry take a healthy slurp, his eyes flickering worryingly as he tasted it.

'Coffee all right?' Sean asked.

'Er . . . no. It's fine. Fine.'

'Good . . . Not Scotland, though. I think you'll find it a bit cold up there, sweetheart.'

'I want to stay in London,' she said angrily, eyeing Sean. 'It's not fair that I should be chased. Look, why don't we just go to the police?'

'No!' said Harry and Sean simultaneously, making them both half-smile. 'We do that,' said Sean, 'we lose control of the situation.'

'That's right,' said Harry, looking into his drink, blinking slowly. 'We need to keep on top of it.'

They talked over a few possible locations, Harry giggling at his own joke that if you really wanted to be safe from Bohra, go to live in Turkey. He was giggling a lot by the time he'd finished his second cup of coffee.

'Listen,' he started to say. 'No hard feelings, right, between you and me? You understand how it is, don't you? You've got a difficult job, don't get me wrong. I respect you, no, wait, that's bollocks, respect isn't the right word, but I hate the way it's all so . . . ach-trish-nal. Any more coffee?'

'Sure.'

Harry shouted at him through the open kitchen door as Sean leaded another mug for him. 'But listen, what I don't understand is why you spend so much time on, you know . . . Sweet Bill. I mean, what is he? He's nothing. Small time. Like fucking amoeba time. But Bohra, he's up to his neck in everything, that's what my brother told me anyway. He knows what's going on, or that's what he reckons. Why don't you go after that bastard?' he asked, lovingly accepting another coffee.

'I hear you, mate,' said Sean. 'It'd be nice to put one over on Bohra, wouldn't it? You reckon, mate?'

Harry nodded and took a gulp. 'Fucking right,' he replied. 'I'd give anything to see that fat bastard squirm. Anything. He trashed my brother's shop. Did I tell you that?'

Sean watched as Harry put the rest away, trying to tell the story of the attack on the shop. The effect of the rum was evident now. Sean reckoned his moment had come. He needed the spiv still to be able to remember what was going on.

'Good coffee,' Harry said, carefully placing his cup down and pushing it along the table in front of him.

Sean knew he had him right where he wanted him. 'So he trashed the shop?'

Harry nodded. 'Went in there, gave my brother a heart attack, I'm not kidding.' He gritted his teeth as he spoke, suddenly overcome with emotion.

Sean nodded, thinking it was strange to exaggerate about something like that.

'Went in there and . . . threatened my old man. My old man?' Tears were actually starting to well up in Harry's eyes. 'Do you know how that made me feel?'

'Angry.'

'You're fucking right, angry. I want him to pay for that, for what he did.'

'What if I told you there was a way we could get to him, do him over, hit him where it really hurt?'

Harry waved a hand. 'I'm in,' he proclaimed. 'Anything.'

Sean leaned forward on the sofa now, drawing Harry in towards him, until he could smell the battery acid on his breath.

'What're we going to do?' Harry asked.

'We're going to rob him. You and me.'

29

....

Harry had listened to the plan carefully, although there were innumerable distractions, chief among them the instability of the room around him. Generally, though, he felt happy, buoyant even. The plan that Thingie (what was his name again?) had come up with seemed utterly foolproof, an utter piece of piss, not a problem. He'd said that Harry's cut would be enough to pay off Bohra, and then some.

The idea was for Harry to distract Bohra, get him and the twins away, while Whatshisface snuck in and nicked Bohra's money. Easy as pie. They'd asked the girl where she thought Bohra kept his money and she said that Bohra was always funny about who went into his office. She'd described the layout of the room. There was a bed in there apparently.

'I know where his money is,' Harry had interrupted. 'Under the bed. I know a million blokes like Bohra. Always under the bed with them. Scared of banks. Under the bed. In shoeboxes, probably.'

'OK,' Thingie had said, satisfied with that. 'You call him and tell him you want to meet him. Somewhere public . . .'

'Dogtrack?' Harry suggested.

'Fine. But we need a good reason for you to call him, something that won't make him suspicious.'

'Like what?'

'You'll have to think of something.'

Thinking was hard at the precise moment. 'Yeah, but like what?'

'I don't know. Just blag it. That's what you do for a living. That's what you're supposed to be good at, isn't it?'

Harry sat back, blinking hard. Thingie, Immigration Boy, seemed to have all the answers, like he'd done this kind of thing before.

So Harry was supposed to call Bohra and get him out of the office long enough, keep him delayed while the blag came down. When Thingie (what was his name?) had done the nicking, he'd contact Harry to let him know the coast was clear.

'How am I supposed to know when that is?'

Thingy had produced a case with Home Office markings on it, from where he'd given Harry a small plastic box with an LCD display.

'A pager. Ain't you heard? We've got mobile phones south of the river as well,' said Harry, laughing at his own joke.

Sean shook his head. 'No phones. Too risky. Phones cause complications.'

Harry made a face, turned down his mouth but just shrugged. 'But they'll hear it go off, won't they?'

'No. You see here?' he'd said, and with Harry still holding the pager he pushed a button on the side. Harry laughed, almost dropped the thing as he felt shivers pass up his wrist and arm.

'It vibrates,' Thingie had explained. 'When you feel it, you'll know the coast is clear. We'll meet back here and split the money.'

Brilliant, thought Harry, as he drove down the dual carriageway towards New Malden, the bottle of Australian fizzy on the passenger seat next to him, vaguely aware of the speed cameras going off every half-mile.

He turned into Carla's street, saw there was no sign of the cab outside, and parked. Getting out, the cold evening air was like a kick in the teeth. He shook his head a couple of times and blinked. Being alone with his thoughts suddenly seemed shitty.

Walking quickly up the drive, he rang the bell.

Carla took a while to come to the door.

'Surprise!' he said, thrusting the bottle of sparkly at her before he had a chance to see she'd been crying.

She smiled at him weakly. 'Harry, what are you doing here?'

'I came to see you. To celebrate. But if you're—'

'Celebrate what?' she asked, laughing a little.

'My escape,' he said. 'I've got your money.'

'Where?'

'Tomorrow. All of it. I promise.'

He was aware of speaking loudly, and she nervously glanced up and down the street before letting him in, when he made his customary lunge at her. She gestured at resistance but was laughing and managed to kick the door shut behind them as they both tumbled to the floor.

'Why are you crying, baby?' he asked her as they relaxed.

'You been drinking?'

'No,' he replied. Then, on reflection, 'Maybe. What's the matter?'

'We had a fight. He left early for his night shift,' she said quietly. 'He's got a temper, if you didn't guess.'

'It should have been me,' Harry moaned, nuzzling his head clumsily between her breasts. 'Should have been me.'

When he looked up her eyes were filling again. 'Don't say that, Harry,' she whispered, pushing her fingers through his hair. 'Don't.'

'Why not, if it's the truth?'

'That's exactly why. Come upstairs.'

Her kisses, long and pleading, different from normal, began to sober him up. There was an anxiety about her attentions to him that suggested a kind of panic. 'Here's to escape,' she'd said as they clinked Paris goblets of fake champagne. Maybe that was what she wanted, to go back in time with her little brown boy, to take solace in lust from life's difficult stuff. Looking down at her in her hot underwear, kneeling on the bed, running her tongue down his stomach as he stood before her, he wondered if things could have turned out differently.

As she started to unzip his fly, she felt the bulge in his trouser pocket.

'What's that?' she asked, reaching in and extracting the pager he'd been given.

'I'll show you,' he said, leaning forward to push the button on its side, making it purr and hum in her hand. 'It's a vibrator,' he said, jumping on her.

30

....

Sean rose early, his day already planned after a sleepless night. In truth, shutting down his life here in order to start a new one elsewhere wasn't going to take that much doing. What had once meant exclusion and loneliness was now a convenience. He posted a month and a half's rent to his landlord with a brief note saying he was vacating, but offering no explanation, paid off his credit card, packed a few clothes and black-bagged the rest for the rubbish men. Then he went out, leaving Ranjita with strict orders to get a cab, go to Croydon and spend the whole day at the multiplex, even if it meant seeing the same movie twice. He didn't want the Bombay spiv coming back, saying he had cold feet and changing his mind on them now. That was why Sean had insisted on using his old Home Office pager. No contact, no numbers being stored in his phone's memory, no chance for afterthoughts. He'd have to go through with it or face the consequences of Sean dropping him in it with Bohra. Simple as that.

He went out and cleared his current account, pleasantly surprised by how much all his overtime had earned him. He went to a used-car dealership, bought a Honda for reliability, paying in cash, then went to pick up the maps he needed and a couple of books.

At about three o'clock he made the call from a public box.

Five rings before it was picked up.

'Yes?' said a voice, middle-aged and mellow, with a hint of surprise. The sound of it sent Sean's memory reeling.

'It's me,' Sean said. 'I need to meet.'

A silence. Sean heard the man breathe sharply through his nose. The way Sean remembered him doing.

'Sorry. I think you have a wrong number.'

'I *need* to meet.'

Another pause.

'Very well. Where and when?'

31

....

Harry made the call at about three o'clock from the payphone outside Jay's room.

He felt knackered and still had the remnants of the headache he'd woken up with that morning. Or rather been woken with, Carla forced into a slap to the face to rouse him and get him out before Darren made his reappearance. He'd dressed quickly, his head a dark grotto of self-pity and regret. In the chaos of Carla's insistence at his hurried departure, he didn't remember what that nagging commitment was until he was back in the motor.

He'd gone back to the flat and tried to sleep it off, but even after four Nurofen the reggae pulse in his skull wouldn't fade. After a few hours he'd got up, showered, bought a pound of jellybeans and gone back to the address where the plan had been hatched last night.

Nobody home. Of course.

That was that, he'd told himself on the way to Dad's to prize open the safe in Jay's bedroom with the combination he'd been given. Now he knew he'd have to go through with it. He couldn't afford to take the risk that Immigration wouldn't be going ahead. If he did get collared by Bohra, then there was nothing to stop him spilling the fact that Harry had known where the girl was, something that probably wouldn't go down all that well.

So he'd got out of the lift on Jay's floor, the envelope with the eleven grand in his inside pocket giving him a false sense of security. The battery on his mobile dead again, he'd gone straight to the payphone.

'Mr Bohra?'

'Harry Boy.'

'I need to see you.'

'Good news, I hope.'

'There's something I need to discuss with you.'

'What would it be, Harry?'

Harry paused, swallowed. 'I've got something for you. Be at the dogtrack. Nine. Got to go.'

He hung up and looked over his shoulder. He calculated, hoped, that would be tantalising enough. Now he had to face Jay, not having done anything about finding a replacement for the shop . . .

An idea came to him through the ache in his brain. It was perfect. He put another twenty pence in the phone and called the office, marvelling at Carla's studied aloofness.

Harry sat by Jay's bed, his mobile recharging at a power point probably meant for a dialysis machine, both of them staring up at indoor truck racing from some giant hangar deep in the Bible Belt.

'Who's winning?' Harry asked after a while.

'It's not a race, it's an exhibition,' explained Jay. 'Some of these trucks weigh, like, four tons.'

'So what's the point of it if they're not racing?'

'Man and machine,' sighed Jay.

Harry offered him a jellybean.

Jay declined. 'You know them things make you constipated?'

'You're lying in hospital giving out health advice?'

'Least I'm not constipated.'

'How do you know they make you constipated?'

'I read it.'

'Where?'

Jay threw a magazine at Harry that had been lying on his bedside table under a copy of *Asian Eye*.

'*Men's Health*? I'm impressed. Where did you get this?'

'There's a girl comes round selling magazines. They didn't have *The Grocer*.'

Harry shook his head. 'What were they thinking?'

'You get the money?' Jay asked, after a pause.

'Yeah,' said Harry patting his chest where the bundle sat.

'I know how much was in there.'

Harry nodded.

On the screen, a truck overturned taking a corner.

'Finally,' said Harry, 'some action.'

'I suppose,' Jay said, picking up the magazine and leafing through it. 'I suppose I don't really want to die.'

Harry looked at him. 'You're not going to die.'

'It's just that sometimes . . . I'm lying here and wondering what exactly it is I've got to live for, Harry.'

Harry was stunned. 'There's no reason why you should feel that way,' he stammered. 'Maybe, have you ever thought that you spend too much time behind that counter, that you need to get out, meet some people, meet someone . . .'

'There's nobody else,' pleaded Jay, sniffing hard. 'That's it. There's only me. And I'm not paying anybody else,' he added, wiping his eyes, pulling himself straight.

'Listen,' Harry said. 'There's somebody coming to pay you a visit. Somebody who I thought might be able to work in the shop. If you play your cards right, she might do it for less than the minimum wage.'

'Who? Who?'

'Hang on.'

Hearing the lift doors open, he got up and put his head round the door. A large woman with a young, round, pretty face walked out, dressed in a white sari and headdress, looking in both directions. She carried some flowers and a biscuit tin.

'Smarten yourself up,' he hissed at Jay before stepping out and approaching her. 'Miss Sharma,' he greeted her.

'Oh, Mr Verma,' she said on seeing him. 'As soon as your secretary told me, I came straight down. I was so sorry to hear your brother was ill. I'm not intruding, I hope?'

'Not at all. In fact, you've come at a perfect time. I have to leave him for a while, but he's so been looking forward to meeting you.'

He led her in. 'Jay, this is Miss Sharma. This is my brother, Jay.'

She sat down next to him. 'When I heard that Mr Verma's brother was ill, I thought I must come down . . .'

'I mentioned that you were interested in helping out in the shop.'

'Oh, yes. Absolutely. I'd be delighted to help out, if it's OK.'

Jay tried to open his mouth, but was interrupted by her again.

'Oh! Where are my manners? Here, I brought you some flowers and these.' She handed him the biscuit tin, which he opened.

'Cakes,' he said with awe. 'Cakes, Harry.'

'Oh, yeah,' she beamed. 'Cooked them myself. My auntie's recipe. All the way from Ahmedabad.'

'You're from Ahmedabad?'

'Yes.'

'That's in Gujarat,' Jay patronised Harry.

She giggled as Jay carefully put a sweetmeat into his mouth, purring at the taste of sugar.

'Home-made penda. Nothing like home-made,' he said. 'You do understand, if you worked in the shop, I couldn't afford to pay you much?'

'Of course, I quite understand. Whatever you think.'

Harry had never seen such compatibility. He could tell that Jay was already thinking of marriage. For then, as they both knew, he wouldn't have to pay her anything at all.

32

....

Nearly eight o'clock.

Sean sat in the Civic as it grew dark, parked down a side-street, watching Bohra's place, one of a row of once-grand Victorian terraced houses, any charm eroded by standing on what was now a busy main road. On his lap was the map Ranjita had drawn him of the house's interior. Even with Bohra out of the house, he still had to be quiet, as the women would be in the back. Ranjita reckoned the easiest way in was through the basement. Unlike virtually every other on the street, this house hadn't been converted and so there were no stairs leading down, only an eight-foot drop covered with a metal grille. Then he'd have to get in through the window there, smash the glass if necessary and make his entry that way.

He was smoking a cheap cigar, for reasons not even he was sure of. Keep his hands busy, probably. He didn't really care much for the taste, making him lick his lips continuously. Sitting there, just waiting, he was acutely aware of the sounds he was making: the rattle of his keys dangling from the ignition when his thigh brushed them, the creaking of the fake-leather upholstery with even the slightest move, his unsteady breathing.

He heard footsteps. In the far wing mirror, he saw two youths, both wearing sweatshirts with hood pulled over their heads, marching along the pavement. Quickly he flexed an arm, pushing his elbow down on the lock. The other doors locked automatically.

The two boys walked past, laughing at something one of them had said, not even registering his presence inside the car. Just two kids. Sean felt stupid. But he didn't unlock the car.

They told you . . .

Don't get out of the car . . .

He'd been waiting an hour and a half when Bohra stepped out of the front door. Alone.

Ten seconds later, a grey people-carrier with a nasty dent on the driver's side pulled up outside the house. Sean made out two heads inside. If Ranjita was right about Bohra never going anywhere alone, least of all a meeting on neutral ground, that must be the twins. When the van moved off, Bohra was gone.

After another twenty minutes he got out of the car.

33

A funny thing started happening while Harry waited in the Popular Enclosure at Wimbledon Dogtrack.

He started winning. Not just winning, but winning big. Long shots, reverse forecasts, straight forecasts, tricasts, winning from the bookies, winning on the tote. A brick of notes clogged his pockets. But somehow this was fate's last kick in the teeth. He watched it heavy-eyed, waiting for Bohra. Tonight, winning felt just the same as losing. His luck in picking one scrawny dog out of six that barely had a name, that was luck he couldn't afford to waste, luck he needed to keep Bohra occupied for long enough to make the plan work, the real reason he was there, knee deep in dog people. It seemed inevitable that he would turn up, smell a rat straight away and leave. Harry had to think of something, had to blag him into staying for his own sake, but with what?

He looked on and cursed as dog 5 got his nose in front on the line and just pushed out number 3. He looked down at his ticket: 5 to beat 3, a winner.

'Shit,' he muttered.

'Harry boy,' came the familiar voice from one step behind, accompanied by a stabbing tap on the shoulder.

Harry hadn't been looking out for him, knowing that their agreed time wasn't until nine o'clock. The next race was only the 8.30, so if Whatshisface wasn't in position, he wouldn't have seen him leave, might not know he had even left until he came back. Stupid fucking greyhound luck.

'You're here early,' he said, spinning around. On the extra step up, Bohra, dressed in a sheepskin coat with grey track pants tucked into white socks and trainers, looked huge.

'You like the shoes?' was Bohra's reply, lifting a foot to show Harry yet another pair of spanking-new white trainers with blue flashes. He stuffed a mint into his mouth and dropped the wrapper on the floor. 'Never been here before.'

'Right. Well, it's very . . . South London.'

Bohra looked around, inspecting the scene, his face wrinkling.

'Where are the boys?' Harry asked.

'You think we go everywhere together?' Bohra looked puzzled.

'Yes,' Harry laughed nervously.

Bohra looked concerned, miffed even. 'They are through there,' he pointed inside. 'Playing fruit machines.'

Harry nodded, caught a glimpse of a knee-length white puffer jacket and a V-sign directed at him.

'So,' Bohra asked. 'What is it?'

Harry faked misunderstanding. He needed to start playing for time. 'What is what?'

'So the dogs just run around the track?' Bohra asked, restless.

'Oh, right. Yeah, well, that's the basic idea.'

'How many times?'

'Just the once, usually.'

Bohra looked perplexed. 'And people bet on that?'

Harry looked out into the track. 'Yes. They do.' He had to admit it seemed strange, put that way. He was struck with panic that Bohra's brilliantly empirical analysis would lead him straight out of the stadium, shaking his head at the stupidity of it. Across on the other side of the stadium, he saw that the dogs were parading in their faded trap colours for the next race, prize money of sixty quid.

'Gambling.' Bohra shook his head. 'Gets people into trouble, doesn't it, Harry?'

Harry glanced at him but saw he was looking around, probably with a view to rounding up the twins. 'You said you had something for me?'

Shit!

'That's right.' He blinked fast in an attempt to get his brain to go up the gears. He had the girl? No. He had the girl but he'd lost her? No. He knew where the girl was but needed more time? No, no, no . . .

Think of something!

He grimaced, remembering what Immigration Boy had said to him the night before. What Harry now realised was that he was expert at blagging himself *into* situations but hopeless at getting out of them. His bluff had been called. He had nothing except the money Jay had lent him in his inside pocket. But if Bohra was leaving to find his house being burgled by Harry's accomplice, he might as well just keep a hold of it to help pay for his reconstructive surgery.

Bohra hesitated, prolonging his agony. 'Harry?' he asked.

'Yes, Mr Bohra.'

'What exactly are them dogs doing?'

The question was genuine, childlike almost.

Harry shrugged. 'They're parading. That's what they do just before the race. So you get a chance to get a look at them, see if they look fit, ready to race.'

'And that tells you which one's going to win?'

Harry couldn't resist a pained laugh. 'Not entirely. There's the form, how they've run in the past, how quickly they come out of the traps . . .'

'Traps?'

Harry pointed. 'Those are the traps. That's where the race starts. You see, they're going behind now. The traps fly up and they fly out. Race'll be off in a minute,' he added, turning to head to the tote. Bohra stood his ground. 'You're not going to have a bet?' Harry asked him.

Bohra looked unsure. 'I . . .'

It dawned on Harry that he had no idea what to do, how to place a bet.

'I'll put one on for you. You only have to bet a pound, if that's all you want. Just for fun. Pick one.'

'Which one?'

'Any one.'

'How do I choose?'

Harry revelled in Bohra's naivety, his fear even. He was reluctant because he didn't want to appear foolish in an alien environment. Suddenly, Harry saw through him, saw the sham of culture and community was nothing more than a way of making the world smaller, scaling it down to match his mind. Christ, he didn't even have the savoir-faire to rise to a night at the greyhounds. Looking up at him, Harry wondered why he was afraid of this chump.

'It doesn't matter,' said Harry. 'It's six dogs running like buggery around four bends. It's a lottery. Pick a colour you like. Or a number.'

'Seven.'

Harry clicked his tongue. 'There's only six dogs.'

'Oh, four, then. Four.'

He gave Harry a pound, who went off to the tote desks inside. He was a little pleased with himself, pleased at his short-term victory in keeping Bohra there for at least this race, thinking that every few seconds would count, praying for the moment when Thingie gave him the signal that it—

Oh, no!

He patted all his pockets for the reassuring bulge but knew that he didn't have the pager, hadn't had it all day. He must have left it at his flat when he'd tried to have a kip.

Fuck!

Now he had no way of knowing when it was safe to let Bohra leave. He left the queue and joined the back again, to kill a couple more minutes.

When he went back outside, the last dog was going in. Harry handed Bohra a voucher.

'One pound, dog 4, on the nose.'

Bohra took it and inspected it with satisfaction. 'What will I win?'

Harry checked the flashing tote boards. 'It's an outsider. You'd get about eight quid back.'

Bohra peered down at Harry's hand. 'Which dog did you go for?'

'I had a little punt on dog 2. A fiver,' he said, slipping the £200 win slip into his pocket.

The stadium lights flashed, and in front of them the hare whirred past on its rail.

'Come on, four,' Bohra whispered.

The traps sprang open. Harry cursed as dog 2 got a flyer, took a length lead within the first fifty yards, a quartet of the others packed tight behind it. Number 4 dawdled in its black jacket, out of the race before the first bend. But at the bend the pack had closed a stride and Harry's dog suddenly, inexplicably lurched out, meeting the rest of them almost at a right angle.

It was chaos. The writhing pack of bone and sinew slammed itself into the advertising boards at the track's edge, snarling and snapping, while on the inside dog 4 lumbered by and was halfway down the back straight by the time a couple of the others had extricated themselves. Even then, it was a close-run thing with the pursuers eating up the ground between them and the leader which, though tying up badly, just managed to hold on for the win.

Harry looked on in disbelief. Total carnage on the first bend was nothing new at Wimbledon, but this, this was divine intervention.

Next to him, Bohra roared, arms aloft, punching air.

'Yeeeeeees! Yes! Yes! Number four! Number four! Bad luck, Harry boy. You must be gutted, aye? But I had a feeling about number four. Call it instinct, but I knew exactly how the race would happen. I think I have a gift for this. Bad luck, Harry boy,' he laughed.

But Harry was happy. A sudden change to bad greyhound luck meant better luck elsewhere. And looking up into Bohra's eyes, he knew that he didn't have to worry about keeping him there. One freakish win on a walking Chinese dinner and the fat git was hooked.

34

· ·

There were no lights on at the front of Bohra's house. Having walked down the path and ducked off to the side, Sean saw that the overgrown garden at the front would give him enough cover from the main road. The iron grille over the well in front of the basement window was too heavy to pick up so, grabbing it with both hands, he pulled it up a couple of inches and slid it back far enough to allow himself to drop down. He made the jump carefully, still feeling the twinge in his knee as he landed, reminding him of his pursuit of Sweet Bill. He wondered where he was now, probably out and about again with the help of the Bombay spiv. Jesus, he thought, inspecting the window that led to the basement, encrusted with grime, how did he know he could trust him? He had no choice in the matter, that's how far things had gone.

Sean had to admit that he didn't do trust that well.

He pushed the window hard, felt the frame rattle. Pushing up hard, it gave a little way, far enough for him to get his hands in underneath. Planting his feet firmly, he pushed up with a groan. The window budged a little, but Sean guessed that damp and time had warped the wood so far out of shape that it was a lost cause. Rummaging in his rucksack, he pulled out a towel which he wrapped tight around his fist. He stood waiting for something loud, an articulated lorry maybe rumbling down the road outside. Two minutes he waited before the sound of a bus, engine coughing, gears grinding, brakes squealing, gave him his chance.

He punched the glass hard, once, twice, then waited for the sound to fade. No voices, no footsteps above.

Quickly, he began to pick the remaining jags of glass from the edges of the frame, the ancient putty hardly bothering to resist, until he had a clear space to get through.

Going in legs first, he jumped down on to an abandoned old settee, almost catching the back of his ankle on a protruding spring. He used the torch he'd brought to check Ranjita's map. She'd never been down here, but she knew where the set of steps leading up emerged. Sean could see the stairs curling away at the far end of the room, an ocean of precariously piled junk to be navigated first. He surfed defunct white goods, furniture and dozens of cardboard boxes to make it across, painfully aware of any sound that might carry up through the floorboards.

He climbed the stairs slowly, once again checking the map to see where the door from the basement figured in the overall scheme of the house. He would come out on the opposite side of the corridor to Bohra's office, which was about ten yards further down.

He turned the handle and opened the door a few inches.

The corridor was unlit. Peeking through, Sean got his bearings. There, away to the right, at the front of the house, was the door to Bohra's office.

Sean knew this was the dangerous part, the weak point in the plan. From the top of the basement stairs to the door he wanted was a matter of six or seven hurried paces, but between those two points he would be harshly exposed. He pushed the door out a little further, expecting a Gothic creak to give him away. None came. Now he had enough room to draw his body half out into the corridor, still holding the handle, ready to propel himself forward.

He looked left and saw the closed kitchen door, light spilling from around its edges. Sean knew there were four women who lived in the house: the unfortunate Mrs Bohra, plus her daughter and the twins' wives. That said, their numbers could be swelled at any time by relatives or friends and at least one of Bohra's heavies, there to protect them from the mythical Turkish threat. He tried to pick out distinct voices, heard maybe three. One was dominant, complaining. Ranjita had told them they always congregated in the kitchen, where it was warmer.

Peering up, he could see no lights on elsewhere in the house. He froze as the kitchen voices suddenly died down, a lull in the conversation followed by the silence of familiarity. He waited, eyes rolled to the ceiling, concentrating on every sound, but heard no movement. One of the voices started up again, said something short, pithy. A laugh followed, slightly guilty Sean thought, and the babble started again.

With front teeth dug hard into his bottom lip, he extended his foot out, applied pressure to the linoleum-covered floorboard beneath.

No sound. He held the position for a moment, mouth open, feeling the strain in his calf. The next step would put him in no man's land. He felt the skin around his entire body shrink and tighten, willing himself on but holding, holding, delaying the moment.

Make your fucking move.

He stepped out just as the handle on the kitchen door rattled and it began to open. Sean's fingers reached for the handle but grasped only the sweaty air around his palms. He was out, no way back. Through the widening gap as the door gently continued its outward swing, he saw a middle-aged Indian woman framed by the light. She was looking down, attending to the zip on her overcoat. The shock threw Sean into action. Instinct grabbed him, sharpened his options down to the one chance he had. Leaning across, he pushed at the door he had emerged from, the change in his balance assisting him to fall into the corner behind the kitchen door as it swung fully open.

He stood rigid, a breath caught in his throat, arms across his chest, staring at the detail of his own palms only an inch from his face. Standing uncomfortably, his hip jammed against the dado rail, he fought an overwhelming urge to rebalance himself. He heard a heavy footfall stop directly behind him, maybe a foot away, and a low male growl of exasperation. This must have been Bohra's grunt, on-duty to protect the ladies. Behind him, the Bohra women organised themselves at a funereal pace to go out, Sean agonisingly aware that if they closed the kitchen door behind them as they passed through, he was fucked. But after an exhortation from the senior voice, there was a sudden, excited rush down the corridor to leave and the door was left open behind him.

It was thirty seconds after the front door slammed shut that he dared move. Despite the need to swallow hard and wriggle to free his shirt from the film of sweat on his back, he knew that he had plenty of time as long as the Bombay spiv kept his end up. From what he'd heard, he knew that the women would be away for a couple of hours and was well fucking grateful that they didn't have their own word for 'bingo'.

Even so, he still stepped slowly down to the door of Bohra's office, tried the handle. It wouldn't open. Sean stared disbelievingly at the Yale lock facing him before rolling his eyes. The room was locked and she hadn't mentioned it? Sean tried not to think where this would have left him if it hadn't been bingo night.

Taking one, two steps back, he charged the door, kicking down hard on the lock, which gave at the first attempt.

He was in. Switching on the torch, he scanned the room. There was a desk but no chair, a filing cabinet, shelves adorned with rows of accounting books, a framed, large-scale map of South London on the back wall and there, to Sean's right, the bed.

He moved to it and dropped on to his stomach, lifting the blanket that lay draped over its side. There, underneath, were dozens of shoeboxes. Sean smiled quickly. *Fuck me*, he thought, *the Bombay spiv was right.*

Now it was a question of finding the right one. But he'd have anything he came across in the meantime. Putting the torch on the floor, he slid three piles of boxes out first, four in each pile.

He opened one, then another, and another.

He couldn't fucking believe it.

Shoes. In every box. Trainers, all brand new.

'Reebok,' said a voice from the door in a weird singsong. 'Adidas, Nike, Reebok.'

Sean leaped to his feet and charged the slight frame. The bearer of the voice stepped back but too late. As Sean got him by the collar and pulled him into the room, he drew his arms tight around his head and issued a low moan.

'Who the fuck are you?' Sean hissed, but the moan had gone up an octave or two and was now more like a long, monotone squeal.

Sean dragged one of the arms down with his free hand.

'Who the fuck . . .?'

He stopped himself before he could finish repeating the question. As he'd shaken the featherweight frame, the heavy fringe parted and he saw the flickering eyes, rolled halfway up into the boy's head.

Sean knew who it was. He squinted in disbelief. She'd sat there while they'd planned the fucking thing. Sean let go and sat down on the bed, dragged a hand hard across his forehead.

'Reebok, Adidas, Nike,' said Ranjita's husband.

Sean looked up at him. 'Where's the money?' he asked, dog tired, his anger still there but unfocused now, distracting.

Sean saw the eyes dance, flash by him.

'Reebok best, Adidas second, Nike last.'

'OK,' said Sean, regretting the need to be threatening but prepared to go there. 'Where's he keep the money?'

Sean hadn't expected the boy to start laughing. That's how he interpreted it anyway, the staccato noise coming from the back of his throat.

'What?' Sean asked.

'Shoeboxes,' said Ranji. 'Funny.'

Sean watched, as if in a dream, as he shuffled across the darkened room to the map of the city and drew it upwards to reveal the front of a big black safe.

'Big shoebox.'

Sean rose quickly, got rid of the map from the wall to inspect the thing properly.

'Where's the combination? What's the combination?'

Suddenly the boy was agitated, his head lolling alarmingly from side to side. Sean took him by the shoulders, trying to be gentle.

'You know the combination?'

'Nike, Nike, Nike.'

'Can you open the safe?'

He was trying to wriggle free. Sean decided to play the one card that might work.

'You need to help me open the safe...Ranjita wants you to open the safe.'

The boy stopped moving and started blinking fast, mouth wide open. Sean chose to go a little further. 'She told me you could help us. Ranjita asked me to ask you. She needs your help.'

The boy raised his hand and pushed a finger to his temple. He made a strange fast ticking sound with his tongue. 'I hear it,' he said. 'Just do it. Just do it . . .'

Sean's eyes widened as he saw the boy turn to the dial and begin turning it, staring off into space. The sound of the lock was uncannily like the one that had just emerged from his mouth, perfectly recorded and reproduced. Sean had heard about this kind of thing but now marvelled at its practical uses as, with a pronounced clunk, the safe door loosened itself.

Sean moved in, aware of Ranji retiring to the bed and the fascination of his father's trainer collection, taking off his own shoes and putting a pair on.

The safe was deep, going maybe two feet back, but there wasn't that much in it. On one side there was money, some bundles of cash, grubby bundles of fivers and tenners. Made at any other time, the discovery of exactly how small-time Bohra was would have been satisfying. But not now. There might have been twenty-five, thirty thousand, but Sean had expected more, a fuck of a lot more.

He'd have the money, but Sean concentrated his search elsewhere. In the other half of the safe, the right-hand side, there were documents, papers, envelopes. Sean started rifling through them: deeds to properties, life insurance papers, copies of *Investors Chronicle*. Beneath them was a pile of envelopes, thickly packed. Sean pulled out their contents. They were photographs, the ones Ranjita had told him about, all of young women, mostly Indian or Thai-looking, amateurishly shot in various states of undress or performing sexual acts. These were another of Bohra's insurance policies, Sean guessed, pictures taken of his working girls which he would threaten to send home if any of them decided they might like a change of career. He went through them, fearful of finding one of Ranjita, discarding them faster and faster on the floor as he went. He stopped when he reached the last few, which were of a different subject, a series in black and white, of Bohra and another man, taken from a distance.

Sean looked at these last few open-mouthed for a few moments before stuffing them inside his windcheater. He carried on searching the safe, pulling out more of the envelopes.

'Got to be here,' he muttered. 'Has to be here.' He began spooning envelopes, papers, cash out of the safe and on to the floor.

Sean stopped. There at the back was a small tea caddy. Grabbing it, he pulled off the lid and turned out the contents.

They fell out in a bundle.

Passports. About a dozen, attached together by an elastic band. Sean thumbed through them quickly. Most of them were purple, but there at the bottom was a blue one, which he pulled out and opened.

Ranjita looked up at him, a picture taken in India before her marriage, smiling the smile of opportunity.

He thumbed through. There, on page eleven, her Schengen visa, still valid. At least she'd got something right. He had what he'd come for.

Sean shoved them all into his back pocket and started to fill the rucksack with money. He paused to speak to the boy.

'You should go back to your room. Tell them you saw or heard nothing. You go back to your room now.'

Ranji didn't move, just sat, staring at the pair of trainers he'd put on, the laces hanging loose. Sean approached him and dropped to one knee, starting to do them up for him.

'You make sure you don't tell them. You didn't see anything, hear anything. You mustn't say that you did...Ranjita says thank you. She said you were brave.'

No response.

'There,' said Sean, knotting up the second shoe. 'New shoes. Now it's time to go,' he added, hauling him up.

Sean started to watch him go, felt almost overwhelmed with pity for him. What had Sean done to help him? Nothing. But consciously, ruthlessly, he bit off that emotion and spat it out, turning back to the safe to empty it of cash. Only when his back was fully turned did he hear the dull thud that sent Ranji reeling back into the room, legs buckling, hands clutching his head.

Out in the corridor stood Crazy Horse, one hand raised, holding his trusty brickphone.

'You wanted to know what it was for,' he said with a dry chortle.

'Why am I not surprised to see you?' Sean said, which made Eric cock his head in slight puzzlement.

Ranji issued a low moan.

'I only tapped him,' said McCleish, staying out of the room. 'How did you get here?'

'Greatrix. He told me you were shooting your mouth off—' he shook his head '—speaking out o' turn. I felt I had to take the matter up with you personally, so I paid you a home visit, you know, like I would on some toerag illegal. Except a toerag illegal would have had better locks on his doors, I reckon. By the way,' he went on, reaching for something out of Sean's view, 'did you know you had this under the stairs?'

He dragged Ranjita forward by the hair and threw her into the room.

'I'm sorry, Sean,' she sobbed. 'I'm sorry.'

'If you've touched her . . .' started Sean.

Eric sucked in a breath.

'Oh, you'll have to forgive me. I think I might have touched her at some point. But I don't think she's marked. I was quite careful about that, because I remembered a little rumour I'd heard about a girl who'd gone missing, whose family wanted her back and they'd pay through the nose to get her back. But I arrive here to find . . . this. I mean, how much trouble can one bloke get himself in?'

Sean stepped towards Ranjita slowly, her face masked by her hair.

'You got to Cougar, didn't you?' he said. 'You got him to come up with that bollocks about me.'

Eric stepped into the room. 'Come on. I was in a corner. I knew you'd shoot your mouth off. No honour. So I just got my retaliation in first. They brought up Lagos, I bet?' he asked, twisting a smile.

Sean didn't respond.

'Still playing the innocent? Fucking persistent, I'll give you that.'

'What's the point in me saying anything when everyone's made their minds up already?'

'Ah, fuck off. You were in it up to your eyeballs.'

'Whatever you say,' Sean shrugged.

'You know what it is?' Crazy Horse laughed. 'You coughed it, I'd think better of you for it.'

Ranji struggled to get up but Eric stepped across to throw him back down.

'And as for you, ya wee shite. Wait until your father finds out about this.'

Sean reached Ranjita and pulled her up, clinging to him.

'I'll tell you what,' Sean said, choosing to gamble. 'You want chapter and verse on Lagos, fine. I'll cough if you do.'

'What about?' asked Eric, intrigued.

'That you're Bohra's inside man. That you're the one been feeding him intel for the last year, shafting that operation against him.'

Eric smiled. 'A guess?' he asked.

'No.'

'Then how?'

Sean nodded down at Ranji. 'He told me,' he said, immediately regretting it.

Eric cocked his head. Sean prayed he didn't hit the boy again.

'Not likely.'

'But it's true, isn't it?'

Eric couldn't hide his mischievous pleasure. 'You shouldn't believe everything you hear.'

'Why'd you do it?'

'You've got some nerve asking me that, Lagos Boy. If you must know, there was an arrangement. He gave me some information on some of his business rivals who I shut down for him. Turks, mainly. Jesus, what is his problem with the fucking Turks?' he asked, directing the question at Ranji before facing Sean again. 'Got any proof?'

Sean looked crestfallen.

'Of course not,' said Crazy Horse, passing the brickphone from hand to hand as he moved closer. 'Another empty threat. You're not very good at this, are you? It's decision time, mate.

Either you stay until Bohra gets back and I tell him that you've been plugging his daughter-in-law or you leave her here and take your office disciplinary like a good boy. You'll do time for it, of course. But you being an immigration officer, they might put you in the asylum wing at Rochester. There's a couple of tasty boys I put away in there. I'm sure they'd be more than happy to go over their torture stories with you one more time.'

'Eric,' said Sean, stepping back. 'We can come to an arrangement here. Why don't you let us walk? The money in the safe – half's yours.'

Eric stopped. 'Are you trying to bribe an immigration officer, sonny? Tsk tsk.'

'Jesus. Have you seen how much is in there? Look.'

Letting Ranjita fall, he moved to the safe, pulling the door right back. 'Look.'

McCleish came nearer, more out of an academic interest than any great surprise. 'Lot of money,' he nodded.

'You could stay, say that you burst in on a robbery, but that they got away.'

'And who's supposed to have done this robbery?' Eric asked with a contemptuous sniff.

Sean tried to think. 'Anybody, erm . . .'

Ranji garbled something, sounded like 'taxi'.

'What?'

He got up on to his knees, eyes closed, clutching his side. 'Tu-urks. Tu-urks.'

'Turks?' repeated Sean.

Eric thrust out a bottom lip, sanctioning the theory with a nod and a laugh. 'You know what? I'd reckon he'd actually buy that. But you know what I'm thinking? That would constitute a favour. I don't do favours.'

'I'm not asking for favours,' said Sean, his heart racing now as he reached inside his windcheater. 'You'll do it for this.'

Quickly, he pulled out one of the black and white photos he'd stashed of Bohra handing out money to who else but the man himself.

'Did I say I didn't have proof? I lied,' he said, slipping it on to the shelf in the safe to give Crazy Horse a good view.

McCleish's face contorted into a snarl, and he lunged for the picture with his right arm, but too slow as Sean stepped back and slammed the safe door into it, catching it on the elbow with a snap as he tried to twist it away. Crazy Horse screamed, a sound like ripping tin foil, tried to pull it free with his other hand, but Sean kicked out at it, catching the wrist and sending the brickphone flying before pushing his body weight into the door one more time, feeling the bone give way like a cardboard roll. When he released it, Eric slid down the wall, clutching his shattered limb, only to take a kick in the guts from Ranji, who was himself bent double.

Sean crouched down and waved the rest of the photos at him.

'Disappointed in you, Eric. Dangerous to underestimate someone like Bohra,' he said. 'He had the shit on you to use any time he wanted. So listen, I'm going to do you the favour. Here's your chance to punish the bastard. I'll put the money in your car and these pictures go with me. You put a stop to Cougar and we're even.'

Eric snorted. 'You can't stop him. You'd have to kill him.'

'I mean it, Eric. If I get a sniff of trouble, they go straight to the Gasworks. Deal?'

Sean guessed right that there was no more potent threat for Eric than disgrace among his Chaucerian disciples.

Eric groaned, teeth gritted, eyes closed. Sean feared he might pass out. He grabbed his arm. It felt like a sockful of nuts. He twisted it. McCleish growled.

'Deal, Eric? All that money and Bohra with no leverage on you, not forgetting the time you'll get off work with a twatted arm. You can start enjoying it, doing all those things you've been promising yourself. Except golf, I suppose.'

Crazy Horse coughed. 'Never liked golf.'

There was a hint of admiration in Sean's laugh as he wiped a bead of perspiration off the end of his nose.

'And Cougar?'

'I heard the Piper's looking for him. Maybe he'll find him.'

'So we have an arrangement?'

'You are one sick bastard,' growled McCleish, as Sean threw more of the bundles of cash into his rucksack. 'You'd better give me a shot to the face. Make it look better.'

'You sure?'

'Yeah. Look better. Use the brickphone.'

'Here, give it to me,' Sean said to Ranjita. 'Take as much money as you can get in your pockets.'

She handed Sean the phone, all business.

'Ready?' he asked Eric.

He nodded and Sean dealt him a blow across the face. His head lolled forward for a moment and then snapped back, revealing a cut lip and a burgeoning bruise on his cheek.

'Fuck. That hurts,' he commented. 'Fucking Turk bastards.'

'Tu-urks!' shouted Ranji. 'Tu-urks!'

Sean reached into his pockets for his car keys.

'OK. The money'll be in your boot. You ready?' he asked Ranjita. 'We're going out the front door.'

He watched her leave, stop at the door for him. Sean leaned forward to whisper something in Crazy Horse's ear.

As he got up to leave, Eric gave his best approximation of a whoop. 'I knew it!' he shouted. 'I fucking knew it!'

'Tu-rks!' shouted Ranji.

'Fucking Turks!' echoed Eric McCleish.

As they went out into the night, Sean was sure he could hear him laughing.

★

Eric's car was parked outside the house on the main road. Sean opened the boot, took out the Bohras' passports before throwing the bag in, shut it and threw the keys through a gap left on the driver's side window.

'Are we going back to the flat?' Ranjita asked as he got into the Civic.

'No. Change of plan,' said Sean, looking in the rear-view as he shot the car out onto the road.

'What are we going to do about Harry?'

'Who?' He remembered the spiv. 'Shit.'

'You said he'd get a share.'

'The shares have gone down.'

'Yeah, because you gave that bastard half the money.'

'I had to! We had to get out of there. Fuck!' said Sean, trying to think. 'Can we send him his cut, your lawyer friend?'

'Don't have his address.'

'All right, all right. OK. We'll leave it somewhere for him and use the pager to tell him where it is.'

She nodded.

'Ring the number and tell whoever's on the line the pager number, it's written there, and tell her the message for him. Don't mention money. Say there's a package or a parcel or something.'

'OK. Pull in here.'

'What? At the lido?'

'I know where to leave it for him.'

He did so, knowing he risked getting stopped by the Old Bill as a kerbcrawler.

'How much did he want?'

'He owed ten thousand,' she said.

'All right, give him what you've got and some of this,' said Sean, pulling some bundles out from inside his jacket.

'That's nearly all we've got,' she pointed out.

'It's OK. I'm sorting the money out.' Quickly, she grabbed some sheets of an old newspaper from the back seat and wrapped two of the bundles in it before getting out of the car. Harry watched her disappear into the darkness, trying not to think of how little of the money he had left, how much faith he was putting in one man to help him. Something irritated him about the way she ran, almost skipped back a few seconds later.

As he reversed out, she picked up his mobile phone.

'Yes, hello, it's for number . . .' She read out the pager number. 'Yes, message is, Harry, lido, three bins from car park. That's all.'

She hung up and smiled at Sean, who didn't smile back.

'You found my passport, right?

He concentrated on the road.

'We're getting away?' she said. 'Now?'

'I have to meet someone on the way.'

'For the money.'

'Yeah,' said Sean, grimacing. 'Try and sleep.'

35

....

Harry had stayed until the last race with an increasingly excited Bohra, who was picking up the basics pretty quickly.

'That 5 dog,' he was saying as they left, still inspecting his racecard avidly, the literature he'd seized about owning a greyhound stuck under his arm, 'not much of a trapper, running above its grade. You reckon, Harry?'

'Makes sense to me.'

The twins dawdled behind, punching each other and jumping away at intervals of a few seconds.

'When's next meeting?'

'Tomorrow, I think.'

'You coming?'

'No, I'll give it a miss.'

Bohra turned to follow the twins towards the people-carrier.

'Mr Bohra,' Harry called.

Bohra turned back with a smile.

'The reason I called you today.'

Bohra looked aside, then back.

'I had something for you.'

He drew the envelope with Jay's money inside and threw it across the few feet that separated them. 'What I owe you. So we're even.'

Bohra had made an ungainly catch. He looked down at his money, his chin doubling, trebling. 'Where did you get this?' he asked, peering into the envelope.

'I earned it.'

'I pay you more again to find her.'

Harry gave a tired laugh. 'She's gone. Gone. Gone. Pretty gone,' he said, recalling the words of a song he remembered. He turned and left.

'Harry . . .' Bohra called after him.

Harry kept walking.

'You want to go halfers on a dog with me . . . ?'

He waited until the people-carrier had driven out of the fenced car park and off before heading in the opposite direction for his rendezvous with the girl and Thingie, taking a long route to make sure he wasn't being followed.

When he saw the light off in the flat, he wasn't worried, presumed that was just a precaution. He'd given them enough breathing space to rob Bohra twice and still have enough time to Artex the ceiling. They were probably in there, sipping Blue Nun and counting up the dough by candlelight.

He did start to worry when he saw the door had been broken in. One little push and it folded back. He slowly climbed the stairs in darkness, peering into the sitting room, faintly lit in a sodium haze by the nearest streetlight.

Nobody home. And they'd left in a hurry, a drink spilled across the floor, the coffee table overturned, lying on its side like a fallen horse. He sat down in his coat to wait.

After ten minutes of rumbling silence his mobile went off, making him jump.

'Yes?'

'Lawyer?'

Not Mad Anwar. *Not now*, thought Harry. 'Hello.'

'No fucking hello. My nephew fucking deported now.'

'When?'

'Tonight. Eight o'clock. They put him on plane to Lahore

and you do not one fucking thing about it. And me, I got boxes everywhere . . .'

Harry closed his eyes. 'I'm sorry. I did try to make rep—'

'You try nothing. Immigration say they get not one call from you. You are fucking swindler. You gave me guarantee. Absolute guarantee. Remember? Now I got boxes everywhere . . .'

Harry stood, suddenly up for it. 'Why don't you try lifting them yourself, instead of getting your fuckwit relatives to do it for you? Lazy bastard.'

'You are bastard! I paid you two hundred and fifty!'

Harry stood, starting to enjoy himself now. 'Listen, pal, I wouldn't represent you at a cycling proficiency test for that!'

'Fuck you. I call *Watchdog* about you. *Crimewatch*, better. First, though, I pay someone twenty quid to come round and kick your head in.'

Click.

Harry threw himself back down on the sofa, exhaling hard through his nose. It didn't matter; none of it mattered if they turned up with his share.

They weren't coming, of course.

Shafted again.

After an hour of waiting, he got up, unplugged the TV, carried it down to the car and drove off with it.

Beyond midnight he drove to the office to get Baseeq's file and destroy it. Just in case Mad Anwar did get ideas above his station and decide to pay the Law Society Ethics Committee twenty quid to kick his head in. As he reached the door to the building, stopping to fumble for the right key from his chain, it dawned on him that Bohra would have been home by now and seen the carnage to his assets. At that moment it seemed barely credible that he wouldn't put two and two together and be flying around in the back of the people-carrier looking for Harry's scalp.

He found the right key and held it to the lock.

A noise behind him made him turn.

Nobody there. It had sounded like a scraping, like a foot dragging. Harry shook his head. Probably just an urban fox pulling a tramp behind a skip for supper.

As he put the key in the lock, he heard it again, but this time it was coupled with the dog whistle in his ear that signalled impending violence.

The blow, when it came a nanosecond later, was the hardest thing he'd ever felt, like he imagined being hit by a car would be. He'd been struck across the back, heard his kidneys shriek as he buckled beneath a second impact to the backs of the legs.

Over soon, he told himself, *it'll be over soon*, covering his head with his arms and curling into a ball. If it was Anwar behind this, Harry had underestimated his speed of action. If it was Bohra, then maybe it wouldn't be over *that* soon. He could hear the grunt of his attacker as he came in for a third go, smacking him across the shoulder blade. Harry felt something crack, but he wasn't sure where; his whole body was just one shrill lump of pain. There was a lull, but Harry sensed that his attacker was readying himself for the big one. Opening one eye, he saw the cricket bat swoop in a parabola and smash his left knee over long on for six.

Harry screamed, he screamed, screamed, screamed until he felt himself being rolled over and a hand shoved on to, *into*, his mouth.

Through his tears, he thought he saw a yellow tanktop.

'You touch her again, you little Paki bastard, and I'll fucking kill you!'

Darren stood up and made to fling something right at Harry's head. Harry screwed his body away, sending another electric shock through his knee, heard the sound of something smash on the path next to him.

'Look what the fucking tooth fairy left under my pillow.'

There, inches from his face, as he turned back, open-mouthed, was what remained of the pager. He blinked hard to read the message on the illuminated display.

. . . HARRY . . . LIDO . . . THREE

'Lido . . . three,' Harry mouthed as he passed out.

36

. . . .

Sean checked the time again.

4.56 a.m. Still waiting.

He stood on the filling station forecourt next to a dustbin, ripping up the Bohra family's passports one by one and chucking the pieces in. That would guarantee them a good head start.

Across the roundabout where the services were located, he saw the first light of dawn creeping over the countryside, illuminating the mist that clung to the contours of the land like a layer of icing. If he looked away to the left, he could just about make out the spot where the land gave out and, somewhere below, the sea began. He'd forgotten the chill of mornings like this, mornings that meant the start of long journeys, mornings where anything seemed possible.

He stood and waited in the cold, turning every so often to check through the windscreen that she was still there, sleeping in the passenger seat, the denim jacket used as a blanket, pulled up to her neck.

Don't get out of the car . . . , he remembered.

Oh, Maria . . .

From the direction of the sea, he heard a lorry, a big ten-wheel monster, coming down the road, the first one off the latest boat from Calais. It passed Sean and slowed as it reached the roundabout, but instead of moving off it stopped. The hazards went on.

Sean saw a twitch of the tarpaulin hanging over its back, then another as a head poked out. Quickly, the tarpaulin was pulled back and a dozen men, maybe more, jumped off the back and scarpered in various directions across the dew-soaked fields. The last one, a little fatty, was still in the process of climbing down when the lorry set off again.

Sean watched impassive. The scene had no drama for him after . . . how long was it? . . . fifteen years of being in immigration. The only job he'd ever known.

At least he was out of it. That was something.

'Bloody disgrace, really,' said a voice behind him, well spoken.

Sean spun around. A few feet away was a man, mid-fifties, lean, grey hair meticulously parted, Barbour buttoned up all the way.

'Beautiful morning,' he said. 'I'd forgotten about mornings like this until I came back.'

'Sorry about the short notice.'

'Fair old drive from Devon. You've got my wife thinking I'm having an affair.'

'Sorry.'

'Truth is we could probably do with a little excitement.' The man took a deep breath. A sign, Sean knew, that the mood was about to change. 'I can't say I was particularly pleased to get your call,' he said, interrupting a response from Sean with a wave of his hand. 'I had thought our understanding was quite clear.'

'Circumstances,' said Sean by way of explanation.

'There are more discreet ways to contact somebody.'

'I'm sorry, but I don't have a lot of time. You think your phone is . . . ?'

'I doubt that. But I don't care for having my position jeopardised unnecessarily.'

'No.'

'You're in trouble?'

'I'm getting out. I need my money.'

'What money is that?'

'My share.'

'What makes you think I've got it?'

Sean didn't answer.

'You understood our arrangement, Carlyle,' the man went on. 'No contact was, may I remind you, one of its keystones.'

Sean rolled his tongue across the front of his teeth.

'I'm risking everything that I worked for,' the man went on.

'What about what I risked? What about the fucking price I paid?'

'I'm conscious of that. But I don't have the money, as you well know.'

'I don't know! You have to help me.'

The man turned down the corners of his mouth. 'I'm not certain that I do. Whatever mess you've got yourself into isn't of my making. However . . .'

Sean drew in a cold breath.

'. . . I could give you a little cash.'

'How much?'

The man pulled out an envelope. 'There's five thousand here.'

Sean reached to take it but the man stepped back. 'You appreciate that you would forfeit your right to the rest of the money?'

'For five thousand? You're joking?'

'No. If I give you this, then our previous arrangement is null and void.'

Sean muttered a sour laugh, shook his head. 'You just happened to come out with that much, even though you didn't know what I wanted.'

'Hardly a surprise that it was money. Hardly a surprise that you're in a position of weakness. What would surprise me was if you had a choice. Do you?'

'No,' said Sean, utterly drained. 'When did I ever have a choice?'

'What exactly was it you were expecting?'

Sean shook his head, the wind making his eyes water. 'I don't know. I thought you could make arrangements for me, set me up somewhere else.' Articulated out loud, he realised it sounded ridiculous.

The man proffered the envelope with a shake of the head. 'Rather naive of you. I'm sorry. You expected too much. I was just a humble penpusher, you know that.' He thrust it out again. 'Why don't you take it? Then we can go our separate ways.'

Biting his lip, Sean took it, fatigued at his own capitulation, held it in both hands. 'They gave you a hard time after I left?' he asked.

The man shrugged, a little more relaxed. 'I suppose they tried. They had nothing, of course. I don't think they ever really grasped the scale. They couldn't think past the idea of handfuls of grubby naira being handed over behind the bikesheds. Typical civil service mentality, which I suppose is why they're all so happy with their piddling Foreign Office pensions. In all honesty, they rather lost their taste for it after . . . what happened. It seems rather ghastly to be advantaged by such a terrible thing.'

Sean looked into space. 'That was Maria, I suppose. God knows how many times they warned her . . .'

'Don't get out of the car. I know.'

As he and Ranjita sat in the queue to board the ferry, surrounded on all sides by beaten-up old transit vans stinking of spilled beer, Sean let the story go, let it spill like drool down his chin.

'While I was in Lagos, there was an investigation into a big visa-selling scam there. I mean big. I wasn't behind it, that was a Foreign Office bloke . . .'

'The one at the garage?'

He nodded. 'But he offered me a lot of money if I let it look as if it was me, to deflect attention from him. I mean a lot of money. A share of his profits. The chances are I would have been put away for a while, but they wouldn't have been able to touch the cash – that was all being hidden, invested to get back later. That was how it was supposed to happen. Now it's all . . . Maria, she didn't know anything about it, but one day they went round to the American school where she was working, started asking her questions. She flipped out, said she was leaving. She never really liked it out there. We had a row, which delayed her catching her flight. It wasn't the end of our marriage. At least, I don't think it was. She would have waited for me . . .'

He sniffed.

'Because she was late, the driver took a short cut off the main road. They were driving through this shantytown, going too fast, and a child ran in front of the car. They hit him.'

Sean tapped the steering wheel gently with his fist.

'When you arrive out there, one of the first things they tell you is, if you hit anyone, don't stop, drive on and sort it out later. Whatever you do, you don't get out.'

'She got out?'

'There was a crowd waiting. Feelings were running pretty high. Some anti-West bollocks being stirred up by the opposition. Because it was a child and because it was Maria . . . she got out of the car. They took her . . .'

He sucked hard on his bottom lip.

'They cut her to ribbons.'

For five thousand pounds. He'd managed to end up with less than Crazy Horse or the Bombay spiv. That was some fucking going.

Ranjita reached out and stroked the back of his neck as he cried.

'Poor boy,' she said. 'But that is the past. Now you must look forward.'

He breathed deeply, recovered himself a little, unhappy with the Joyce Grenfell tone in her voice. Like she wasn't listening.

'Two weeks before I started in Lagos, we took a holiday down in southern Spain. The very southern tip.'

'Is that where we're going?' Uninterested, she sounded.

He nodded, looked across at her. He saw there was a bump on the bridge of her nose, an imperfection he'd never noticed before. She sat, eyes facing straight ahead, looking a bit haughty, he thought.

'There's a town there, Tarifa,' he said. 'You sit on the beach on a clear day and you can see Africa. Because it's at the point where two oceans meet, there are two winds, the Levante and the Poniente. They fight it out every day,' he explained, turning on the ignition like the vehicles around him. 'That's why it's perfect.'

'For what?'

'Windsurfing. We're going windsurfing,' he said quietly, as they rolled forward.

In the general haze of his misery, there was something troubling him especially, something stinging him, something from back at Bohra's house. It was preying on his mind, eating him up. One thing that she'd gone through with an arranged marriage to an autistic boy, one thing she'd neglected to mention that detail. But to be there, back at the house and not even speak to him . . . It was like she hadn't even seen him.

How could you be so . . .

As they hit the ramp and he glanced over at her again, Sean knew that it could never work out. Of course not.

He felt like a drink.

37

....

Harry sat on the bench, crutches laid out next to him, his bad leg stretched out in plaster before him, trying to sit still to minimise his pain. Cars came down Tooting Bec Road towards him, each one looking as if it was going to slow down and make the expected turn on to the tarmac of the lido car park. Not yet.

He'd woken up in Accident and Emergency, just as they were trying to straighten his knee out. He'd been lucky, the doctor told him, that the damage wasn't greater, which made him momentarily thankful for the run of losing dogs he'd had after Bohra's arrival at the track the night before. Swings and roundabouts.

They'd wanted to keep him in, but after a few hours' sleep he'd checked himself out. He had an appointment to keep. On his way, he went to see Dad, had to call him down out of bed. Or rather Miss Sharma, already established behind the counter, had brought him down.

'Pissed up?' Dad asked, in English, on seeing Harry's leg.

Harry looked hurt. 'Why do you say that? It could have been anything. It could have been police brutality.'

'Nonsense. This is a civilised country.'

'Anyway, I fell down some stairs.'

Dad gave him a strange look, almost proud, Harry thought, before raising his arms and turning to Miss Sharma. 'That's it. We're all bloody crocked. All the Vermas in the wars. Good thing you came along when you did.'

'I'll make a cup of tea,' she suggested. Dad appeared delighted with the new help. They both commented on how much the shop had already benefited from a woman's touch even if, as Dad pointed out, she was no Julia Roberts.

'Thing is,' Harry said, adjusting his balance, 'she's going to get kicked out of the country unless she finds a status here.'

'Like what status?'

'Like marrying someone.'

Dad looked shocked. 'Harry, you haven't . . . ?'

'Not me,' he laughed. 'I was thinking about Jay. I thought maybe you'd suggest it to him.'

Dad thought for a moment. 'You want me to tell him to marry this girl?'

'Just an idea.'

'Only to keep her in the country? Is that legal?'

'It's a loophole.'

'That would be a marriage of convenience?' he asked disapprovingly.

Harry shrugged and looked down. 'I just thought . . .'

'Still, a woman to be around the place . . .'

'And she'd work in the shop for nothing. And, Jay, you know . . .'

'You're right,' Dad said. 'Beggars can't be choosers. We'll go down to the hospital tonight.'

But now Harry was sitting on the bench, waiting. He shivered in the cold and felt the aches spring up all over himself. He cursed his one oversight. If only he hadn't given Carla a piece of vital communicative equipment for her to use as a clitoral stimulus, then this never would have happened. The little things, he told himself, shaking his head ruefully, which hurt like hell.

He glanced down at the newspaper on his lap and carried on reading the news article in the *Evening Standard* about the shooting in Balham:

The victim has been named as Leslie Philip Montgomery, a Jamaican national, who, at the time of the attack, was on bail, charged with drug offences. The police have interviewed a number of witnesses but have come to no conclusions regarding the motive for Montgomery's murder. The possibility of the execution-style attack being gang-related has credibility, as the victim was wanted in Jamaica and elsewhere for gang-type offences. Initial enquiries are focusing on the murdered man's reason for being at the Spatchcock public house. Police believe he was there for an appointment, but the identity of the person he was there to meet is unknown. Enquiries are being concentrated in this area. Police sources would not be drawn on whether Montgomery was in the United Kingdom illegally, nor would the dead man's lawyer, Daniel Le Gall, who had made the successful bail application yesterday on his client's behalf. In a statement, Mr Le Gall said he was shocked by the incident . . .

Harry smiled wryly. Danny Legal could afford to lose the odd client, although Harry hoped that the circumstances were enough to wipe that smug grin off his face for five minutes.

He looked at his watch. It was 3.10. Where were they? He'd been there well before time. LIDO . . . THREE. The message couldn't have been simpler. And yet they were already ten minutes late.

Looking to his left, he saw Conrad, the familiar tramp, coming up the path, stopping to have a root around in the bins that lined it every twenty yards.

Then he heard footfalls on the grass behind him. He spun around to look, but there was nobody on that side. When he turned back, he saw a young man standing by the end of the bench, hunched against the cold, dressed in a denim jacket and jeans over a black T-shirt.

'Hi,' he lisped. 'I've seen you around. My name's Martin. Are you looking for a friend?'

Harry picked up a crutch.

'Piss off!' he shouted, lunging out with it. 'Can't a man just sit on a park bench around here?'

Martin scuttled away, not before expressing the hope that Harry never walked again. In an attempt at defiance, Harry hauled himself up on his crutches and looked around from that elevated position. Still no sign.

And then the awful thought struck him. Three meant three in the morning. They'd been waiting for him at three in the morning when he'd been lying asleep in a doorway with his leg snapped like a chopstick. He closed his eyes and groaned once before setting off down the path.

'All right?' he asked the tramp as he approached him, but with his head inside one of the bins the gentleman traveller barely even offered him a grunt. As he straightened up, he seemed more interested in some fish-and-chip packet he'd found in there, still wrapped in newspaper.

Harry crossed the common slowly and clambered on to a bus that led down to the Broadway. He was grateful for the bulge next to his thigh, the five thousand-plus in cash he had left from what Jay had lent him. As long as he had that, he didn't have to think too hard about the future, about going back to work, whatever work was going to be. In truth, he was more worried about seeing Carla again, making sure she was OK.

Looking out of the window, he saw that there had been a fire on Upper Tooting Road. A kebab shop, completely gutted. And then, about two hundred yards further down, the Ataturk Doner House (of which he was an occasional patron), that too had been ravaged by flames, left black and hollow inside. A coincidence, Harry wondered, or just a bloke who'd copped one stale pitta bread too many?

He hauled himself off the bus at the Broadway and headed to the bookie's. On entering from the street, he saw that they'd completed the stairlift. He looked down the daunting steps. How long would they take him, particularly when he remembered the good thing running in a maiden at Lingfield in two minutes?

Standing there, he suddenly felt sorry for himself like never before. How had he, Harry Verma, turned himself into such a fucking victim? Was it rubbing off on him from the people he represented, from the victim production line he'd spent the last six years working on? *Fear of my life*, boss. He'd heard it spat out casually a million times, as if it were the answer to a phone-in competition, an all-purpose Get Out of Jail Free card, available to all.

Except for him. He had constant reminders of the piece Darren had taken of him. Now he had to wait and see if Bohra and Mad Anwar were coming for theirs. No asylum from that.

From below, he heard Tommy pontificate on the lacklustre performance of the champion jockey. Harry inspected the stair-lift again and was in the process of gathering his crutches to sit down on it when he heard a tap on the glass of the door behind him.

She looked beautiful but pale, offering him a sad smile. Slowly, painfully, he negotiated himself back out into the street, scanning her for any signs of violence.

'Hey,' he said.

She surveyed him with a little shake of her head. 'Look at the fucking state of you. I always said you were trouble, Harry Verma.'

He stared at her then sighed. 'I haven't got your wages.'

She blinked and then dropped her eyes, encouraging him to do the same. Harry looked down at the buggy with her baby son asleep in it. And next to it, a suitcase.

'Come on, Hopalong,' Carla said to him. 'Let's go home.'

Fiction
Crime
Noir

Culture
Music
Erotica

dare to read at serpentstail.com

Visit serpentstail.com today to browse and buy
our books, and to sign up for exclusive news and
previews of our books, interviews with our
authors and forthcoming events.

NEWS   cut to the literary chase with all the latest news about our books and authors

EVENTS   advance information on forthcoming events, author readings, exhibitions and book festivals

EXTRACTS   read the best of the outlaw voices - first chapters, short stories, bite-sized extracts

EXCLUSIVES   pre-publication offers, signed copies, discounted books, competitions

BROWSE AND BUY   browse our full catalogue, fill up a basket and proceed to our **fully secure** checkout - our website is your oyster

FREE POSTAGE & PACKING ON ALL ORDERS ... ANYWHERE!

---

sign up today - join our club

Why not get a laugh out of Danny King's Diaries, published by Serpent's Tail?

The Burglar Diaries

'One of the few writers to make me laugh out loud. Danny King's brilliant at making you love characters who essentially are quite bad people' David Baddiel

'An absolutely hilarious, laugh-out-loud book by someone who has been there' Bruce Reynolds, mastermind of The Great Train Robbery

'Occasionally hilarious, if morally dubious, *The Burglar Diaries* is well worth buying – and definitely worth half-inching' *GQ*

'This is the sweet-as-a-nut, hilariously un-PC account of the jobs [Bex] has known and loved — the line-ups, the lock-ups and the cock-ups. If ever there was an antidote to *Bridget Jones's Diary* this is it. *The Burglar Diaries* is the first in a series. Long may it run' *Mirror*

Meet Bex — he works funny hours. He's your average small-time housebreaker, working the streets of suburbia, stealing what he knows (and he doesn't know that much).

Bex and his long-time partner in crime Ollie are not the sharpest tools in the box, so they get into more than their fair share of scrapes. But they stick together, have a laugh, and make enough cash to stay in the pub all weekend. A confident and lippy raconteur, Bex frequently shares his thoughts on life that are as dodgy as he is and offer an hilarious insight into the mind of the petty criminal.

Burglars, fences, petty villains, dope heads, bent coppers, angry homeowners and one long-suffering girlfriend; you'll meet them all in *The Burglar Diaries* and like every one of them. Just watch your bag, that's all . . .

The Bank Robber Diaries

'Humorous but horrific, and you know you shouldn't laugh . . . A guaranteed success' *The Bookseller*

'It's low on morals but big on laughs, so if you can thieve one, by all means go for it!' *BBM*

'Danny looks set for a long and healthy career going straight . . . to the top of the best-sellers list' *Penthouse*

'*The Bank Robber Diaries* is the best (and funniest) British Crime novel since *The Burglar Diaries*, which was also written by Danny King' *Ice*

'A second tale of wickedly un-PC caper crime' *Publishing News*

'Extremely funny' *FHM*

'King spends his free time writing for a top-shelf grot mag and hanging out with some "tasty" geezers. He's also written a couple of excellent books about the non-legit lifestyle choice, *The Burglar Diaries* and *The Bank Robber Diaries*' *Loaded*

'The characterisation is — well, superb. All the people in it are believable whether you like them or not, and the reactions of them and the smaller players is extraordinarily well conceived and compellingly written . . . if you liked *The Sweeney* and *Two Smoking Barrels*, you'll like this' *Shots*

'I'd like to make a withdrawal' . . . Chris Benson idolises his older brother Gavin. In fact, everyone looks up to him. But then they have little choice when they are lying on their stomachs in the middle of the Halifax with a gun shoved in their face . . .
When Gavin gets sent down for a fifteen-year stretch the somewhat unprofessional trio of Chris, Sid and Vince are left without their ringleader. As if Chris hasn't enough to deal with already with his adulterous partner Debbie spending money faster than he can nick it, his lovelorn, sexually frustrated sister-in-law to 'console', and the Neighbourhood Watch scheme to look after . . .

The Hitman Diaries

'Once again the comic genius and hilarious one-liners have you warming to the anti-social protagonists of Chris, Sid and Vince; more cock-ups than hold ups . . . a thoroughly un-pc but rewarding novel' *BBM*

'It's blokeish humour ahoy in this thoroughly enjoyable tale . . . King's writing is sharp, his comedy as black as Donald Rumsfeld's heart and he has a real penchant for dialogue as spoken by criminals . . . the book's hitman protagonist himself [is] a piece of work so nasty he makes Osama bin Laden look like Claire Rayner' *Maxim*

'The action flows as thick as the blood and the jet-black humour will leave you wondering whether to laugh, cry or vomit' *Jack*

'An action-packed tale of murder, mayhem and dating . . . it'll have you hooked' *Mayfair*

For Ian, being a hitman is just a job. Good money, security and a never-ending supply of contracts. It sometimes causes problems with his lady friends but, by and large, they are understanding and accept his frequent absences. Ian faces a moral conflict when given a contract to get rid of Janet, the love of his life, the only woman to really understand him. And moral conflicts are not something that Ian can cope with.
The Hitman Diaries continue Danny King's unique take on what makes low-life characters tick.

The Pornographer Diaries

First there were *The Burglar Diaries*, next *The Bank Robber Diaries*, then *The Hitman Diaries* . . . and now Danny King puts to good use his many years as an editor of top-shelf magazines.

Godfrey Bishop works for a soft porn magazine. He talks to the models, he reads hundreds of filthy readers' letters, he organises the photoshoots and even gets to direct the action. He has, according to his non-porn friends, 'the best job in the world'. But not for Godfrey Bishop who finds sex on the job well hard to come by.

Chuck into the mix a twelve-girl orgy, a stable of alcoholic co-workers, an angry, argumentative feminist, an obsessive nutty reader who thinks Godfrey is trying to scupper his chances of marrying the magazine's centre-spread girl, and you have Danny King's funniest novel yet.